THE GEEK GIRL'S GUIDE TO Cheerleading

CHARITY TAHMASEB
and DARCY VANCE

Simon Pulse
NEW YORK LONDON TORONTO SYDNEY

SIMON PULSE

An imprint of Simon & Schuster Children's Publishing Division

1230 Avenue of the Americas, New York, NY 10020

Text copyright © 2009 by Charity Tahmaseb and Darcy Vance

Chapter opener illustrations of pom-poms copyright © 2009

by istockphoto.com

SIMON PULSE and colophon are registered

trademarks of Simon & Schuster, Inc.

Designed by Mike Rosamilia

The text of this book was set in Adobe Caslon Pro.

Manufactured in the United States of America

2 4 6 8 10 9 7 5 3

Library of Congress Control Number 2008944280

ISBN: 978-1-4169-7834-3

For my cheerleaders: Bob, Andrew, Kyra, and Abby.
And for my mom, who never said a word about the pom-poms.
—C. T.

For Matthew—this book wouldn't have made it without you.
And for Dr. Kerstin Stenson, the mighty Maureen Crowley,
and the Head and Neck Cancer Team at University of Chicago
Medical Center—Matthew wouldn't have made it without you.
—D. V.

Acknowledgments

Two! Four! Six! Eight! Who do we appreciate?

No one writes a novel—or makes the cheerleading squad—without a little help along the way. We'd like to thank:

Our parents for reading to us and for instilling in us a love of books.

Our families for putting up with countless hours of writing, revision, IM chats, and general preoccupation.

The Granada Drive Gang for helping us navigate the ever shifting landscape of what's cool.

Cheer coach Jodie Slavik for reminding us that cheerleaders are people too and for teaching us the proper length of an insanely short skirt.

Our writing friends, especially those at Writers Village University, in particular Pat, Jen, Helen, Marli, Maria, and Dennis; all the gals in the Wet Noodle Posse; the Yahoo Teenlit Authors Group; and Sara Wealer.

Our fabulous agent(!), Mollie Glick, and our equally fabulous editor, Jennifer Klonsky, for guiding us through this process, providing feedback, and teaching us more about writing in one year than we'd learned in the previous ten.

A special thanks goes to Amy W. Without her—and her question to Charity on a cold day in November during French class—this book would not exist. That question? "Have you ever tried out for cheerleading?" The rest, as they say, is history. So, Amy? Thanks for asking.

It is a truth universally acknowledged that a high school boy in possession of great athletic ability must be in want of . . . A bowl of oatmeal.

At least on a cold November morning in Minnesota. And maybe a carton of orange juice on the side, but definitely not a girlfriend. Jack Paulson, mega basketball star and crush extraordinaire, did not date. Just ask any girl in the Prairie Stone High School junior class. The cheerleaders, the preps, the drama queens, the band crew, the art nerds, the skater chicks, the stoners, the loners, the freaks, the cool and the not-so-cool, all of them had tried.

Including me.

I was hoping to try again that day, if only my best friend, Moni, would show up already. Ever since her parents divorced and her dad moved to Minneapolis, it was like he took Moni's punctuality with him. She'd been totally unreliable. So I wondered, could I pull it off? Could a lone geek girl linger by the cafeteria door in a casual manner? Not likely. You see, every school has a danger zone. At Prairie Stone, ours occupied the space in the lobby that was an equal distance between the cafeteria, the gym, and the girls' bathroom. It was the spot where all the popular kids hung out. A place the rest of us tried to avoid. Moni and I called it the gauntlet.

We discovered that term last year, in word origins class. In case you're wondering, *gauntlet (noun) = a form of punishment where the victim must endure suffering from many sources at the same time*. It comes from the Swedish word *gatlopp*. In Sweden, apparently, they used to punish reprobates *(n. those who are predestined to damnation)* by making them strip to the waist and then run between rows of soldiers who were armed with sticks and knotted ropes.

That sounded about right.

And so I stood at the edge of Prairie Stone's gauntlet, close enough to the gym to sniff the delicate aroma of sweaty socks, near enough to the cafeteria to catch a whiff of oatmeal—and the promise of Jack Paulson. One more step and I would officially enter gauntlet girl territory.

Chantal Simmons, the queen of cool and gatekeeper of popularity at PSHS, stood at the apex of it all. She turned her head in my direction, her blond hair flowing in a way rarely seen outside of shampoo commercials. Her glance made me consider climbing the stairs to the balcony and crossing over the top instead of pressing my way through—but only a coward would do that.

Which is to say, I've done it plenty.

Chantal had a radar for weakness. One wrong move and she'd find yours and use it against you. Forget those sticks and knotted ropes. Chantal could annihilate the hopes and dreams of your average high school junior with just a whisper. And once upon a time, back in the dark ages of childhood and middle school, Chantal Simmons was someone I had told all my secrets to. In retrospect, that was kind of like arming a rogue nation with a nuclear bomb.

No risk, no reward, I told myself. If I wanted an early-morning glimpse of Jack Paulson (and I did, I really, really did), then I needed to cross into enemy territory. Alone. But before I could step over that invisible boundary, someone called my name. Someone short, with a mass of yellow corkscrew curls poking out beneath a QTπ cap.

"Bethany!" My best friend, Moni Fredrickson, bounded up to me, still in her winter jacket, her cheeks pink from cold and her glasses fogged. "Brian just called me on my cell," she said. "They're in the Little Theater. They have Krispy Kremes. Brian said he'd save us one each, but you know how that works."

Of course I did. It is another truth universally acknowledged, that high school nerds in possession of a great number of Krispy Kremes must be in want of . . .

Nothing.

At least not until they shook out the last bit of sugary glaze from the box. Then it was total *Lord of the Flies* time while they searched for more. We had to get there before they tore Brian limb from limb. Moni pulled me along toward the Little Theater and away from the gauntlet. I glanced over my shoulder, sure Chantal was still glaring at me.

But she wasn't. No one was. Not a single gauntlet girl or wannabe peered in my direction. Instead they'd all turned toward the cafeteria, eyes fixed on a tall, retreating figure—one with dark spiky hair and a Prairie Stone High letter jacket. Jack Paulson. He didn't look back at me—not that I expected him to. But then, he didn't acknowledge Chantal, either.

Jack Paulson = Totally Girlproof.

I stumbled along behind Moni and wondered, *What would a girl have to do to get a boy like that to notice her?*

If there was such a thing as gauntlet girl territory at Prairie Stone, then the Little Theater was dork domain. Chantal Simmons might rule the lobby, but a few steps down the hall Todd Emerson (president of the chess club, co-captain of the debate team, editor of the school paper, and all-around boy genius) maintained a benevolent dictatorship over the academic superstars and the techies.

In other words, a bossier boy never lived.

Todd was Harvard bound. Or Yale bound. Well, certainly *somewhere* bound. Somewhere that was far snootier than (what I was sure he already thought of as) his humble beginnings. He was one of those kids who wouldn't return for a school reunion until he managed to make a billion dollars or overthrow a minor country.

A bright purple and gold notice hung on the door to the theater, instructing all who entered to LET YOUR SCHOOL SPIRIT SHINE! and inviting us to attend a call-out meeting for the winter varsity cheerleading squad. As if. I passed through the doorway, gripped the handrail, and followed Moni down the small flight of steps, my eyes adjusting to the semidarkness.

The Little Theater had killer acoustics, something Todd took advantage of up on the stage.

"Can you believe they denied Carlson's request for new desktop publishing software?" he thundered. "You know what they—" Todd broke off mid-rant. "Hey, Reynolds, how long does it take you to lay out the newspaper every month?"

I tried not to roll my eyes about the newspaper—or about Todd calling me by my last name. It was this thing he did, like I was a rookie reporter to his big-city editor in chief.

How long did it take for me to lay out the newspaper? "A while," I said. *Forever* was a better answer, but Todd was wound up enough. The computers we used were ancient, the software even older. I sometimes thought that cutting and pasting—with real scissors and glue—might be faster. Mr. Carlson, the journalism teacher, had been lobbying for upgrades for years.

"Guess what they bought instead?" said Todd. He gestured wildly from the podium. "Come on. Just guess."

I heard the sound of someone's stomach rumbling and the barest click of a Nintendo DS. I looked around at the collection of smarty-pants misfits that made up our "clique." These were the kids who lived to raise their hands in class. That no one offered a guess was a testament to the power Todd wielded over the group.

He pounded the lectern. The crack of his fist against wood echoed through the theater.

"They bought new"—Todd stepped out from behind the podium for effect—"*pom-poms*." A look of disgust rolled across his face as he approached the front of the stage. "For the varsity *cheerleading* squad."

I glanced at Moni. She crossed her eyes at me and pointed toward the seat that held the Krispy Kreme box. Todd glared, daring someone, anyone, to speak.

A throat cleared behind us. "Well, I highly approved of the new outfits last year." This was Brian McIntyre, Todd's sidekick, mellow where Todd was high-strung, soft-spoken where Todd was loud. Brian was one of those boys whose looks froze in fourth grade. He had a roundish face and full cheeks, with sweet blue eyes and hair that flopped over his forehead. People constantly underestimated him, which was why he cleaned up in debate, at chess, and in the Math League.

"The cheerleaders had new outfits last year?" Todd asked.

"You didn't notice?" Brian sounded genuinely puzzled.

Moni paused before biting the doughnut she was holding and raised an eyebrow at me. I'd known her long enough to catch the meaning of that look: *When did Brian start noticing cheerleaders?* Not the best development, especially when you considered that somewhere around homecoming, Brian and Moni had gone from "just friends" to something a touch friendlier.

"I guess it doesn't matter how big a boy's brain is," I whispered, "it can still be derailed by an insanely short skirt." But Moni wasn't paying attention.

"Whatever," she said to the group. "There's nothing so special about cheerleading. I mean, even Bethany and I could do that."

"Do . . . what?" Todd and I said at the same time.

"You know. Ready . . . okay!" Moni bounced on the balls of her feet, like she might break into a display of spirit fingers at any moment.

"You mean," I said, going along with it (because annoying Todd was my favorite sport), "you and me trying out for the varsity cheerleading squad?"

"Who says we can't?"

Ummm, *technically*, no one.

Todd knelt at the edge of the stage and frowned down at us, his oversize dork glasses slipping down his nose. "You have got to be kidding."

Yeah. What he said.

But out loud, I agreed with Moni. "Think about it, Todd. We could petition to expand cheerleading to support the debate team. The chess club, even. You know, *Gambit to the left, castle to the right, endgame, endgame, now in sight!*"

Moni giggled. Brian, still lazing near the back of the room, snorted in appreciation. A few of the other guys took up the cheer.

You know how in Greek mythology, Medusa could turn anyone who looked at her into stone? At that moment she had nothing on Todd Emerson. Lucky for me, the bell rang. Or maybe not so lucky—Todd and I shared first-period honors history.

We all filed from the Little Theater and straight into the heart of the gauntlet, together. Todd had this theory about strength in numbers. It was one of the reasons he collected the nerds, the debate dorks, the third-tier drama geeks, the lowly and lonely freshmen, and invited them all to his house for Geek Night every Saturday. As a combined force, we could breach the gauntlet. Whereas if any one of us tried it alone? Suicide.

And it worked. Mostly. Chantal Simmons stepped back immediately, but then, she probably didn't want smart cooties on her three-hundred-dollar coral-colored peep-toe pumps.

Some of the boys still chanted the chess cheer as we passed a few members of the varsity basketball team. Seniors Ryan Nelson and Luke Vandenberg stood with Jack Paulson. All three of them looked up, like the chant was their cue to rush the court and play. Only Jack seemed to notice we weren't cheering for them. He frowned.

I wanted to turn, go back and tell him that we weren't making fun of him. But it was too late; the crowd had already taken me along in its tide. Maybe I could explain when I saw him in Independent Reading class.

Oh, who was I kidding? I could barely respond when Jack

graced me with a few words across the classroom aisle. I'd never be able to explain, not now, not then. Even so, I turned around for one last look. Instead of Jack, I locked eyes with Todd. He handed me a Krispy Kreme—a slightly battered Krispy Kreme, but one from the middle of the box. It was still warm.

"Checkmate," he said.

The bank's time and temperature display flashed: 10:46 P.M./29°. Only in Minnesota could it be this cold just four days past Halloween. All of us—me, Moni, Todd, Brian, plus assorted members of the chess club, debate team, and Math League—shivered outside the Games 'n More video store.

Light spilled from the warm movie theater lobby a few doors down, but I knew the huge sign on its door read NO LOITERING. It was the strip mall and hypothermia for us. And there were still seventy-four frigid minutes before the midnight release of the latest shoot-'em-up video game.

What a way to spend a Saturday night.

We huddled together on a bus-stop bench. Todd lounged on my right—in his Nietzsche "that which does not kill me, makes me stronger" mode—pretending that the cold had no effect on him. Brian sat to Moni's left. Every five minutes he scooted a millimeter closer to her. The rest of the guys took turns standing in line. Apparently some geeks were more equal than others.

But that was no surprise. In these boys' world, status was measured in grade point averages and frag counts. Todd and Brian were at the top of both those lists. And Moni and me? We weren't there because we were dying to buy some dumb video game the first second it dropped.

"The category is famous first lines," Todd said. "You go first, Reynolds."

Of all the books I'd read (1,272 since I started keeping count) I couldn't think of a single opening line. I was pretty sure that meant my brain was frozen.

"I've got one if she doesn't," a member of the chess club offered.

"It's Reynolds, numbnuts. She's got one," Todd said in my defense. Some of the animosity I'd felt toward him for moving Geek Night from the toasty confines of his basement to the icy tundra that was Prairie Stone Plaza softened.

"Okay, how about," I began, but my brain was still iced up. I'd have to go with my fallback—an oldie, a goodie, my favorite. "'It is a truth universally acknowledged, that a single man in possession of a good fortune must be in want of a . . .'?"

"Too easy," said Moni over the top of her gas-station cappuccino. "C'mon, guys," she said. "You have to know this one."

"Uh . . . it's . . . it's . . . ," Todd struggled. "Give me a second . . . er . . . Brian?"

"Is that your final answer?" Moni snorted, causing the steam from her cup to fog her glasses and loosen a curl so that it fell onto her forehead.

Brian grinned at her, or did until a burst of giggles echoed down the plaza.

The late movie had just let out, and a group of kids hurried to their cars. Clouds of breath billowed ahead of them, partially hiding their faces, but the giggle sounded like Cassidy Anderson, the "Omigod!" was unmistakably Traci Olson's, and the clipped, condescending "Check it" could belong to none other than Chantal Simmons.

"What was the question again?" Brian asked, his attention focused near the theater's exit.

I repeated, "'It is a truth universally acknowledged, that a single man in possession of a good fortune must be in want of a . . .'?"

"A . . . cheerleader?" Brian answered, his face still turned toward the movie crowd.

Now it was Todd's turn to snort. "Yeah, that's it. Final answer."

I thought it was funny, but Moni's face fell. She hopped to her feet and took a step away from the group.

"What'd I say?" asked Brian. His round cheeks, already pink, grew red.

"Cheerleader, good one." Todd leaned across me and smacked Brian on the arm. "Can I quote you on that?" He made a show of pulling out his iPhone to record Brian's words and probably the latitude and longitude at which they were uttered.

"Moni, come back," I said. "Please."

"Yeah," Todd said, a little too loud. "Besides, it's my turn next, and I've got a good one. 'A long time ag—'"

"*Star Wars*? Again?" I wasn't the only one who groaned.

"Okay," Todd said, "how about: 'In the week bef—'"

"*Dune*," I interrupted.

"No way, Reynolds. There is no way you could've known that."

Todd was way more predictable than he liked to believe. So was Moni. She still stood a few feet away, her arms crossed over her chest, a glare aimed at Brian.

"Really, Moni. I'm sorry," Brian said as he started to stand. His voice rose in volume and pitch, drowning out me, and even Todd. "I don't know what I said that was so—"

"Trouble in Nerdland?" A pair of teal, pumpkin, and tan ballet flats appeared only inches from my feet. I didn't have to look up to know who it was. No one in Prairie Stone had a finer shoe wardrobe than Chantal Simmons.

Todd sputtered but gave up before saying anything coherent. Brian froze, half-sitting, half-standing, his posture apelike. Moni tapped a toe but didn't say a word. I kept my eyes on the sidewalk. It was better that way.

Chantal and crew stepped off the curb, and a few freshmen math whizzes stared after them. No one said a word until the girls were inside their car and slipping down the frosty street. Then one of the boys let out a low whistle.

"Cheerleaders," his friend said wistfully.

Moni threw her cappuccino into the trash. The cup rattled, and a couple of boys jumped.

"Really, you guys," she said. "What have they got that we haven't got?"

"I assume that's a rhetorical question," said Todd.

When Brian joined the chorus of heh-heh-hehs, Moni scooped up her mittens and her Sudoku book and clomped down the sidewalk. I hurried after her. Brian tried to follow, but Moni shot him a look that, I swear, dropped the temperature another ten degrees.

"I'm serious," she said when I caught up to her. "What *do* they have that we don't?"

She stopped in front of Waterman's Women's Wear and made a slow turn in the display window's reflection.

I didn't know what to tell her. I was pretty sure we weren't ugly. Moni was bouncy and petite, curvy in the right places. I was taller and a little too thin, but not in a size-zero-starlet sort of way. Moni's bright blond curls were the opposite of my straight, dark bob. I hugged myself against the cold. "Maybe it's the pom-poms," I said.

"Yeah." Moni pushed her arms straight forward, then pulled them quickly back. She thrust them up in the shape of a V, then did a swivel-hipped pivot thing and checked her reflection once again.

Just when I thought she was going to go all Dance Dance Revolution on me, she stopped and stared at our images in the glass.

"Maybe."

The following Monday morning, Moni's brain seemed as fogged over as her glasses. I had to remind her twice before she pulled off her Camp SohCahToa hat and stowed it in her locker. At lunch she walked right past our meet-up spot and would have glided into the gauntlet if I hadn't grabbed her shoulder.

It wasn't until last hour that I really started to worry. Most of the geek squad had been excused from eighth-period classes. We were all in the Little Theater, up on the stage, getting ready to start practice for the National Honor Society induction ceremony. Mr. Wilker, the NHS advisor, had just assigned each of us a sophomore inductee to shepherd through the program when the door to the theater opened.

Cassidy Anderson (senior, cheerleader, gauntlet girl) stepped inside, bringing in a thin stream of light with her. The radiance followed her as she bounced down the aisle to the foot of the stage.

She handed Mr. Wilker a note. "Thank you, Miss Anderson," he said, then turned his attention back to our group under the lights.

"Um," Cassidy said, "I sort of need that right away."

Mr. Wilker paused and glanced at the note. "My grade book is back in the classroom. I'll have to check that first."

Moni left her sophomore and nudged me. "I bet she needs proof she's not flunking," she said. "Cheerleading tryouts, you know."

No, I did not know. I didn't really care, either. Except that Cassidy still hadn't left. Every second she delayed practice made it more likely I wouldn't have a chance to finish my Life at Prairie Stone column before the newspaper staff meeting after school. I stole a glance at Todd. If I didn't turn in my column, he'd make my life miserable. That is, if he could pull himself out of the hormone-induced rapture that seemed to coincide with Cassidy's arrival.

Dork.

And he wasn't the only one. While Mr. Wilker negotiated with Cassidy, I took a look at the boys onstage. Their combined IQ was probably close to thirty gazillion, but no one would believe it if they saw them in this state. All that chest puffing and gut-sucking-in-ing, and Brian—was he actually slobbering? Really. They might as well have been Neanderthals.

I turned back to Moni, certain that she'd spit out a suitably scathing, sarcastic remark. Instead she blinked, then turned her head from Brian to Cassidy and back again. Beneath us, Mr. Wilker attempted to get the practice under way again.

"Cassidy," he said finally, "I'll meet you in my room after school."

"But—but—," Cassidy whined. She blew a bubble with the gum she was chewing. After it popped, she huffed, "I guess you can just have someone bring it to me."

Fifteen male hands shot into the air as if powered by rockets.

Cassidy turned and headed up the slope toward the exit. When she opened the door, the lobby lights framed her body in silhouette and accented the shine of her hair. She paused as if posing, then whipped around to address us.

"Hey, losers," she said. "Take a picture next time. It might last longer."

With that, the door whooshed closed and plunged us all into darkness.

"That's it," Moni whispered at my side. "We're going to do it."

"Do what?" I whispered back.

"Try out for cheerleading."

"What!" I said, forgetting for a moment how good the acoustics in the Little Theater could be.

"Miss Reynolds?" said Mr. Wilker. "Something you'd like to share with the rest of us?"

I shook my head, but on the inside I was thinking of all sorts of things I'd like to share with Moni, the main one being, *Was she out of her freaking mind?*

2

Welcome, Prairie Stone Cheer Candidate!
You are about to embark on the most exciting experience of your high school career: becoming a Prairie Stone High School varsity cheerleader! If you've been attending tryout practices (and I know you have), then put your fears aside. You're ready for the next step. Cheerleading involves hard work, commitment, and sacrifice, but remember the *fun*! And most important: Let your school spirit shine!
GO PANTHERS!!!!!

Two weeks later Moni and I stood in matching purple shorts and gold T-shirts outside that same Little Theater. It might be debate dork domain most of the year, but once in May and once in November, the Prairie Stone High School cheerleading squad takes it over for tryouts. From behind the closed door came stomping, clapping, and a way too enthusiastic, "Ready? Okay!"

I *still* couldn't believe I was doing this.

"It's a conspiracy," Moni said. "I'm telling you." She licked her fingertips and used the spit to gel back a wayward curl.

"A *cheerleading* conspiracy?" I asked.

"Exactly! I mean, jeez, Bethany, you've seen me do the splits."

I had. It was not pretty.

"This was your idea," I reminded her.

"Yeah, well, no one said anything about splits."

True.

Also true: I had let Moni haul me to the cheerleading call-out meeting without protesting—much. But I figured that would be the end of it, especially once we met Sheila. Sheila Manning, the Prairie Stone High cheerleading coach, probably did high kicks while she was still in the womb. How could anyone be that perky?

Another truth: I did take the information sheet when Sheila handed it to me. I needed a bookmark for my honors history text. That was the last time I saw it until Moni called me the night before the first tryout practice.

"Don't forget to shave your legs," she said.

"Huh?"

"It says we're supposed to wear shorts."

In November? In Minnesota? Still, a girl's got to have some pride, if not common sense. I shaved my legs and crawled to the back of my closet to pull out the box marked SUMMER CLOTHES.

The first time I suspected Moni had more on her mind than just aggravating Todd or even winning over Brian came the next day, in German class. We were supposed to be conjugating the verb "should" (*soll, sollte, gesollt*) but all she could talk about was cheerleading. Even worse, she seemed to have developed some sort of *strategy*. Could cheerleading tryout practice even *have* a strategy? But I nodded my head and let her go on because, well, with her parents' divorce and her dad moving to Minneapolis, I felt like I had to be there for her. Somebody *sollte*.

Of course, I never thought "being there" meant matching purple shorts and gold T-shirts. And I certainly never thought it meant *cheerleading* tryouts.

After school, on the first day of tryout practice, I'd left a note on the big whiteboard in the newspaper office: *Late—B*, and headed to the main hall outside the gym. I figured I'd be back in time for the staff meeting. I mean, how long could it take to learn a stupid cheer?

Longer than you'd think. Especially when your best friend goes all earnest on you and says, "If we're going to try out, then we should *really* try out."

I raised an eyebrow at her. "More strategy?" I asked.

That's when Moni gave me what I like to call her Moni Lisa smile. Mysterious and compelling, it made her whole face light up. All she had to do was turn it on you, and next thing you knew, you'd forgotten that what she was suggesting was a bad idea. If someone could capture that smile on oil and canvas, her portrait would hang in the Louvre. For sure. Bottled, it would be worth millions.

"I think it's important," she said, "you know, for the experience. The more we put into this, the more we'll have to laugh about when it's over. Just think of Todd's reaction."

That was one thing I didn't want to think about. Todd would kill me if he knew I was memorizing dance moves to the school song instead of writing my next Life at Prairie Stone column for the paper.

But for Moni and for "the experience" I put Todd's reaction—and my misgivings—out of my head. The truth was, if anyone but the wannabes had shown up at practice, not even friendship would've kept me there. But the Prairie Stone elite had opted out of tryout practice. So Moni and I opted in.

I worked on my straddle jumps while Moni perfected her round-offs. And the next day, when it was time to practice the dance routine, I put way more into it than I normally would. I kept up with Moni's ridiculous faux fervor, shimmy for shimmy, all week.

It was simple. It was easy. It was fun. Nothing about it mattered, not even the stares and giggles from the other girls. That is, until Moni found out about the splits, which was right before the official tryouts started.

"Sheila could've mentioned it earlier," she said to me now.

I agreed. The cheerleading coach had been vocal on every requirement except that one. No doubt Sheila took one look at the assortment of Prairie Stone High cheerleading hopefuls and decided to separate the girls from the . . . geeks. *Of course* cheerleaders did the splits. Everyone knew that.

I pulled a sheet of paper from my back pocket and unfolded it.

> Cheer candidates are required to perform a cheer, the school song with dance, and a jump sequence. Candidates will also answer an interview question. Scores will be based on the following point system:
>
> Showmanship: 20 points
>
> Performance of school song and dance: 15 points
>
> Crowd-leading ability: 15 points
>
> Coordination: 10 points
>
> Interview question: 5 points

"See?" Moni said. "I don't see splits on there at all. Where do you think they fall into the scheme of things? Coordination? Showmanship? It's not fair."

"You're right. It's not fair. Let's quit," I said, and tried to saunter off casually down the hall.

Moni grabbed my hand. She turned me around, and I saw something close to panic in her eyes.

I sighed. "I can do the splits," I said.

"What?" Moni jerked and her blond curls swung, the way they did when she was surprised, or happy.

"I can do the splits."

"Front and back, or sideways?" Moni asked.

"Both, actually."

"No way! Since when?"

Ever since Madame Wolsinski's modern dance class wasn't as lame as it sounded. Modern dance isn't all running around a stage flapping your arms, but did I want to explain that to Moni? A grunt, a groan, and a desperate cry came from inside the Little Theater. Any explaining would have to wait. We were up next.

"I'll do the splits," I said, a sudden pulse beating in my throat. "Your round-offs are good. You could—"

"No, wait. We'll wow 'em with a ginormous finish." Moni's enthusiasm was back.

"Ginormous?" I asked.

"And you should do the splits sideways—looks more painful. I can do a round-off over the top of you." Moni bounced on the balls of her feet. "How does that sound?"

"Dangerous?"

"They'll never know the difference."

Oh, sure, I thought, but before I could say anything more, the door swung open. Kaleigh Bartell and Anna Crouse staggered out, faces flushed and sweaty. Anna looked close to tears. Kaleigh was limping.

"Good luck, guys," said Kaleigh. Halfway down the hall she added, "You're gonna need it."

The door to the theater closed behind me, shooing me into the darkness. Moni was already halfway to the stage when I hurried to catch up to her. Mrs. Hanson, the guidance counselor, scrutinized us over a pair of half glasses that sat on the tip of her nose. Sheila Manning tilted her pretty head to one side and tapped a perfect tooth with a pencil eraser. Ms. Bailey, the family and consumer sciences teacher, was the third judge. She had her arms crossed over her chest and stared almost but not quite at the ceiling.

"I'm curious, girls." Mrs. Hanson scanned the judging sheet in front of her. "Why did you two decide to try out for cheerleading?"

The tone in Mrs. Hanson's voice made the question seem a lot less like *Why do you want to be cheerleaders?* and more like *What the hell are you doing here?*

I looked over at Moni. This was her idea, after all. She opened her mouth, only to clamp it shut.

"Maybe you should start your routine," Sheila suggested. "You can answer the interview question later." Like stalling with round-offs and splits would help.

The more I sweated and kicked my way through the dance, the more it burned me. Not just my muscles, either, but the whole idea of it. Why *shouldn't* we go out for cheerleading? Moni and I had as much right as anyone else, didn't we? And hey, who said a geek girl couldn't see how the other half lived?

I sang loudly during the school song, and mostly on key, too. When it came time for the ginormous finish, I slid sideways to the floor and Moni vaulted over me. We didn't budge. Not even when Sheila gave Moni a "come on, you can do it" nod. I just smiled and planted my elbows on the floor and my chin on my fists. Moni didn't waver, didn't even attempt the splits.

Silence. Stares. Well, who could blame them?

"Very nice, girls," said Sheila at last.

I struggled to stand, my legs wobbly. Sweat coated my upper lip. I gave it a swipe with the back of my hand.

"That was, uh, nice," Mrs. Hanson echoed. "Very . . . spirited."

Oh, yeah. We had loads of school spirit.

"So," she continued, "what made you decide to try out for cheerleading?"

There it was, that question again. And there was the usually talkative Moni, silent. Again.

Answers swirled in my head. Why was I trying out? To jerk Todd's chain. To make Moni happy. But besides that, maybe I was doing it to prove I could, that *anyone* could. Maybe I was striking back at the long-held tradition of Prairie Stone High cheerleading being nothing more than a popularity contest. Or maybe it was because so many people thought I shouldn't—or couldn't. As if being able to diagram a sentence—or in Moni's case, solve quadratic equations in her head—made us incapable of doing a herkie.

Those were all good reasons, but not the ones Sheila, or Mrs. Hanson, or the bored Ms. Bailey wanted to hear. I shifted my weight, and the sole of my sneaker squeaked against the floor.

"School spirit?" I said. The acoustics in the Little Theater made my words rebound on me like an accusation.

Mrs. Hanson arched an unbelieving eyebrow. Sheila beamed. Ms. Bailey doodled on the notepad in front of her.

"Very well," Mrs. Hanson said. "You girls are through."

We dashed up the aisle, out the door, and into the hall. I took hold of Moni's shoulders and stared into her too-bright eyes. "We are never, *ever*, doing that again."

Amazingly, after all that, I still had time to slip into the newspaper office and catch part of the weekly staff meeting. But one look at Moni told me she wouldn't be satisfied until she read the tryout results in black and white. Or purple and gold—Coach Sheila probably wrote exclusively in the school colors.

The same went for everyone else, or so it seemed. Even though Thanksgiving break had officially started at last bell, twenty girls loitered in the lobby. Sure, a few pretended to study the trophies in the cases, but most of them made no pretense at all. They just sat outside the Little Theater, eyes narrowed, expressions grim.

"How long does it take to copy last year's roster?" I asked.

"At least the view is good while we wait," Moni said, and nodded her head toward the open gym doors. The varsity basketball team was practicing there—a worthy diversion, in most everyone's opinion—or at least the opinion of the girls peering inside. Were they any different from Todd or Brian going brain-dead over cheerleaders?

"So I'm missing newspaper to watch a bunch of jocks?" I said.

"Hot jocks," Moni corrected.

"Conceded. Still—"

Moni held up a hand and continued as if I hadn't said a word. "Did you see Jack Paulson today? I think he's grown five more inches since September."

Jack had played on the varsity team since our freshman year. Now that he was a junior, he stood a head above even the tallest senior. Did I see Jack Paulson? What kind of question was that? *Of course I saw Jack Paulson.* Everyone saw Jack Paulson. He was . . . well, *Jack Paulson.*

The door to the Little Theater opened a crack. A hand with perfectly lacquered nails emerged and taped a sheet of paper to the wall.

Most of the girls sprang forward. It must have been mass hysteria or something, but my feet carried me toward the list. I stopped before I got too far, though, vowing not to give it any more attention than it deserved.

Kaleigh came up behind Moni and me. "You guys heard, right?"

"Heard what?" I asked. Moni ducked her head.

"There are three slots up for grabs," Kaleigh said.

"Twelve," I corrected her.

Kaleigh tipped her head to one side and squinted. "Twelve?"

"Technically, all positions on the cheer squad last for just one season. 'Veteran cheerleaders are encouraged to reapply but cannot be guaranteed a spot on the team.' It says so right here."

I offered the info sheet to Kaleigh for inspection. She waved it off, rolled her eyes, and turned her attention to Moni. "Dina, Traci, and Chantal can't cheer this season. Traci and Chantal are banned, and Dina . . ." She trailed off.

And Dina . . . Until that moment I'd almost forgotten about the party last August, the keg of beer, and the accident that sent shock waves through the school. Dina was still in physical therapy and being homeschooled. Now Traci and Chantal couldn't cheer?

Of course they couldn't—Prairie Stone High School had a zero tolerance policy. I hadn't put two and two together before now, but apparently Kaleigh—and Moni—had.

"So," Kaleigh continued, "*anyone* could make the squad." She skipped a few feet ahead. "Well, almost," she tossed that last comment over her shoulder before bolting for the list.

Moni huffed and walked in a tight circle. "One of these days, I'm going to slap the lip gloss right off her mouth."

"You *knew*, didn't you?" I said.

She shrugged and gave me another Moni Lisa smile. "I know *this*," she said. "We really need to check that roster."

"Please. Moni." I reached out to stop her. "I went along with this 'for the experience,' but even with Chantal out of the running . . ." I shook my head, frustrated. "You didn't fall and hit your head during one of those round-offs, did you? Girls like us, we don't . . ." I sighed. Girls like us didn't do a lot of things, and cheerleading was at the top of that list.

Moni turned, pointing toward the trophy case, then the Little Theater, and the gym. "Think about it." Now she pointed down the hall, toward the cafeteria and the gauntlet, that spot where Chantal, Traci, and their minions hung out. "Without them *anything* can happen."

"So it's what?" I said. "A cheerleading paradigm shift?"

"Now you sound like Todd."

Yeah, it was something he'd say. Todd was forever talking about things like that. He was really into politics, and he didn't restrict his opinions to the national level, either. According to Todd, politics and politicians were everywhere. Especially in high school.

Kaleigh burst through the crowd around the roster, arms in the air, a victory dance in progress. If she had a football, she would've spiked it.

"Uh-huh, that's right. I did it. I'm the—"

"Man?" Moni suggested.

Not even Moni could bring Kaleigh down. "Made the squad, which is more than—"

Another girl broke through the crowd, red blotches already sprouting on her cheeks. She tried to hide her expression, but I saw it. "Anna?" I said.

Kaleigh whirled. "Oh God, Anna. I didn't even look. . . ."

That was Kaleigh for you—the kind of girl who'd start celebrating before checking whether her best friend made the squad.

I watched Kaleigh trail Anna down the hall toward the junior lockers. A lone figure stood near the end of the corridor. Blond.

Lean. In the kind of outfit that sneered at Minnesota Novembers. *Chantal?*

Once Chantal and I had shared the barre in Madame Wolsinski's modern dance class. We were a two-girl front against the others, with their whispered insults and snobbish exclusionary tactics. But that was before Chantal metamorphosed into the darling of Prairie Stone High. Before I reached my full geek potential.

"You know," I said to Moni, "this wasn't supposed to matter." And yet, somehow—

"It doesn't," she said, but her voice sounded hollow.

And that ache in my stomach? That didn't matter either.

I tugged Moni by the sleeve. "I think we're going to need the real thing after this—white chocolate mochas with whipped cream. Maybe even extra whip." I stepped forward, but Moni stopped me.

"It was my idea. I'll look." She slipped into the crowd and under the arm of a red-headed senior. Moni stood on tiptoes, fingers pressed against the posted roster. She stayed like that for way too long. Moni could speed-read; she liked to run through digits of π in her head—for fun. She probably had the entire list memorized in two seconds.

A whine rose up from within the crowd. I braced myself; we were definitely going to need the extra whip. But it wasn't Moni, and it wasn't a whine. The tone transformed into a high-pitched shriek. Next thing I knew, the redhead had a handful of Moni's T-shirt. I rushed to save my friend, but the girl grabbed me, too, then pulled us into a group hug . . . one that grew to include the entire brand-new Prairie Stone High School varsity cheerleading squad.

And there Moni and I were, right in the middle.

In the sea of squeals, Moni bumped me and I bumped Kaleigh, who had returned (it seemed) from hastily consoling Anna. Kaleigh gave me a look, then bumped both of us back. Moni and I stumbled to the outskirts of the squad.

"No. Way," I said.

"Way!" Moni nodded, curls flying.

I pointed at Moni, then back at myself, because a strange fear had stolen my voice. We *both* made it?

The flying curls bounced into place. For the first time since her parents divorced, Moni looked serene. Content, even. When at last she nodded, I had to wonder, How much did this cheerleading thing really mean to her?

Sheila emerged from the Little Theater and dropped pair after pair of purple and gold pom-poms into the mob.

"Here you go, girls," she said. "Take them home. We'll do uniforms on Monday, but this is the best way to let everyone know you made it."

I looked down to find gold in my right hand and purple in my left. How could I take these . . . *things* home? My parents didn't even know I was trying out. All I'd said was that I was staying after school with Moni. That was normal enough. Between class projects, painting scenery for the school play, and working on the newspaper, I stayed late all the time. Sure, I had extra-curriculars. There wasn't much else to do in Prairie Stone. But *cheerleading*?

The thud of a basketball stole my attention. It bounced across the lobby and straight toward my feet. I trapped it, barely, between purple and gold fringe. Then I looked up.

Jack Paulson.

He held out his hands to take the ball, and they tangled with mine in the pom-poms. His skin was warm, and I tried not to count the number of times his fingers touched mine. (One, two, three . . . swoon . . . four times?) He laughed. His normally dark brown hair was black and spiked from sweat. Jack wasn't just cute and talented. He worked hard—harder than most boys on the team.

Too soon, the basketball escaped the pom-poms. Jack held the ball against one hip, an arm draped over it to keep it in place.

"You make the squad?" he asked.

I wanted to say . . . something. At that moment, though, the only thing in my head was that stupid chess cheer from a few weeks ago: *Gambit to the left, castle to the right, endgame, endgame, now in sight!* That would be worse than lame. I held the pom-poms out as if they could speak for me.

"Well, congrats," said Jack. "Looks like I'll be seeing you at the games."

"Paulson!" came a voice from the gym. "You're up! Get your butt back in here."

Jack glanced over his shoulder at the gym; then, barely turning toward me, said, "See ya." And took off.

"See ya," I croaked.

"Oh . . . my . . . God." Moni came up behind me. She was sounding more like a cheerleader every minute. Frankly, it was a little disturbing.

"I just knew it," she said. "This cheerleading thing is going to pay off. Big-time."

"What?"

"Hello! Jack Paulson. *The* Jack Paulson. He's going to be *seeing* you at the games?"

I glanced at the gym, then inspected the pom-poms. They couldn't possibly be a Get Out of Geek Free card, could they? They couldn't. "I think he meant 'you' as in everyone on the squad," I said. "You know, the collective."

"Yeah. Right. A collective of cheerleaders." Moni snorted. "A pod of whales, a colony of rats, a pride of lions—"

I stopped her before she got to her favorite—a coffle of asses.

It didn't really matter if we were cheerleaders, right? Except, maybe it did. The possibility of it tightened around my heart. Jack Paulson was . . . well, Jack Freakin' Paulson, and totally unattainable. One of the many places geek girls didn't go. Not even ones with pom-poms.

"Girls," Sheila said. The empty pom-pom bag at her feet looked like a deflated balloon. "Can I talk to you two?"

It wasn't like we had a choice. She bounced forward, winter

coat fluttering at her sides, and planted herself in front of us. It was an impressive move, considering the weight of wool, the canvas tote, and those killer boots. Sheila Manning could probably strike terror in the heart of the meanest mean-girl cheerleader. I resisted the urge to cower behind Moni.

"You're new to cheerleading, aren't you?"

Wasn't that obvious?

"Well, I think a bit of fresh blood might be—" Sheila tucked a lock of glossy auburn hair behind one ear. "A good thing. And honestly . . ." Hands on hips now, she continued, "You two were the only ones who looked like you were having any fun out there. Your school spirit just shines." Sheila dug through her tote and pulled out two spiral-bound books. "But I think you might want to acquaint yourself with this before the start of practice next week." She handed us each a book, and I took a quick glance at the title: *The Prairie Stone High Varsity Cheerleading Guide* by Coach Sheila Manning.

With that, Sheila headed for the entrance. She halted at the door, though, nailing us with a look. "And Moni, sweetie, you really need to work on your splits."

Only when the second set of double doors whooshed closed did we dare to look at each other. "I've got spirit. Yes, I do," Moni said, straight-faced. "I've got spirit. How about you?"

"I'm not sure," I said. "That thing about fresh blood, you think it's anything like fresh meat?"

"Oh, no. It's much better." That sly Moni Lisa smile flitted across her face. "This changes everything," she added.

"Yeah, right."

"Don't you get it? *We* made the squad. Next thing you know, Todd and Brian will go out for football."

The co-captains of the debate team? Football? Brian was destined to win a Nobel Prize. Todd would go into politics, or make a gazillion selling used cars—like his dad. More likely both.

"*I* have a better shot at the football team."

"All I'm saying is," Moni spread her arms wide, "we are a beacon of light to geek girls everywhere."

"Viva la geek?"

"Cha-yeah. We're like the cheerleading weapons of mass destruction."

"You mean everyone's scared of us, but we don't really exist?" She was right about the nonexistence part, if nothing else.

"No," Moni said, "more like—"

"A cheerleading new world order?" Sheesh, I really *was* starting to sound like Todd.

Moni scooped up her pom-poms and shook them at me. "Exactly! Welcome to the revolution, bay-bee," she said before she twirled, stumbled, and landed on the floor.

"Nice splits."

"I'm serious, Bee." Moni gathered up the pom-poms and gave them another good shake. "This means . . ."

I waited for her to finish, but her eyes got that faraway look. What did cheerleading mean, *really*? It meant walking through the halls in a purple and gold cheerleading uniform. Okay, I guess I could do that. It meant Jack Paulson would be "seeing" me at the games. Oh, I could definitely do that. It meant being invisible was no longer an option. That was tougher. But for Moni, sure, I could do that.

A *thump, thump, whoosh* came from the gym, and I felt a lump in my throat. Boys' basketball was a big deal. No, a huge deal in Prairie Stone. Some towns had football. Up north, it was hockey. But here it was basketball. The school devoted weeklong celebrations to it. Social life revolved around it. Most years a slot in the state tournament was almost a sure thing.

It was the only reason anyone tried out for the winter cheerleading squad. Cheering for wrestling? Not cool, despite the presence of several hot seniors on the team. Helping out at girls' gymnastics meets? Please. But basketball. Pep rallies. Banners. The band. The boys on the team. And at the center of it all?

The cheerleaders.

Gah. I knew exactly what this meant. It meant all those people, up in the stands, and the boys out on the court. It meant I was going to have to sing, dance, and cheer, in front of everyone.

While wearing an insanely short skirt.

3

I stood at my locker with my winter coat buttoned all the way
to my neck and took a pre-weekend inventory. German,
history, and English books: check. Permission slip for the
Victorian holiday field trip: check. A set of purple and gold pom-
poms . . . check? I had no idea how I was going to get these things
through the door, never mind tell my parents that I was now a
Prairie Stone High School varsity cheerleader.

I contemplated the possibility of not telling them—ever. I could leave the pom-poms here, sneak my cheerleading outfit to and from school, and change in the locker room. Then it was just a matter of explaining my sudden interest in basketball, gymnastics, and wrestling. Oh, sure. That would work.

"Hey, Bethany!" Moni called. "My mom's here." I reached for the folder where I kept ideas for my Life at Prairie Stone columns and disturbed a slim paperback near the bottom of the stack: *The Art of War* by Sun Tzu. Todd had made everyone on the debate team and newspaper staff read it at the beginning of the year.

A book on military strategy might make sense for the debate team. But the newspaper? Still, maybe something in it would be useful. I gathered everything up, slipped the loops for the pom-poms over my wrist, and ran down the hall. All the while, my mind raced even faster than I did. There had to be a way to get the pom-poms inside the house without my parents noticing.

In the car, Mrs. Fredrickson's expression went from disbelief to near ecstasy when she caught sight of the pom-poms. Her blue eyes—just like Moni's—went wide. "Oh, honey!" Moni's mom leaned across the seat to hug Moni and the set of pom-poms.

I didn't remember her being this excited when Moni made the regional Math League finals last year. Moni was so busy squealing and basking in her mom's attention that she didn't say a word to me in the car. I unzipped my backpack and pulled out *The Art of War*.

> Whoever is first in the field and awaits the coming
> of the enemy, will be fresh for the fight; whoever is
> second in the field and has to hasten to battle will
> arrive exhausted.

Getting waylaid at the front door with evidence of cheerleader activity was definitely not "first in the field." Maybe the pom-poms would fit under my coat?

We stopped at Moni's house first. When we got to her room, Moni gave her pom-poms a ceremonial shake before arranging them in the place of honor in front of her plaster bust of Archimedes and her larger-than-life-size poster of Orlando Bloom.

She touched the scroll bar to wake up her laptop. Almost immediately, her IM program pinged.

"Oh, it's Brian!" she said. "PQ request. He probably already senses my new cheerleader hotness."

"PQ?"

"Party Quest, Bethany. You still didn't sign up, did you?"

I hadn't, and I wasn't sure I was going to either. For the past few weeks all my friends had gone crazy over a new online role-playing game. The avatars in the game were cute, and if Moni was right, there were tons of guys who played. But the truth was, I found online boys just as intimidating as the real-life ones.

Moni's fingers flew over the keys, but she didn't enter the game world. There wasn't enough time. Twice a month and every other holiday, Moni stayed with her dad, eighty miles north in Minneapolis. Sometimes she left straight from school. Other times, like tonight, she met up with her dad at a neutral location like the Happy Chef just north of town.

Her mom seemed to go a little crazy on those days. Moni never said anything, but I had the feeling I was the buffer zone in the routine. With me around, Moni could finish packing and mentally prepare for her dad's new girlfriend without her mom hovering over her.

Moni logged out, readied her laptop for the trip, and threw a few more things in her bag. At the last minute, she grabbed the pom-poms and stuffed those in as well. She blew kisses to Orlando and Archimedes while her mom paced out in the hall.

"I'll call you from my cell," Moni said when we pulled up to the curb in front of my house. These days, she never used the D-word (for Dad) around her mom. It always made me wonder when her parents would start acting like grown-ups again.

I stood on the front porch until I saw brake lights and the turn signal; then Moni was officially gone. I sighed. Things had been bad enough right after the divorce; but once both of her parents started dating, Moni's spirits had sunk even lower. On weekends she had to put up with Monica, her dad's walking, talking Barbie doll. And lately, Mrs. Fredrickson spent a lot of time in coffee shops with a younger man whom Moni had dubbed "Starbucks Boy."

In comparison, sneaking in a set of pom-poms was a minor problem. Still, I shoved them under my jacket—hoping it just looked like I'd had a big lunch—and opened the front door. Inside was dark, but I caught a whiff of chicken cutlets and my dad's special biscuits. Okay, so he popped them from a can and baked them, but somehow that made them dee-licious.

In the entryway, I dropped my backpack and everything nonessential to my mission. I willed my stomach not to growl and crept up the small flight of stairs to the living room. Three tiptoed steps down the hall to my bedroom, I ran into my nine-year-old sister, Shelby.

"What's that?" she asked, poking the front of my coat.

"Nothing, nothing at all." I race-walked to my room.

"Come on, Bee. Show me what it is."

I shut my bedroom door, shoved the pom-poms under the bed, hung my coat in the closet, then sat at my desk, like nothing had happened.

A few seconds later Shelby poked her head inside. "Let me see."

"What?" I said, a little breathless.

"Beth-a-nee, come on."

I shrugged and glanced at the closet, then pretended I hadn't. Shelby sprang forward, threw open the closet door, and said, "Ah . . . ha?"

I laughed.

"I'm telling Mom!" Shelby ran from the room.

"What?" I called after her. "That I have nothing in my closet?"

Dad yelled from the kitchen. It was time to eat. I waited until partway through dinner to drop the C-bomb. I figured with the carbohydrates from the biscuits making everyone drowsy, I might be able to slip in a reference to cheering between the talk about college politics (Dad), and Science and Math Sisters Club (Shelby), and tomorrow's Thanksgiving dinner at Grandma's (Mom).

Once everyone settled into a rhythm of eating and talking, I plunged in. "Could you please pass the salt?" I said to Mom. "And by the way, I'm-cheering-for-winter-sports-this-year."

My mom sighed. For a moment I thought that was the end of it. I didn't have the salt, but hey, I didn't have any explaining to do either.

"Really, Bee." Mom studied the shaker in her hand before passing it to me. "If you don't enjoy athletics, just don't go to their contests. Taunting the jocks will only make things worse."

"Huh?" Dad, Shelby, and I all said at once.

Mom raised a spear of broccoli on her fork and used it to indicate my dad. "Oscar, you have to agree, nothing good can come from *jeering* at them."

"Dear." Behind his glasses, Dad's expression looked perplexed. "I think she said . . . cheering."

The broccoli fell from Mom's fork. Her brow wrinkled, then she smiled and nudged me with her elbow. "Cheering?" She laughed. "Oh, right. Bethany. A cheerleader. Of course."

I thought she might spurt green tea out her nose.

"That *is* what she said," Shelby chimed in. "Isn't it, Bethany? Isn't it? Isn't it?" Her eyes glittered as they swam from me to Mom and back again to me.

"Well—," I started.

"Well?" Mom echoed.

"Well, yes, *cheer*-ing. Moni and I tried out, just for fun." I shrugged, probably because I still didn't believe it myself. "And we made the squad."

"Do you have real pom-poms?" Shelby gushed. "Can I see them? Will you teach me the cheers?"

"Hold on there, Miss Firecracker," Mom said. "Bethany, honey, are you sure this isn't some sort of—"

"Some sort of what, Mom? Mistake? Joke?" Chantal Simmons and her gauntlet girl groupies probably thought Moni and me making the squad was some sort of hilarious error. But my own mother? I expected my parents would have trouble accepting the "Bethany as cheerleader" concept from an intellectual standpoint. Smart girls like me didn't participate in such frivolous things.

"Why shouldn't I be a cheerleader?" I demanded.

"Now, Bee." Dad reached over to pat my hand. I pulled it away. "I'm sure your mom didn't mean—"

"No, no. Of course not." Mom pressed her fingertips against her closed eyes—a sure sign she was aggravated. "I just . . . I mean, are you *certain* that you . . . and Moni?"

Enough was enough. I picked up my plate and headed for the kitchen.

"Bethany," said Dad.

"Bee, sweetie, come back and finish your dinner." That was Mom.

"I'm not hungry," I said, and stomped to my room.

Later, as I made my way to the bathroom, I overheard my parents still discussing it.

"Our little girl is growing up," Dad said. "It's time she started making her own decisions. And if some of them are poor ones, then, well, that's a learning experience too."

"You just don't know, Oscar. You were never a teenage girl. They can be so cruel."

"You're talking to the man who went through high school as Oscar, as in Mayer wiener. You don't have to tell me anything about cruel. But I don't think the athletic department would—I mean, this isn't a prank, not if the administration is involved."

"Oh." Mom's voice brightened. "I could call the school. . . ."

That was the last thing I needed. And even though Mom hadn't called the school—yet—the shame of it scorched my cheeks. I ran cold water and splashed my face. By the time I returned to my room, they were all there on my bed—Mom, Dad, and Shelby.

Mom smiled weakly. "Someone wanted to see those pom-poms."

I reached under the bed, pulled out the handfuls of purple and gold fringe, and dropped them—one, two—on the floor by Shelby's feet.

"Can I touch them?" she asked.

"Sure," I said. Then, glaring at Mom, I added, "They won't bite."

"Oh, honey, I'm so sorry," said Mom. "It's going to take some getting used to. We've never had a cheerleader in the family before."

Except she said "cheerleader" the same way someone else might say "ax murderer."

Shelby gave the pom-poms a tentative, then a more strenuous, series of shakes. Over the rattle of fringe, I said to Mom, "Please don't call the school."

"But—"

"Please?" I tried to keep the whine from my voice and looked to Dad for help.

In the end, I got it. Sort of. Mom wouldn't call the school, but I had to be available for occasional babysitting. Dad hoped I'd continue to help him with the family website. They both hoped I would keep up my grades. No problem.

Or so I hoped.

After a long holiday weekend of explaining to my geeky relatives—No, Shelby doesn't just have an active imagination. Yes, I really will be cheering this winter. Right, I did say varsity squad. No, they don't have separate crews to cheer for the Brain Bowl team—actually getting a cheerleading uniform seemed beside the point.

That Monday after school, the entire squad stood in the equipment room, in various states of purple and gold.

"It's supposed to be short," Moni said.

"Not this short." I held the microskirt to my waist. "I don't want to show this much leg."

Moni, who was several inches shorter, scowled. "At least you have legs to show."

"I don't care. No one wants to show this much leg," I said.

"Chantal Simmons would."

Chantal. Despite her current status as Queen Bee, the Chantal I used to know would not relish flashing butt shots at the student body.

"I bet Jack Paulson likes leggy girls," said Moni.

"So?"

"So, I'm thinking we need to get you an even shorter skirt."

In less than two weeks, I'd be the one flashing the student body. That felt . . . wrong. At least we were allowed to wear a turtleneck beneath the normally belly-baring vest.

"I'm telling you." Moni shook out a uniform and struggled into the top. "This changes everything. It's like Clark Kent transforming into Superman. Only it's, you know, us."

"It's a bird, it's a plane, it's Wonder Geek?" I held the skirt against my waist again. No way.

Coach Sheila threaded through the group, inspecting each girl, adjusting a skirt here, trading sizes there.

"Sugar, I know it's strange at first," she said, a big-sisterly hand on my shoulder. "But you really need a smaller size." In a single swoop, she swapped skirts. "It's supposed to fall four fingers below the butt cheek."

That was information I didn't need.

"For freedom of movement," Sheila added. "Besides, you wouldn't want to look . . . frumpy."

I inspected the even shorter purple and gold skirt. It was so small, I wasn't sure it qualified as actual clothing. And besides, what was wrong with frumpy?

Sheila moved on to Moni, who now wore the outfit over gym shorts and a T-shirt. "Very cute. I don't suppose contact lenses . . . no? All right. We can work with it."

"You know," Moni whispered, "we could kill her now and bury her under the pom-poms. No one would find her until next fall."

I snorted. *Death by pom-pom.* "A jury of *our* peers would never convict us."

Sheila clapped her hands. "Listen up. We've got a lot of work and not a lot of time. Here's the winter cheer schedule. As you know, we have just under two weeks' prep time before the first game, but we support more than just the boys' basketball team."

Some girls shifted from foot to foot. The veteran cheerleaders stared at the floor.

"We'll be cheering at these upcoming sports events, and I expect you to show up at your appointed time and place. Now." Sheila's sparkle turned fiery—downright deadly even. "I've arranged it with the wrestling coach. We can use the weight room between three thirty and four fifteen. That's not a lot of time. So last bell, you're in workout clothes and downstairs immediately."

The weight room? In the basement? The renovated sections of the school were almost nice, but the basement?

"I want my girls toned!" Sheila cried.

"Remember when I said this cheerleading thing would pay

off?" Moni said. "This wasn't what I had in mind. Brian said a rat ran across his foot down there in gym class."

A rat? From anyone other than Brian, I would take that as a joke. But Brian, mild-mannered math boy, was far too serious to joke about rats, especially after reading *1984*.

"After weight training," Sheila continued above the groans, "it's upstairs to the lobby for stretching and routine work—which is what we'll do right now!"

Right now? In the lobby? In our scraggly gym clothes?

"Sheila, can we—," a senior ventured.

"Out, out, out. We only have an hour left."

An hour. I tugged at the tie of my faded drawstring shorts. How bad could it be?

Sheila herded us from the equipment storeroom, down the hall past the locker rooms, and into the lobby. The doors to the gym were wide open, and the varsity basketball team ran some kind of shooting drill inside. Sheila started us with a warm-up routine. I wasn't sure how it happened, but the basketballs stopped thumping in the gymnasium. We'd finished stretches and were working our high kicks when the boys gathered at the doors to watch.

How bad could one hour be? Pretty bad. Humiliating, even. Right there—standing a head taller than all the other boys—was Jack Paulson. I tried not to look at him. I knew I would trip if I did. Much better to fade to the back. Maybe I didn't know cheerleading, but I was an expert at invisible.

"You know." Moni's words came between breaths. "Now would be a really good time for you to do the splits."

Sheila beamed at us. "Moni, what a great idea. I just love your attitude. Bethany, would you care to demonstrate?"

I cared very much *not* to, thank-you-very-much. How could I stay invisible with my legs splayed across the lobby floor? Moni glanced at me and mouthed, *Sorry.*

Yeah, well, so was I. If Moni hadn't been my best friend for two and a half years I would've . . .

But Sheila was waiting, the other girls were staring, and a hush had fallen over the boys gathered at the gym doors. Humiliation, meet Audience.

My limbs felt numb, but somehow I walked to the front of the group, drew in a deep breath, then let the air seep from my lungs while I eased my legs to the floor—sideways. And since I couldn't feel anything but cold tile anyway, I planted my elbows on the floor and my chin on my fists. A single, long wolf whistle came from the gym.

"By the end of the season, I know all of you will be able to do this," Sheila announced. "Shall we start?"

The rest of the squad slid to the floor . . . or at least tried to. Moni frowned. Maybe it was from pain, but probably it was Sheila, who was crouched next to her, saying, "Breathe, breathe, don't forget to breathe."

I turned my face toward the gym doors, where all the boys still stood. Or rather, all the boys except Jack. Where was he? Did he think I was showing off?

Coach Miller blocked my view and hustled the boys back inside. Only then did I realize that *I* had been the one who forgot to breathe. Now I could feel my limbs again, and each and every muscle was cramped. Standing might require assistance.

Across the lobby, in the gym, Jack tipped the ball through the net, then paused next to senior Ryan Nelson before getting back in line. Together they peered through the doors. And laughed.

At me?

I turned my head, as if I was fascinated by the trophy cases, and stayed that way until the reflection of Jack in the glass vanished.

Maybe because I dreaded actually wearing the uniform to school, the days slipped by. A week later, on Tuesday, there I was, in an impossibly short skirt, ready—more or less—to cheer wrestling that night. According to Sheila, wearing uniforms on game days promoted school spirit. So far, the only thing the outfits seemed to promote was hypothermia. My legs had felt like popsicles ever since I left home and I wasn't sure if my knees could still bend, or if they would simply snap off when I tried to sit.

"I can't believe you betrayed the brotherhood."

I whirled from my locker, the cheerleading skirt swaying with the move.

Todd blocked my way, his arms folded over calculus and physics books and a rumpled plaid shirt. He probably glared, too, but his mop of bed-head hair and those fingerprint-smudged glasses shielded me from the effect.

"Could you say that again?" I asked. "In English this time?"

"This." He waved a hand at the cheerleading uniform. "What is this supposed to be, Reynolds?"

I checked the urge to roll my eyes, then leaned close and whispered in his ear. "They're called clothes. Perhaps you've heard of them?"

He sputtered a few words, but when Moni appeared I was saved somewhat from his wrath. His eyes widened. "Not you, too!"

"You didn't tell him?" I asked her. That wasn't exactly a fair question. *I* hadn't told *anyone*. In fact, I was still hoping no one would notice. And yes, I realized the absurdity of that. Now.

"I thought *you* would," Moni said. "I told Brian."

On cue, Brian emerged from the stream of students and approached our group. As soon as he saw Todd's face, he took a step back and tried to rejoin the masses. Too late. Todd was already reaching to grab his collar.

"You knew about this?" he said to Brian.

"Well . . . yeah." Brian shrugged him off and straightened his shirt. "It's kind of cool, isn't it?"

"No, it is not cool. You can't mess with these things."

"I don't know," said Brian. I watched his eyes scan Moni from the toes of her white and silver Skechers to the purple and gold bows that held back all but the most rebellious of her curls. "I think they look cute."

"They always look cute," Todd said.

A compliment from Todd? Maybe we really *had* entered a new world order.

"Okay, so now they're hot." Brian wiggled his eyebrows. On his sweet, round face, it looked kind of weird, but Moni granted him one of her smiles.

Todd frowned. "Think you can you still rub two brain cells together in that outfit, Reynolds?"

"I aced my German test yesterday," I told him.

"And Mr. Shaffer says I can stay in Math League," Moni added, "even though cheerleading practice is at the same time."

Todd stared. "There's practice?"

The throng of kids carried us along the hall. I found myself walking backward and bumping into other students. Step. Bump. Step. Bump.

"What could you possibly need to practice?" Todd asked. "How to smile like an idiot at a bunch of brainless jocks?"

Step. Bump—and straight into Jack Paulson.

"Hey." Jack spun. "I resemble that remark."

Todd's ears turned red. It wasn't often someone could fluster the boy genius. "Sorry." He adjusted the books in his arms. "I was just—"

Jack slapped Todd's shoulder. "If the Nike fits, bro."

For once I wasn't paralyzed in Jack's presence. I laughed. I mean, *If the Nike fits?* That was funny. I caught the look in Jack's eye as my giggle started to fade. He held my gaze, and his expression changed slightly, in a way I couldn't read.

"See you in reading?" he asked.

Commence para-lyze-ation. I nodded—at least, I think I

did—before he turned to walk down the hall. The bell rang, lockers slammed, and we joined the crowd of students heading for class.

"This doesn't change anything," Todd stated. "It's not going to make you . . . whatever it is you think it's going to make you."

"I don't know," Moni said. "I ran the gauntlet twice this morning without a single comment."

The gauntlet? Well. *That* was a change.

"Really?" I asked. "Twice?"

Moni nodded, and when we passed the chemistry lab, she left us with a wave. Before she crossed the threshold, though, she ran back and caught Brian in a hug.

"Thanks," she told him. Brian blushed and stared after her. It was obvious he was crushing. Moni was too, though from what I could gather, Brian's online game character was moving forward way faster than the real-life boy seemed capable of.

"He gave me a wand last weekend," Moni had said.

"A what?"

"A *wand*, Bethany. That's got to be worth, maybe, seventy-five thousand points."

"Has he asked you out yet?"

"In real life?"

I rolled my eyes. "*Of course* in real life."

"Then . . . no."

I was pondering how long it would take Brian to catch up with his virtual self when Todd poked me.

"Listen, Reynolds, you can still resign, right?"

I turned toward Todd, and a wave of students knocked me into him. We were pinned against a wall, with only millimeters separating me from Todd's massive self-centeredness. "Why would I do that?"

"Just because Jack Paulson, the God of Mount Prairie Stone, condescends to talk to you, *once*, it doesn't mean the natural order of things has changed."

I swallowed the urge to tell him I talked with Jack all the time. More than once, anyway. In the hall after tryouts, in Independent Reading . . . Okay, so really, Jack talked, I mostly stammered. Natural order aside, sometimes we came close to real conversation. But I knew—and so did Todd—that it didn't mean Jack would ask me to the prom, or even sit within ten feet of me in the cafeteria.

"Uh, I need to get to class," I said. We both did. But even though we were heading for the same room, I scooted away from him.

"See?" Todd said. "It's starting already."

His words glued me to the floor. A few students turning in to history smacked into me. "What's starting?" I asked.

"The whole cheerleader thing. Next you won't even sit with us at lunch."

Not at this rate. "Look." I drilled a slightly chewed fingernail against his chest. "You're the one acting like a jerk. Not me."

"I'm just trying to warn you. Nothing good can come from this." Todd flipped his mop of hair and marched into class.

The frost outside was nothing compared to the icicles forming at our history table. Todd actually shielded his face from me with his hand. Where was his sense of irony? Wasn't Todd the one who *hated* high school—the cliques, the politics, the "buddy" shoves into lockers that echoed through the hallway and rattled his jaw? He of all people should get the cosmic humor in all of this. Instead there he was, acting like someone who . . . someone who thought popularity mattered.

I pulled out my notebook and a pencil. I'd gone along with Moni's cheerleading scheme to help her, sure, but that was just the start of it. The more I thought about it, the more I felt like I had something to prove: Popularity *shouldn't* matter. Not in cheerleading and not in anything else, either. Of course, deep down, I worried that it did. My pencil rolled across the table toward Todd's notebook. Instead of stopping it, he picked up his books and let it roll off the edge and onto the floor.

What was next? Would he delete me from his IM friends list? Scratch my name off our shared report? Please. I groped for the pencil, trying not to display my purple butt. What did Todd know about cheerleading, anyway?

When Jack Paulson entered Independent Reading, he looked right at me. Or rather, he looked at my face, glanced at my bare legs, then centered on my face again. Gah. I struggled to hold back a blush. And failed.

He took his seat next to me, stretching his own long legs along the desk in front of him. "I've been meaning to thank you for this." He let a thick book thump on the desk. "At least, I think so. Maybe."

I caught a flash of the library's copy of *The Lord of the Rings* when he hefted it a second time. I'd suggested it to him in one of our almost conversations.

"Wilker says if I get through the whole thing and tell him stuff that isn't in the movies, I'll definitely get a B, maybe even an A."

"That's great," I said, or something equally scintillating.

"My grade point average could use it." Jack grinned. "So, what are you reading—today?"

It was his standing joke. Independent Reading class meant, well, independent reading. There were a few books we read together as a group, but most of our time was spent on books of our own choice—and I brought in a new novel at least twice a week. Sometimes I thought I'd caught Jack staring at me while I read. For him, reading was mostly a spectator sport.

I pulled *Pride and Prejudice* out of my bag and laid it on the desk. It was the second of our class reading projects, and we were due to start on it soon.

"I've already read it," I said, "but—"

The second bell rang, and Mr. Wilker rapped on his desk to quiet the remaining talkers. "Everyone needs one of these before Monday," he announced, waving his own well-worn copy of *Pride and Prejudice*. "We'll begin discussing the first couple of chapters then."

Jack groaned. I glanced his way, and he gave me a weak smile. "I'm on the library's waiting list, here *and* downtown," he whispered. "Who knew that dumb book was so popular?" He laughed, but in his eyes I thought I saw a hint of worry—*about buying the book?* Everyone in Prairie Stone knew about Jack's mom, the cancer, his handyman dad, and the insurance that hadn't even begun to cover all the medical bills.

Jack leaned across the aisle. "So what's it about?" he asked. "I tried looking at SparkNotes—boy meets girl, boy pisses girl off."

"Something like that," I said. "Things get off to a rough start. First time they meet, Mr. Darcy disses Elizabeth." I sat back and held in a sigh. God, did I know how *that* went. The first time I'd laid eyes on Jack, he'd been laughing at me. But that had been freshman year—ancient history, or so I hoped.

"Yeah, I got that part, and I thought maybe with the notes . . . ," Jack said while he watched the front of the room. "But that's not going to work, is it?"

"Not in this class." Lots of kids took Independent Reading thinking it was an easy A. It was anything but that.

As Mr. Wilker continued detailing the sort of questions we could expect on the test, I thought about the time Jack's father had come to my house. It was a Sunday about two years ago, when no one else was available for an emergency involving water pipes, a large leak, and our newly refinished basement.

I'd watched Jack work with his dad that day—we all did at first. Me, Mom, Dad, Shelby; it was kind of like a live-action documentary, only instead of the Discovery Channel, it was happening right downstairs. After an hour, Mom and Dad slipped away, then Shelby and I brought drinks for Jack and his dad. The cola was generic—the only kind Mom ever bought—but Jack didn't seem to mind. He gulped it down, and when he'd finished, his dad smiled.

"Okay, Jackie," he said. "I don't care how pretty they are, we need to get back to work."

I'd peeked at Jack through my bangs, wondering how he'd react. Would he roll his eyes? Look away? Pretend he hadn't heard? Laugh at me again?

None of the above. Instead he winked at Shelby, gave me a grin, and proceeded to squirm behind the water heater, a place where spiders, centipedes, and who knew what else lived. I'd known from the first day of high school that Jack was incredibly cute, which I'd assumed meant he was also narcissistic and mean." Now I had to amend my opinion of him. He wasn't really a stuck-up jerk; he was nice.

After they finished working, Jack drank another cola in the kitchen while our fathers haggled over money.

"Come on, Dale. Let me write you a check," my dad had said.

"Can't let you do that. We hardly did anything," Mr. Paulson countered.

"Except save me several thousand dollars." Dad sounded frustrated.

I remember shuffling from foot to foot while Jack squeezed the soda can hard enough to leave dents. His jaw had a proud tilt, but his body was stiff and his eyes looked afraid. It made me wonder how much they needed the money, and how many of their customers gave up fighting before they ever wrote a check. Finally Mr. Paulson conceded; he handed the check to "Jackie" for "safekeeping," and I saw Jack's shoulders relax.

Since that day, I liked to think I knew something about Jack, something important, something most of Prairie Stone High didn't know. Everyone saw Jack Paulson, A-list jock. I saw Jack Paulson, a boy desperately trying to hold things together. Somehow, that made him even more appealing.

When Mr. Wilker returned us to our "regularly scheduled reading," I shoved my copy of *Pride and Prejudice* across the aisle at Jack.

"What's this?" he asked.

"Take it."

"But—"

"Like I said, I've read it." I paused. "Plus, I have an extra copy at home."

What sort of freak has two copies of the same book? That was the question in Jack's eyes. He didn't know it, but I was actually the freak who had *three* copies, or was it four? A hardback, two paperbacks, and one copy in a compilation of all of Jane Austen's works. Admitting that would be social suicide.

Jack's expression shifted again. If I was so good at reading, why couldn't I tell what that look meant? "Thanks," he said. He tucked the book under his desk and opened his compilation of *The Lord of the Rings*.

And that was that. I turned back to my desk before it hit me. I had nothing to read. Not a thing. I'd planned on spending a little quality time with Mr. Darcy and hadn't even thought to grab a backup book.

I leaned toward Jack, ready to ask for the book back—just for the hour. But between the time he opened *The Lord of the Rings* and now, he'd switched books. There he was, reading *Pride and Prejudice*. My copy. In his hands. Sa-woon. No way was I interrupting *that*.

A look of surprise lit Mr. Wilker's face when I approached his desk. He granted passes to the library, sure, but if he thought someone was screwing around (and he had a built-in sensor for that), they were screwed, period.

"Bethany Reynolds needs a library pass?" he said. "Should I check for other signs of the Armageddon?"

A wave of laughter rolled through the classroom. But to tell you the truth, I barely noticed. Instead Todd's warning rang in my head.

This doesn't change anything.

4

From *The Prairie Stone High*
Varsity Cheerleading Guide:

At Prairie Stone High, the varsity cheerleading squad
leads by example.

Some things we *don't* do as Prairie Stone High varsity
cheerleaders:

- We *don't* criticize the sport we're cheering for.

- We *don't* socialize with our friends in the stands.

- We certainly *don't* flirt with the participants!
  Our Prairie Stone athletes need to concentrate.

By fifth-period lunch, I knew Todd was definitely
wrong about cheerleading. One thing had changed:
A purple and gold cheerleading outfit made it pretty
much impossible to stay invisible. People noticed. Some did

double takes. A few stopped conversations midsentence to stare after me.

But I worried he was right, too. Despite the short skirt, I was still Bethany Reynolds, geek, and the cafeteria was still . . . the cafeteria. Sure, I'd be there with Moni, Brian, and Todd (assuming he got over himself by then). But other than the gauntlet, no more dangerous territory existed for my kind. It was the reason I'd made *invisible* = *better* my mantra in the first place.

True, in the morning, the cafeteria could be the best place on earth. Its huge bay windows let in a ton of light. The space was warm, with the scent of cinnamon and all-you-can-eat oatmeal. And of course, there was always the sight of Jack Paulson shoveling in two or three bowls.

Something happened to the cafeteria between first bell and lunch, though. The gentle light of morning turned harsh, highlighting every flaw, making the slightest stain (on your shirt, or your reputation) stand out. And today was no different. If anything, it was worse. Moni wasn't at our normal meet-up spot after fourth period. Now I was all alone, in a cheerleader outfit—and it felt like the first day of freshman year all over again.

Until a few years ago, I'd lived my whole life in tiny nearby Edgerton. I'd gone to school there with the same twelve kids since kindergarten. Then my dad got tenure at Prairie Stone State College, and we moved to the city. No more fifteen-mile drives just to go to the library, grocery shopping, the mall. Yeah, Edgerton was that tiny: think gas station, church, bar/restaurant, as in one of each.

On the first day of high school I walked into a big new school, knowing no one. Or almost no one. I'd known Chantal Simmons from years of dance class (another fifteen-mile drive), and that was something. Sure, I hadn't talked to her all summer, but that wasn't abnormal for us. Her family was the sort that vacationed in faraway places like Europe and Mexico, or at least the Mall of America. Mine was more likely to seek out something more "educational" and "authentic"—like Mount Rushmore or even lutefisk-eating contests.

I'd searched desperately for Chantal that first morning. When I finally thought I'd spotted her, I couldn't be certain it was her. Her hair was lighter, more shimmery. Her body was lighter too. Gone were the thick ankles and slightly pouchy stomach. Even her face looked different. And when I smiled at her and waved, there was something tentative in her response. A case of mistaken identity, I'd thought. That girl wasn't Chantal.

But then someone called her name, and her response that time wasn't reluctant at all. She'd spun away from me and greeted the girl with enthusiasm. A tiny crack of doubt opened inside me. But it was the first day. There were schedules to memorize, lockers to open, classrooms to find. Cutting Chantal a little slack wasn't hard. It was mandatory.

So mandatory that I didn't think twice about approaching her table in the cafeteria. There was one open chair, right next to Chantal. I walked over, balancing a tray in my hands. "Can I sit here?" I asked.

"Well," Chantal said. "I guess you could, but—"

Someone snorted.

"But I'm sitting here." Dina slipped into the empty chair, leaving her own free. She pointed to it. "There's a spot over there."

Traci sprang up and dropped onto the open seat. "Oh, look. There's a space over there."

Cassidy joined the game; she scooted over too. "Sit here! Sit here!"

The lunch tray trembled in my hands. No way was I chasing a free spot around the table in some demented game of musical chairs. Without another word, I walked away.

I heard a roar of laughter behind me. And like a sore tooth you can't keep your tongue away from, I couldn't stop myself from looking back. When I turned, I spotted the tallest head in the freshman class. That cute kid, Jack Paulson. He was laughing too.

For the next few days, whenever I passed Chantal's lunch table, someone would call out, "Hey, there's a seat over here." And again, the laughter that made me wish I could sink into the floor.

By the following Monday, the joke was as stale as the bread in the sandwich bar. No one called out, except a girl named Moni, from my Advanced Algebra class. She waved me over to a table in the far corner. I was hesitant still, but when she nodded her head— and gave me that Moni Lisa smile—I knew I'd found refuge at last. At the geek table, with a couple of boys named Todd and Brian.

Would it feel like that today? What if Todd pulled a Chantal? I could see it now: Todd recruiting anyone, the kids so weird that even *they* didn't like to sit next to each other, all so I wouldn't have a seat. As frightening as that was, I couldn't stand in the doorway forever. I took that first step and crossed the threshold to the cafeteria. The volume dropped as I entered. I swear it did. Not to a complete hush, and no one pointed at me, but it still felt like I was being watched. I caught sight of purple and gold, but it wasn't Moni. It was Cassidy, the cheerleading captain. She sat with the other seniors on the squad—and Chantal Simmons. When I walked past their table, they scooted their chairs so their backs were to me.

For real? Was that it? *That* I could deal with. It was almost funny.

But after I went through the food line, things didn't seem so laughable. I still couldn't see Moni or Brian, and I sure wasn't counting on Todd. When someone touched my shoulder from behind, the tray teetered in my hands. But before it could fall, Brian grabbed it.

"Come on," he said. "Everyone's waiting."

"Everyone?"

He tugged at my tray, trying to pull me forward, but my Skechers had excellent traction and we went nowhere. "Bethany, come on," he said. "It's Moni and . . . and everyone. Wait till you see."

I let Brian lead me by the cafeteria tray. What choice did I have? As soon as we reached the table, the reason I hadn't spotted Moni earlier became clear.

It was like that scene from *Gone with the Wind*, the one with

Scarlett O'Hara surrounded by all those men at the picnic. There was Moni, a blond, curly-haired cheerleader version of the perfect Southern belle, enclosed in a circle of adoring geek boys. She turned to one, then another, positively beaming.

"Hey, guys!" Brian said. "Look who I found." He sounded like he'd just returned from an Amazon quest with some sort of treasure. Three of the boys in front of me scattered, leaving their chairs empty.

"Yo, Bethany!" a boy I knew only as Rad Thad said. "Mine doesn't tip." To demonstrate, he ground the chair legs into the linoleum. I picked Thad's untippable seat, and he did a fist-pumping thing that might have been embarrassing—if I hadn't been so flattered.

For once no one got into an argument about the latest Dungeons & Dragons campaign. No one mentioned the symbolism in *Naruto*, either. Instead one boy shyly showed me his manga drawings. I compared notes from Independent Reading with a second boy. He whispered how *Pride and Prejudice* was secretly one of his favorite books, then begged me not to mention it. He had his "street cred" to think of. I put my hand over my heart and promised. A third boy asked how my latest Life at Prairie Stone column was going.

Maybe Moni was right. Maybe there was something about donning cheerleading uniforms that transformed us. We were celebrities. Okay, so we were nerd celebrities, but still . . .

Just as I was thinking I could get used to it, Todd's shadow fell across the table. He clutched a thick book to his chest and glowered with all the charm of Darth Vader. "Your column is past due," he said to me. "The rest of you, impromptu debate practice, Little Theater."

A few kids looked his way but didn't appear all that enthralled about either debate or practice. When no one snapped to attention, Todd added, "Now."

Rad Thad jumped up and ran, but toward the soda machine and not out the cafeteria door. When he returned, he handed Moni a fresh Diet Coke.

Todd folded his arms over his chest and cleared his throat. "I said, Little Theater. Now." This time only Brian glanced at Todd, and he motioned for him to sit.

"If anyone is interested in doing something serious," Todd declared, "something real, you know where I'll be."

"Todd—," I began. I was about to explain about my Life at Prairie Stone column, but Todd blasted me with a killer look, one that held every ounce of disgust he could muster.

"I said something serious, something *real*, Reynolds." With that he spun, took a few long strides, and collided with Rick Mangers.

Everyone at Prairie Stone knew Rick, even if they didn't really *know* him. He was senior class royalty of the highest rank. Todd stammered an apology, but Rick wasn't listening. Instead he pushed Todd out of the way, sending him careening into a garbage can. The book Todd was carrying toppled inside. Todd blinked, then rooted through garbage while Rick laughed—or did until a group of girls strolled by, then Rick followed. Todd's book, *The Decline and Fall of the Roman Empire: Volumes 1–3*, was streaked with ketchup that looked like blood. He turned and marched out of the cafeteria. Without thinking, I sprang up to go after him.

Brian put a hand on mine. "Don't," he said. "He's so pissed right now, he'll probably smear that ketchup on you, then go back through the line for mustard."

I stared after Todd and willed him to turn around. This space, the geek table and its comforting, abiding acceptance, belonged to him—and him to it. There was no skirt short enough to change that.

That night I tucked the pom-poms under my arm and took the school steps two at a time. The wind lifted my long winter coat. Icy air whooshed straight up my legs and made my breath catch in my throat. I turned at the doors, in time to see the brake lights on our ancient Volvo flicker, then Mom was gone. For a minute, I felt empty, despite the pancakes we'd eaten for dinner—something Mom did only for special occasions.

Moni stood alone inside the lobby, pom-poms clutched in one hand. The slap of mats landing on the floor and the clank of bleachers rolling out echoed from the gym.

"Where's the rest of the squad?" I asked.

"You got me." From her coat pocket, Moni pulled the cheer schedule. "There's supposed to be six of us here: Kaleigh, three seniors, and us."

"So what do we do now?" We looked at each other. Both of us had been counting on the seniors to help break us in.

What the Prairie Stone High wrestling team lacked in student support, it made up for in parental sponsorship. Tons of moms, dads, and grandparents filed in to cheer on the boys.

"Hey, there's Mrs. Dunne," Moni said. "My mom knows her." She dashed off but returned a minute later, looking more confused than before. "Mrs. Dunne says wrestling doesn't have cheerleaders. She looked at me like I was crazy."

So much for counting on the seniors. I peeked at Moni's cheer schedule, although I already knew it by heart. *No cheerleaders?* That didn't make sense. Dread crept into my stomach, and it was like that dream I always had around final exams. The one where I was late for a test and couldn't find the classroom. Wrong place. Wrong time. Just plain wrong.

We inched inside the gym. Two young girls grinned up at us. One reached out to ruffle the gold and purple fringe of our pom-poms when Moni and I walked by.

Otherwise, we really could've been invisible. Parents rushed by us without a glance. The coach turned his back on us as we approached. The wrestling team huddled in one corner, stealing looks at the two of us. At least that meant we weren't totally see-through.

A lone boy wearing a Prairie Stone High Athletics sweatshirt over his purple uniform stood and turned in our direction. A second later I saw who it was. Rick Mangers. He walked straight for us.

My thoughts went to the cafeteria earlier that day, and my heart rate doubled. This couldn't be good.

Rick put an arm around each of our shoulders. "Ladies, perhaps I can be of some assistance?"

I waited one beat, and then another. Between the two of us, Moni was always the one to talk to guys first. But tonight her wide-eyed stare and open mouth made her look like she was hypnotized.

Uh-oh. Like I said, not good.

I cleared my throat. "Well, see, we're just not sure what to do. I mean, we're new to this cheering thing and . . . we've never been to a wrestling game before. When do the cheerleaders usually get here?"

"They're called meets, and I've been coming to them since my oldest brother was on the team," he said. "Believe me, no one's *ever* cheered before."

"You're kidding." I looked to Moni for support, but she continued to stare, her eyes slightly glazed. I pried the schedule from her hands and pushed it toward Rick.

He released me then, but kept his arm around Moni.

Double uh-oh.

"I can tell you this," he said, scanning the roster. "The rest of the squad won't show. You might as well go home."

In theory, I suppose we could have. That seemed to be the unofficial cheering procedure for unpopular sports. Sure, we could call Sheila to ask for help—but ratting out the others on the squad? Probably a bad idea.

"What," I said, surprised at the words coming from my mouth, "what if we stayed?" After all, no one knew unpopular like me and Moni.

Moni snapped out of her stupor and nodded.

A strange look crossed Rick's face, but this one I understood. He was impressed. "You want to stay?" he asked.

This time we both nodded. Moni even managed to shake her pom-poms a bit.

"Well, in that case . . ." He led us over to the other boys, who let out a cheer of their own. While a few freshmen played keep-away with the pom-poms, Rick covered the basics: Never block a parent's view, especially a wrestling dad's view. And never slap the mat. *Never.* One of the wrestlers might think it was the referee.

Rick retrieved our pom-poms, walked us to the far side of the gym, and gestured to a corner where the yellow mat ended and the hardwood began.

"You should be out of the way here," he said. "I'd better go warm up." He strolled away, pulling off his sweatshirt as he went. I had no idea one boy could have so many muscles.

"Whoa," breathed Moni. "He's hot."

Yeah, I thought. *And he knows it.*

"He was totally nice, too," Moni continued, still breathless. "Can you believe they call him Rick the Prick?"

Actually, I could. "Shh. Don't say that." With our luck, his mom was behind us in the stands. But it was true: Rick did have that awkward nickname. And according to gossip, he didn't just *know* about the name, he *embraced* it.

"Didn't you see what he did to Todd today?" I asked.

Moni gave me a confused look.

"In the cafeteria?" I prompted. "Talk about being a—"

"You know," Moni said, as if I hadn't spoken. "Speaking of nicknames, there's something about that wrestling outfit. . . ." She gave me that sly half grin.

I couldn't believe this. "What about Brian?" I asked.

"What about him?"

"I thought you and—"

"In real life?"

"No, in la-la land, or whatever you call it."

"Oh, in the game he's a serious mack daddy. But then he stops over the other night to return a book he borrowed and I think, cool, the boy finally figured out an excuse to spend some nonpixelated time with me, right?" Moni rolled her eyes. "He spent the whole time talking to my mom." She shook her head. Poor Moni.

And poor Brian. Ever since the two of them went from just friends to . . . whatever they were . . . I could tell he didn't know what to say or how to act around her. The game was probably an easy way out.

"What about the wand?" I asked. "That was something."

"Yeah. That's what I thought. But tell me this." Moni looked grim. "Where is he right now?"

If he were as smooth as Rick the Prick, he'd be in the bleachers behind us, supporting Moni's cheerleading debut. Okay, this was Brian. Smooth had never exactly been a quotient in his formula. But if he wasn't here, where was he?

"Home?" I guessed. "The library? Over at Todd's?"

"Ding, ding, ding," said Moni. "He's gone over to the Dark Side."

"What?"

"Todd got to him. I went online before dinner and suddenly Brian's telling me that the wand is just a loan." She huffed in disgust.

A staticky version of "The Star Spangled Banner" began playing, and everyone stood. Fixing Moni's love life would have to wait. When the song ended, two boys walked onto the mat, taking stances opposite each other.

"What exactly are we supposed to do now?" I asked Moni. "Do we cheer?"

"I guess. But what?"

During all the prep for Friday's big game, I'd memorized dozens of cheers. Problem was, only two were for wrestling. "Let's do that takedown one," I said.

"Ready?" Moni whispered. "Okay."

Together we chanted, "Takedown! Takedown! Two points!"

There was a takedown, all right. But judging by the crowd's response, it was for the other team.

Moni cringed. "Bad timing?"

"How are we supposed to know when to cheer it?"

"I don't know . . . the Internet?" Moni offered.

I gave Moni a quick look before raising my eyebrows at the new and highly unusual position the wrestlers had taken. "The what?"

"I found a cheer site the other day while I was surfing at my dad's."

"A cheerleading site?" I didn't know which was more disturbing, that such sites actually existed, or that Moni was surfing them in her spare time.

"I'll print some cheers off tomorrow. I think they had a whole page for wrestling."

After a moment—and another takedown—I asked, "Just one page?"

"Yeah."

That would help. But really, knowing what the boys were doing out there on the mat would be even better. "You know what they should have at cheerleading tryouts?" I said. "A quiz on—"

"On all the sports!" Moni's face lit up. "Exactly! How else can you know when to cheer?" To emphasize her point, she slapped the mat.

Moni's eyes went huge. I sucked in my breath. That creeping dread? It returned, only stronger. At any moment a wrestling dad would probably drag us from the gym by our hair ribbons. We waited, but aside from a quick glare from the boys on the mat, nothing happened. The first match ended, and I couldn't tell if we had won or lost.

Somehow, Moni and I worked up a routine. "Victory, victory, that's our cry!" was an old standby, and we took turns giving each boy a personalized cheer as he left the mat. "Way to go, Logan!" "Way to go, Steve!" "Way to go, Rick!"

I was in the middle of a straddle jump for a senior named Mark when Jack Paulson walked through the gym doors. My ankle crumpled on the landing, and I knocked into Moni.

"What the—" Moni paused, then squealed. "Oh, my God!"

Jack climbed the bleachers and selected a spot where his long legs could stretch out unhindered. From a white paper bag, he pulled mini-cheeseburger after mini-cheeseburger and washed them all down with a half-gallon carton of milk.

"No way anyone can eat that much," said Moni.

"I think it's skim milk," I pointed out.

"Oh, sure." She gave me a look and crossed her eyes. "That makes all the difference."

"What's he doing here, anyway?"

"I heard he shows up at the girls' basketball games too." The kids in Math League were huge gossips, and Moni heard things before the rumor mill even had a chance to get rolling. "He's just cool like that."

I tried to turn my attention back to the match, but Jack was always there, teasing my peripheral vision. His dark hair, his bright red Chuck Taylor All Stars. A flash of milk carton. Okay, so maybe that part was a little gross. It was also . . . endearing. So much for Todd's God of Mount Prairie Stone theory—Jack Paulson wasn't some deity, he was a mortal boy who drank from milk cartons. He probably left the toilet seat up too.

But Jack never left his heavenly perch in the stands, not even when the meet ended and others around him were pulling on their coats. A couple of skinny wrestlers flashed us smiles as they headed for the locker room. Rick sauntered past and gave us a thumbs-up. He scaled the bleachers and plopped down next to Jack.

I grabbed Moni by the wrist. "Come on, let's go."

"But—" Moni pulled away. "What do you think they're talking about?"

"Not us."

"Then why are they staring? Gah, don't look." Moni bent down, pretending to tie her shoe. "Okay, now look. Are they still staring?"

I shook my pom-poms as though the fringe was in desperate need of fluffing. Mid-shake, I darted a quick glance toward the stands. Rick and Jack were, in fact, looking our way.

"Yeah." The pom-poms slipped in my hands. "They're still—oh, my God. Jack's standing up. Hurry, let's get out of here."

Instead, Moni switched to her other shoe. "Just in case. Wouldn't want to trip on my laces."

"Stalling is so middle school," I muttered.

Jack strolled forward. "Hey." He raised the milk carton in a toast. "Nice job tonight."

Moni sprang up, shoes apparently in order. "Thanks! Did you see Bethany's jump?"

He nodded. "A little trouble on the re-entry?"

Great. More humiliation. But Jack looked seriously concerned as he asked about my ankle. *Seriously* concerned.

My heart stopped.

It didn't start up again until he asked twice if I was okay. I gulped, looking to Moni, hoping she'd rescue me. But Moni opened her mouth to speak, then froze. A half second later, Rick came up behind Jack.

"So, Paulson," said Rick. "You tell 'em?"

Moni seemed to be in a Rick Mangers–induced coma. "Tell us what?" I choked out.

"About the bet," Rick said, and Jack frowned. "You know, the one about—"

Jack stared at his shoes. "C'mon, man, that's not—"

"Fair to tell them about it?" Rick interrupted.

Jack looked up, panic on his face.

"I don't remember any rules that said we couldn't, come to think of it." Rick ruffled Moni's pom-poms. "I don't remember any rules at all. Ladies." He held out his hands to indicate both himself and Jack. "We have this bet."

Jack immediately went back to inspecting his shoes, but Rick continued on, completely at ease. Like I said, he was smooth.

"One of us thinks you'll be here to cheer for the next home meet," Rick explained, "and one of us thinks this was an . . ."

Jack looked up again. Something Rick said had seemed to erase the tension from his jaw and around his eyes. He smiled. "An anomaly," he added. "One of us thinks this was an anomaly," he clarified, tilting his head toward Rick and winking.

"Ooh. Big word for a jock." Rick gave Jack a shove. "You

studying for the SATs or something?" He reached out and caught one of Moni's ringlets and watched it spiral around his finger. The curl sprang back when he let go, and continued bouncing as Rick walked toward the locker room.

With Rick gone, Moni regained her composure—and her voice. "So what did you bet?"

"Fifty bucks."

Fifty dollars? That was a lot, or at least, it was a lot to me. I was sure it was to Jack as well.

"Our mere presence is worth fifty dollars . . . ," Moni mused. "Money in your pocket."

Jack smiled, but there was that unreadable look again.

I fought to connect my vocal cords to my brain. "And all we have to do is show up?" I asked.

The tension returned to Jack's eyes for a split second. "Well that, and—"

"And what?" I asked. "How do we help you win?"

"Telling you would be against the rules." He left us with that and headed for the boys' locker room.

I pushed down my own tension and called out to him, "Wait a minute. I thought there were no rules."

Jack smiled and waved before turning into the hallway.

"Whoa," Moni said. "What did I tell you? This cheerleading thing? Paying off. Big-time."

5

From *The Prairie Stone High
Varsity Cheerleading Guide*:

Time to take center stage—or court. Pep rallies are
your chance to really let your school spirit shine.
Dedicated fans will always attend a big game, but
what about the fair-weather fan? Now's your chance
to convince them. Get out there and make heads turn!

For the first time all year, Moni managed to arrive at school
early the next morning, and we headed up to the library.
If I thought she was taking the cheerleading thing too
seriously, well, here was the proof. She scanned the nonfiction
shelves for books on basketball, wrestling, and even gymnastics.

Meanwhile, I was working frantically on my latest Life at
Prairie Stone column. Todd was right; it was overdue. And, after
his supreme obnoxiousness yesterday, I didn't want to prove that

the only thing cheerleading really *could* change was me—*into a slacker*. But by the time I'd come home from the wrestling meet, I could barely lift a pencil, never mind write a whole column.

At least I already had my interview—a senior who split his day between Prairie Stone High and Prairie Stone State, where my dad taught. I hadn't known it before, but Jarrod Scott was taking one of my dad's classes, Intro to Psychology.

Moni hurried back and forth, pulling books from the shelves and plopping them on the table where I sat. I held the digital recorder to my ear. I'd listened to the entire interview twice but kept coming back to one quote: "We were talking about change in your dad's class and how we resist it," Jarrod said, "even when something good happens to us."

It was an interesting idea. I thought I could write the column around it if I got rid of the "dad" part. That had been weird, talking to someone in my dad's class, and I didn't need that information printed for all of Prairie Stone High to see.

Moni rushed up to the table, an open book in her hands. Her eyes were bright, and the reference section of the library was way too quiet when she asked, "Did you know that in ancient Greece the men wrestled naked?"

The librarian coughed. I clicked off the digital recorder.

"Listen to this. They anointed wrestlers with olive oil," Moni read. "After that, they were dusted with powder to make them easier to hold." She slammed the book shut. "Whoa. Now that's a sport I can get behind. Too bad they don't anoint these days."

The librarian coughed again.

"That would *so* be a cheerleader's job." Moni collapsed into the opposite chair like all of it—the oil, anointing, and powder—was just too much.

"I suppose you'd get Rick Mangers," I told her, "and I'd have to anoint a bunch of skinny freshmen."

The librarian coughed for a third time, and I thought I might have to use the Heimlich maneuver on her.

Moni flipped through the book's pages. "Thing is, wrestling? Really complicated. I still don't get all the rules."

"I think the first rule is to use plenty of oil."

Moni snorted. I looked over at the librarian, waiting for her to give me the international sign for "I'm choking," but the kind of torso usually found on Greek gods blocked my view.

"Oil for what?" a voice asked.

I didn't need to look up to tell who'd addressed us. I'd know Jack Paulson's voice anywhere. Maybe if I turned my eyes back to my column, he'd disappear. Then Moni and I could go back to our ridiculous debate over ancient Greece and skinny freshmen. And maybe I wouldn't have to employ the international sign for choking, this time for myself.

A hint of a smile lit Jack's face. Had he heard the whole thing? "Whatcha reading?" he said.

"I believe they're called books." Rick Mangers appeared. He bopped Jack on the head, then crossed his arms over his chest and focused on Moni.

"Oh, yeah," Jack said, "those things that collect dust at the bottom of your locker."

Rick used a finger to lift the cover of Moni's book on wrestling. "What do you say, Paulson? They cheer the whole season and we go double or nothing on that bet?"

"You're on."

"That's—" *One hundred dollars*, I started to say, but we could all do the math. At least I was pretty sure we all could. No one else seemed to think this raising-the-stakes thing mattered, especially not Jack. He just stared at my chest.

Not that there was much to stare at. Then I remembered my accessory du jour, the SUPPORT YOUR LOCAL MASTER*DE*BATER! pin that Brian had foisted on me in the hallway outside the library.

"It's—," I started again, but really, there was no explaining something like that. "I mean, I was wondering if you could lend me your copy of *The Lord of the Rings*? I need a book for reading today."

"I suppose you've already read everything else in here," Jack said.

Of course. We were in the library. Surrounded by books. Now probably wasn't the time to admit I'd already read *The Lord of the Rings*—twice. "Well, there's this." I held up a book on basketball. "But technically it's not a novel."

Jack took a step back. "You two are really serious, aren't you?"

"We've been talking." I glanced across the table, but Moni was under Rick's spell and didn't meet my eyes. "It doesn't make sense to cheer for something we don't understand. We think cheerleading tryouts should include a quiz."

Rick burst out laughing. "It's going to be an interesting season. I'll be seeing you girls later." Moni watched Rick swagger from the library. When he hesitated near the magazine racks, she hopped up to walk him to the exit.

Jack gave me that same mysterious look, the one I could never read. He stuck his hands in his pockets, stared at the floor, and said, "See ya in class."

He left before I could say good-bye. When the library's double doors shut behind him and Rick, Moni nearly ran back to the table. "How much do you think they heard?"

"Like it matters?" I said. "I'm always saying stupid stuff around Jack." Maybe the cheerleading uniform was a Get Out of *Smart* Free card.

"It doesn't matter. I think he's into you."

"No way."

"Way. How many times has he shown up where you are in the last few days? Come on, instead of breakfast in the cafeteria, he's at the library, before school? When's the last time Jack Paulson even stepped foot in here?"

"Oh? So that explains why Rick couldn't find his way back out?"

A blush washed over Moni's face. "C'mon, Bee, Rick's so totally cute. Do you think there's any—"

"He's got a reputation as a player," I warned her. But it was more than that, really. Something told me he *enjoyed* having a reputation. And that bothered me.

"I know." Moni sighed. "But does it matter?"

Maybe. Maybe not. I liked giving people the benefit of the doubt. If only this bet between him and Jack didn't seem so much like a joke. Geek girls or not, I didn't want either one of us to figure into the punch line.

If the librarian hadn't coughed one more time, I might not have noticed the odd look she gave me when I checked out the book on basketball. And later, if Todd hadn't glared, I might not have noticed that I followed him from honors history into the wrong classroom. My mind was on Jack—and that bet. Only when I rushed into Independent Reading late, and Jack aimed his eyes my way, did I come back to the present.

Like Jane Austen might say in *Pride and Prejudice*—such fine eyes. No one with eyes like Jack's could do anything deliberately cruel.

"Your tallest five," Coach Miller said to Sheila.

Moni and I stood with the rest of the cheerleading squad just outside the gym doors. It was the Friday of the first basketball game. Royalty was the pep rally's theme, and the Student Council had decked the gym in school colors.

"It looks ridiculous for a tall boy to be escorted by a short girl." Coach Miller sent the smaller girls a disapproving look. "I'd like to maintain a sense of dignity."

Dignity? Of course. That must be the rationale behind the

paper crowns and the oh-so-dignified shiny, plastic, purple robes. Kings of the Court, get it? Moni poked me in the ribs, and we both tried not to snicker.

Inside the gym, each class packed its own set of bleachers, freshmen at the end by the doors, with seniors near the front. I heard the band play the opening notes to Pink's "Get the Party Started." The cheerleading squad was supposed to be dancing to that. Instead we fluffed our pom-poms in the lobby while Coach Miller and Sheila negotiated.

"All right. We can work with it." When Sheila pinched the bridge of her nose, then tipped her head toward the gym, I caught the disappointment in her eyes. We'd all worked hard on that dance routine. The only reason we were any good was Sheila's unrelenting faith that we could be. That, and the fear she'd go ninja on us if we screwed up.

"Let's see." Sheila bit a perfectly painted nail and looked us over. "Bethany, Kaleigh, Cassidy, Elaine, and Brianna. Line up by height, girls."

Kaleigh bolted to the front of the line, even though I was taller. And we both knew it. I fell in behind her anyway.

"Actually, Kaleigh," Sheila said, "Bethany's got at least an inch on you."

"But look." Kaleigh waved a hand between her head and mine, showcasing her teased ponytail, and I could've sworn Sheila swallowed a smile.

"Hairstyles don't count, sweetie," said Sheila.

I traded places with Kaleigh, who "accidentally" pushed me from behind. I stumbled forward into the gym and finally grasped the reason behind Kaleigh's attitude: There stood Jack Paulson, a paper crown on his adorable head, waiting to be escorted by the tallest girl. Of course. As the tallest boy, he'd be first. Duh.

I teetered on the balls of my feet and fought for balance. Never mind the entire school, I didn't want to trip in front of Jack. I adjusted my skirt and walked a mostly straight line toward him. When we met, I took his arm the way Coach Miller had instructed. Jack grimaced, but a shiny purple robe and paper crown could do that to anyone. Right?

A long, plum-colored, construction-paper carpet wound its way across the gym floor to the place of honor beneath the basketball hoop. My Skechers touched the carpet in tandem with Jack's high-tops. At that moment Coach Miller threw up a hand to halt us.

I squinted to see the holdup. Coach Miller seemed to be having the same type of conversation as he'd had with Sheila, only this time with the band director.

Jack swore under his breath. "I can't believe he's doing this. He's making the whole school wait."

When he didn't elaborate, I whispered, "For what?"

"For us," he said.

"I don't think the whole school minds," I said.

"They should."

On the band director's cue, the members of the Prairie Stone Jazz Band lowered their instruments and dug through their music folders. Light glinted off Brian's trombone while he juggled it and sheet music. The crowd murmured, then pockets of chatter broke out in the stands.

"Do *you* mind?" I asked Jack.

"It's the worst part of basketball season."

Really? I glanced at him, not sure I'd heard right. Jack stepped out onto the court every day. He could probably do layups in his sleep and was no doubt personally acquainted with every plank in the honey-colored wood floor. If anyone owned this court, it was him. I looked up at the tension in his jaw and wondered—maybe it was one thing to step out there wearing a jersey and holding a basketball, something entirely different under the weight of a shiny robe and paper crown.

I'd never thought of it that way before, never thought what it was like to walk across fake purple carpets or shake pom-poms and various body parts center court. And I never thought anyone who did those things minded being in the spotlight.

"You know," I said, as the jazz band settled down, "it's either this or honors chemistry."

"Or Rocks for Jocks." Somewhere behind the scowl was the start of a little-boy grin.

"No one wants to be in class," I told him. "Really."

The band director raised his baton. The first strains of Queen's "We Are the Champions" filled the gym, and the chatter died. It was showtime.

"Except Todd," I added. "He'd rather be in class."

Jack laughed. He actually laughed. And reached for my hand. He tucked my arm back through his, and from somewhere inside me, I found the courage to give his hand a squeeze. He laced his fingers through mine and squeezed back.

We were halfway across the gym when he stopped and leaned down. A single word caressed my cheek.

"Thanks," he said.

A wave of dizziness swept over me. "For what?" I managed.

"Just . . . thanks."

Five minutes after the pep rally ended, Moni tackled me from behind.

"Did he kiss you?" she demanded.

"Did *who* do *what*?"

"When you and Jack were walking across the gym," Moni said. "Did he *kiss* you?"

I stole a look over my shoulder. Jack and the rest of the basket-ball team still stood beside the doors. The cheerleaders swarmed around them. With all the squealing, there was no way Jack could hear Moni. Or so I hoped.

"Are you crazy?" I said. "Of course not."

"Sure looked like it to me."

"He was just . . . he was just"—I touched my cheek—"saying thanks."

"Whoa. If that's thanks, I'd love to see how he says you're welcome."

"Did it really—"

"Look like a kiss? Oh, yeah." Moni nodded toward the gauntlet girls. "They thought so too."

I turned and caught Jack looking at Moni and me. Or maybe just me. Then Chantal Simmons curtsied low in front of him and said, "Your Highness," and he turned away.

That snapped me back to reality. In the real world, Chantal was the cheerleader. Chantal was Jack's proper escort. Me? I belonged in the stands, wedged between Moni, Todd, and the rest of the geeks. But thanks to zero tolerance, we were clearly not in Kansas anymore.

Students streamed from the gymnasium, heading for an abbreviated class before lunch. Moni and I fought the crowd and recovered our books. By the time we made it back to the lobby, Jack and the rest of the basketball team had vanished. And so had Chantal. But really, she had just moved several feet across the lobby and was now standing at her spot in the gauntlet.

"Do we go for it?" I whispered to Moni.

"Hey, Jack Paulson just kissed you in front of the entire school," Moni said. "We can do anything we want."

She was right. No one spoke to us—or at us—as we entered the danger zone. At the halfway point, I started to think I could get used to this gauntlet-crossing thing. No more running through the freshman hall to get to German on time. No more climbing the stairs to the balcony or huddling behind tallish jocks to get to the cafeteria. We were almost all the way through when I took my first deep breath since the pep rally. A locker door slammed behind us and shook the air.

"Uh-oh," Moni sang, and nodded her head in Chantal's direction. "I think someone's a wee bit upset with us." She turned and walked a few steps backward.

"Careful," I said. "We're not out of range."

"Have no fear, Super Brain is here." Moni whipped out her calculator, holding it up like a shield.

"What are you going to do, daze her with denominators?"

"Maybe. But first I'm going to pummel her with my Pythagorean theorem."

"Hey, chill. She might hear you," I said. "Anyway, we don't want to stoop to their level."

Moni swung around and tossed her hair. "You are *so* right."

Besides, I *knew* Chantal, knew her from what seemed like a lifetime ago. We shared more than a crush on Jack Paulson. And despite what Moni might believe, a pair of pom-poms didn't change everything. They couldn't even begin to reach across the chasm that had opened between Chantal and me. But with the whole school buzzing, and everyone doing double takes when I walked by, it didn't matter. Much.

Chalk one up for cheerleading.

If the jazz band played "I'm Too Sexy" one more time, I was going to stomp over to the horn section and stuff my pom-poms down the first instrument I saw. From my vantage point on the sidelines, it would be Brian's trombone. He'd been grinning at Moni all night—at least when his mouth wasn't otherwise engaged.

During the game she'd cast him a few smiles, but otherwise played it cool. I kept forgetting to ask if Brian had come to his senses—if he'd given Moni back the virtual wand. More likely Todd was still using the Dark Side of the Force to control Brian's actions.

I stepped in a slow circle, doing a pom-pom shake and Sheila's patented hip thrust. When the band played, we were supposed to dance—no matter what the song selection. According to Sheila, it gave the crowd something to look at.

Todd sulked with the members of the debate team on one end of the bleachers, while Chantal held court on the other.

Oh, yeah. The crowd was riveted. Moni glanced at me and crossed her eyes.

My legs trembled. My voice was hoarse. I'd lost five pounds in sweat since the game started, five pounds that had magically transferred to my pom-poms. Who knew fringe could be so heavy?

And it wasn't even halftime.

If the sweat and the song were bad, having my back to the basketball court was worse. More than once, I turned to watch the game and track Jack's progress up and down the court. Moni would nudge me when one of the senior cheerleaders threw us a dirty look. *Someone* had to follow the game, didn't they? It was idiotic to cheer, "Shoot. Shoot. Shoot that ball for two!" when our team was on defense.

"Oh!" Moni said. "You're not round and orange, you don't bounce—much—but he still noticed you!"

"What are you talking about?" I asked, while trying to cement the sweatiest strands of my hair behind my ears.

"Jack's checking you out."

I turned toward the team and Jack grinned at me, then huddled with Coach Miller and the other boys.

I tried hard not to smile. Jack was famous for his complete concentration during a game. He hated it when girls tried to distract him. Earlier, when he stood on the free-throw line, Kaleigh had shouted, "You're so hot, you can't miss a shot! Goooo, Jack!"

He missed.

For an instant Jack had turned a scowl on the entire cheerleading squad. Whoa. *Serious game face.*

"Way to go, Kaleigh," said Moni, loud enough that everyone heard, including fans three rows deep in the bleachers, who laughed. After that, the squad's mood shifted. When Kaleigh glared at us, the same unbearably hot gym turned suddenly chilly.

At the end of the first half, Chantal picked her way down the bleachers and whispered something to Cassidy. Elaine and Brianna scooted so far down the bench to make room for Chantal that I was bumped off and had to resort to kneeling. Everyone on the squad, except Moni, pretended not to notice. The two of us snuck off for a drink of water as the dance team took the court.

We returned in time to witness the end of their routine. For once, I was glad it was *cheerleading* Moni had talked me into. I might have to flash my purple butt to the crowds, but at least I didn't have to spank it to a song called "Whip It."

In a blur of purple and gold for the Panthers, and red and white for the Wilson Warriors, the boys jogged back into the gym. But it was Jack who had my attention. He'd taken a fall earlier, the result of a foul. I searched for signs of a limp, but he looked good, focused. He stretched and glanced my way again. I gave my pom-poms an extra shake.

The Warriors called the first time-out of the second half. It was our cue to rush the court and try something marginally innovative and generally dangerous. Usually that involved a perilous twelve-girl pyramid or tossing Moni, the smallest of us, into the air.

Cassidy put her hands together in a triangle, the signal for a pyramid, and Moni rolled her eyes. I swallowed a groan. Nothing like having half the squad on my back—literally. But when Moni dashed forward, I followed. It was all part of the deal. No burden was too heavy if it made my best friend happy.

Midcourt, before even turning to face the crowd, I knew. Oh God, I knew. It was me and Moni standing there.

And no one else.

We were stranded, midcourt, in front of the filled-to-capacity stands. Sometime between Cassidy's hand signal and now, the rest of the squad had disappeared. Oh, there they were—on the sidelines, snickering at us. I searched for a friendly face and caught Chantal's smirk, then Todd's told-you-so expression. That said it all.

I scanned the bleachers for Sheila, though I knew she wasn't there. She'd called Cassidy earlier—a flat tire had kept her away from the game. Thanks to that flat tire, Moni and I stood here, at the intersection of geek girl and humiliation.

Moni looked stricken. Her dad was up there in the bleachers. He'd driven all the way down from Minneapolis just to watch her cheer, then take her back for the weekend.

"Tryouts?" The word left my mouth before I really considered it. But what was the other option? We could slink back to the sidelines. Or we could make it look like we planned it all along.

"Shit," Moni swore under her breath, then, "Tryouts. Ready? Okay."

We did the cheer and jump sequence, the one with the ginormous finish. This time I added a herkie before the splits. I stuck the landing for an instant, then slid to the floor sideways. Moni flew over the top of me, a blur of gold and purple and way-too-close-to-my-head white Skechers.

The band didn't play. No one clapped. No one cheered. On the sidelines, Kaleigh frowned. Cassidy looked confused.

Then a whoop came, not from the stands, but from behind us. One of the boys on the basketball team let out a yell so loud, it echoed through the gym. Its owner sounded a lot like Jack Paulson, but I didn't dare turn to look.

The rest of the boys cheered then—from both teams. Their roar felt solid. Like if I leaned into the sound, it might support me. Finally, the crowd caught on. Even Todd joined in, his applause slow and steady. If anyone could clap sarcastically, it was him.

We sprang up and ran off the court.

"They hate us," Moni said, pulling me close.

I looked down the bleacher row at Kaleigh and Cassidy. Their expressions made me think, *If looks really could kill, Moni and I are about to suffer a lethal dose.*

"What do we do?" Moni asked.

What *could* we do? I crouched and scooped up both sets of pom-poms. I passed Moni a handful of purple and gold.

"I guess we cheer."

Not even Jack's best game could save the Panthers. We lost, seventy-five to seventy-two. Moni's dad waited for us in the lobby.

"Well, that," he said, nodding toward the gym and the score-board, "wasn't you girls' fault." He grinned down at Moni. "I'm impressed, pumpkin. I didn't know you could fly. And very cool for the rest of the squad to let you two strut your stuff."

Oh yeah, yay for the rest of the squad—they were the *best*.

Moni rolled her eyes, but that Moni Lisa smile gave her away. With her dad's new girlfriend out of town for the weekend, Moni had her father all to herself. Something, I knew, that didn't happen often enough these days.

"And that Paulson kid." Moni's dad let out a whistle. "If the college recruiters haven't spotted him yet, they will. He tore up the floor."

"He's crushing on Bethany," Moni said.

"He is not," I protested, but Mr. Fredrickson preferred to believe Moni's version.

"In that case," he said, "I'll have to keep my eye on him. No one messes with my girls."

On her way out the door, Moni glanced over her shoulder and mouthed, *Call me.*

Like I would forget. Getting away with a phone call after midnight was easy now that I had my own line. But that was as far as my parents would go—no cell phone for me. I waited in line for the pay phone with the rest of the losers. A bunch of kids from Wilson High gave me funny looks. I looked down to make sure my skirt wasn't stuck in my briefs, but no, *thank you, God*, that wasn't the cause. I supposed they thought all cheerleaders came equipped with cell phones. Then I followed the group's eyes from me to the gym doors. Of course. They were wondering what was going on. Over there, a group of cheerleaders stood alongside the football players, and the rest of the high school royalty, waiting for the dance to begin. And on the other side of the hall—the only cheerleader. Me.

Even the lamest kids knew how it worked. Sure, cheerleaders put in an *appearance* at the monthly dances sponsored by the Student Council, but that was only pre-gaming. The crowd would end up someplace like the old gravel pit, when the weather was warm, or Rick Mangers's house when it was cold.

And clearly, I wasn't invited.

Someone behind me brushed my leg. The touch of denim against my bare skin freaked me out. I shrugged on my coat and the wool heated up immediately, trapping my sweat. I felt totally out of place. Worse, everyone in the world must have forgotten to charge their cell phone batteries. The line for the pay phone was endless. Whatever the cause, while I waited, the Student Council cleared the gym, pushed back the bleachers, and got the DJ's sound system set up.

The doors to the gym whooshed open and closed once the dance started. Snatches of music burst into the lobby, loud, then muted, then loud again. Halfway into sophomore year, Moni and I had given up on dances. Even if the debate dorks went, they never wanted to dance. Or worse, they thought it was cool to do the robot.

I'd just hung up the phone when the door to the gym swung open again. Inside it was dark, and I swore the scent of sweat still hung in the air. One song faded, and the DJ cued up something that sounded slow and syrupy. "This one goes out to all the members of the varsity cheerleading squad." Oh, yeah. Sure it did.

Mercifully, the door closed and cut off the squeal, but the sound of it continued to ring in my head. I glanced at the parking lot, willing Dad to arrive, when pounding footsteps from the locker room hallway startled me. I pulled the coat tighter around my legs.

Jack Paulson rounded the corner, and his sneakers squeaked when he skidded to a halt. He swallowed a breath and stared at me. "Nice cheer," he said.

"Yeah, well, it wasn't exactly . . ." *Planned*, I'd started to say. But that would be like shining one of Todd's nerd-a-licious light sabers on my moment of humiliation. "Good game tonight," I said instead.

"We lost."

Well, duh. I knew that. And I knew that boys—especially boys like Jack—hated losing. "But *you* were great," I added.

He shrugged, then stepped closer. I clutched the pom-poms tight enough that the fringe rustled in the quiet lobby. Jack's hair was damp from a shower, and I caught the warm, clean smell of him. Jeans, plain white T-shirt, a Prairie Stone letter jacket in gold with purple trim. All a boy like that needed to look good was a bar of soap. It wasn't fair.

"So." He nodded toward the gym. "You going inside?"

I gave the gym doors a glance before checking the parking lot. Any minute Dad would pull up in our prehistoric Volvo.

"I—my—I mean—" I was babbling. Again. But what was I supposed to say? My daddy was picking me up? So not cool.

"Uh." He swiped at a few strands of hair that had fallen into his eyes. "I guess that would be a no."

The gym doors opened. The music surged. Jack slipped away into the dark and sweat smell. And—I had no doubt—straight into the arms of a gauntlet girl.

"Okay," Moni said. "One more time, tell me *exactly* what he said, word for word."

"I told you. He said, 'You. Going. Inside.' That's all. It's not like he actually asked me to the dance or anything."

Something that sounded like a raging blizzard assaulted my ear. I pulled the phone away and waited for Moni to calm down. "I can't believe you're so stupid about this stuff," she said. "That's how boys *do* it. Especially boys like Jack. That way, when you're dumb enough to turn them down, they can rationalize that they never really asked you to begin with."

How could I argue with that kind of logic? Especially when the very same notion had taunted me all the way home. Tears had blurred my view of the Volvo's headlights, but the frozen dash down the school steps cleared my head and squelched the sob in my throat.

"Lots of cars still here," Dad said.

"There's a dance going on."

He tapped the brakes, slowing the car. "Did you want to go, Bee?"

"No," I said. "I'm tired." At least it wasn't a lie. I *was* tired. Tired of the gym, of cheerleading, tired of the gauntlet, even tired of Jack. It was all just too hard.

"We can recover from this," Moni said on the phone. "We've got a week before winter break, and—"

"Oh, sure. Because nerdy girls always get second chances with the star basketball player." I didn't mean to sound so defeated, but that was how I felt.

"I really think he likes you," said Moni.

"Maybe." Why did everything have to be a maybe? Maybe Jack liked me. Maybe he just had a thing for insanely short skirts. Maybe I hadn't blown my only chance.

"Here's what I think you should do. . . ."

An hour later a list sat in front of me: "Witty Things to Say When Jack Paulson Is Nearby." Somehow, *Is that a jockstrap in your pocket or are you just happy to see me?* did not inspire a ton of confidence. I didn't want to think about it anymore, not tonight, so I asked Moni, "How's Minneapolis?"

"Sucks."

Uh-oh. That meant her dad's girlfriend, Monica, was there. So much for father-daughter alone time. And this wasn't the first time her dad had promised his exclusive attention, then gone back on the deal.

"You won't believe what she did tonight," Moni said. She was going for sarcastic, but I heard the hurt in her voice.

I started to ask what was going on, but Moni was already launching into a rant.

"She told me how great it was that we 'share' a name."

"What?"

"Moni-ca. Moni."

I pointed out that, technically, Moni was Ramona. Though it was spelled similarly, it didn't sound the same at all. She didn't share anything with Monica.

"Yeah, except my dad."

Moni continued to complain, but I didn't mind. It was part of the vow I'd made when her parents announced their divorce. Phone calls until three in the morning. Sure. IMs when Moni was gaming on the computer. Fine. Any time, any place. That was no maybe.

I'd always be there for Moni.

Monday morning I clutched the list and stepped through the door to Independent Reading. I tried to get Jack's attention before class started, but he and Ryan Nelson were revisiting a play from Friday night's game—while Traci Olson batted her eyelashes at both of them.

Mr. Wilker tapped his desk. "As you read today, I want you to pay close attention to the inequities between the haves and have-nots in Jane Austen's era. How do they correlate with today's social world?"

Let me count the ways, I thought.

On Tuesday and Wednesday, despite constant prompting from Moni, I still couldn't work up the nerve to use the list. By Thursday I was either determined—or frightened. If I didn't say something to Jack by the end of the day, Moni threatened to intervene on my behalf.

Thankfully, I spotted Jack early that morning. A gaggle of sophomore girls was knotted at the edge of the gauntlet in front of him, blocking his way to the cafeteria. He looked desperate to find a way through the fray. *What Would Lara Croft Do?* I thought. Every boy on the geek squad worshipped The Divine Ms. L.—the anatomically impossible heroine of the Tomb Raider video games. WWLCD had become a common refrain among them.

I whispered it to Jack as I slipped past. He looked down at me, wrinkles forming across his forehead. He obviously had no idea what I was talking about. The crowd parted before him. Jack took a few steps away, then shrugged. Maybe he hadn't heard me. I decided to give it one more try, for the list's sake.

"WHAT WOULD LARA CROFT DO?"

Before cheerleading this would've come out as a whisper too. Not now. Sheila taught us to project to the very top of the bleachers. With Jack moving through the gauntlet, I meant to raise my voice a little. Instead I raised it a lot. The sophomore girls around Jack froze. A few inched backward, putting a safe distance between them and me. Chantal Simmons had to hold on to her sides, she laughed so much. But Jack's expression was (once again) unreadable as he disappeared into the cafeteria.

I stood there, mortified by my own stupidity. I gave up the idea of following Jack into the cafeteria. *The list*, I thought, *should come with a warning: Say it, don't scream it.*

Friday was the last day before winter break. A snow delay meant a modified schedule—no cafeteria breakfast, no Independent Reading, no Jack. Not to mention no list and no chance of making a fool of myself.

After last bell, Todd trailed me down the hall. He was giving me some terse instructions for my newspaper column when I saw Jack, a full head taller than the rest of the crowd.

Jack waved. I turned to see the lucky recipient and found Chantal. Her manicured hand lifted, but she stopped halfway.

"Hey! Hey, Bethany?" Jack said. I'd never heard him say my name before, and the deliciousness of it made my knees threaten to wobble.

"Sorry about yesterday," he called, and then he was beside me. "I don't play video games much, so it took me a while to get it." He tapped his head. "I've seen the movie. Angelina Jolie, right?"

I nodded.

"What would Lara Croft do," he added. "Good one."

Only if *good* had the alternate meaning of "lame." But with the way Jack smiled down at me, lame might actually be good. Or even great.

"Have a nice break," he said, and raced down the hall.

"What would Lara do?" Todd asked. "You said that? To him?" He steered me to a stop against the lockers. "You think you're one of them now? Because, let's face it, he's not one of us."

"Yeah." Chantal sidled up to us. "Next time you should ask yourself, WWTD?"

Neither Todd nor I spoke, but I guess she could read the question on our faces. *T?*

"What would *Todd* do? He seems to know what he's talking about. This little—whatever you're trying to do with Jack. It's not going to change *anything*." She turned on the toe of her silver and red rubber-soled Mary Janes and marched away.

When she was out of earshot, I asked Todd, "Can you believe she said that?"

"Actually, no." He pushed his glasses up his nose. With a goofy grin on his face, he craned his neck to follow Chantal's progress down the hall. "I didn't think she knew my name."

* * *

Mannheim Steamroller played quietly in the background while my mom tinkered with our new set of LED Christmas lights. She was attempting to sync the flash to the music. At the computer desk, I ran the mouse over the color palette and clicked green. On the monitor, a pudgy eighth-grade Chantal Simmons glowed—chartreuse hair, orange skin, blue lips. And, since all was fair in love and war (and cheerleading), I gave myself a bleach job. Ack. I was *so* not a blonde. I clicked undo and wove a white streak through my black hair. Not too bad. The Cruella De Vil—no, Rogue from the X-Men comics—look could really work for me. If I could just get the parents on board with it.

I dangled my index finger over the delete key. Some of these photos simply had to go, preferably somewhere far away, locked in a vault, maybe buried, burned even. Dad could not be serious about posting them all on his family heritage website.

Still, the older photos were pretty neat. We had ones from as far back as the 1800s. Dad had taught me how to scan them in, then adjust the clarity and brightness in Photoshop. That was pretty cool—until we reached the not-so-ancient history of the Reynolds family. Okay, so an Oompa-Loompa Chantal, well, *that* was funny. Maybe I'd send a JPEG to Moni.

When I heard footsteps behind me, I closed the image without saving. The screen was left scattered with thumbnails of tutus, Madame Wolsinski overseeing rows of leotard-clad girls, and one of two young friends side by side, each with a foot on the barre. The caption on that one read: Bee & Cee.

I felt a hand on my shoulder. Mom bent down to view the screen, her soft laugh brushing my cheek. "I'd forgotten all about that. You know, even the parents were a little scared of Madame Wolsinski. You girls were such good sports; you never complained. I think that's why she liked both of you."

She liked us? I always thought Madame Wolsinski preferred the others in the class, the ones with the moms who clucked and tutted on the other side of the waiting-area window.

"And the mothers!" Mom said, as if she could read my mind. "You do know what it means to live vicariously, don't you, Bee?"

Sure I knew. Vicarious was the SAT Term of the Day a couple of months ago, but I'd heard it long before then. I guess Mom thought I wasn't listening when she filled Dad in every week after dance class. It was funny, really. My parents would rather die than be caught watching a soap opera on TV. But give them a real-life drama starring a dozen simpering stage mothers and their offspring, and they were riveted.

"Chantal . . . oh, what was her last name? Simmons, right?" I knew my mom placed Mrs. Simmons in the stage mom category too. She'd pushed Chantal into everything. Dance class, modeling lessons, sessions with a nutritionist . . . Chantal didn't complain about any of *that*, either.

Not even when her mom showed up before our last recital with a small, beautifully wrapped package. Chantal's lip barely quivered when she opened it to find . . . a pair of tummy-control panties.

"A *girdle,* Oscar! Can you *believe* that?" Mom had said. "For a thirteen-year-old girl."

"Poor thing," Dad had agreed.

Mom leaned closer to the monitor. "Have you heard from her lately?"

I shrugged and prayed she wouldn't ask for more details. Surely she knew we went to the same school. Mom squinted at the screen. "I imagine she's lost that baby fat by now."

And then some. Talk about an extreme makeover. "You wouldn't even recognize her." I no more than whispered it, but Mom picked up my tone of voice immediately.

She squeezed my shoulder. "Want to talk about it?"

I shook my head. What could I say?

Sometimes I wondered what had changed. Was it her or me? Well, Chantal had changed, that was for sure. But it was more than just the weight loss or the wardrobe or the brand-new mean-girl attitude. I'd heard the rumors: nose job, fat camp. To me, it was like someone had forced Chantal into a mold and sliced away all the good parts.

I held my finger over the mouse button, poised to bring the old Chantal back again, even if it was only in pixels. Just then, the Christmas lights flashed bright and the deep bass opening to the high-octane version of "Get the Party Started" sounded down the hall, replacing the delicate carols.

Talk about living vicariously. Ever since I'd made the squad, Shelby had gone nuts—stealing my pom-poms and begging me to teach her all the cheers and dance routines. We'd been "practicing" together nearly every night, but—ugh—my legs were noodles and my feet felt like they were about to fall off.

"I think your sister wants to shake her groove thing," Mom said.

"Her what?"

"Shake it like a Polaroid picture?"

I rolled my eyes, and Mom laughed.

"Bethany," Shelby called.

The very last thing I wanted to do was shake, shimmy, pivot, or kick. I was spending more hours at school during winter break than I did in a normal school week. Both Sheila and Coach Miller were determined to get everyone ready for the rematch with the Wilson Warriors, a game set for the Friday after Valentine's Day.

If the boys won the game, they'd probably go to the regional tournament and have a shot at state. But what exactly were we cheerleaders getting out of the deal? It sure wasn't extra time with the jocks. When we took a break, Coach Miller had the basketball team run laps. When the boys lounged in the lobby, Sheila chased us down to the weight room. There really was a cheerleading conspiracy after all. Its dark and mysterious goal was to keep me from talking to Jack. I carried my "Witty Things to Say When Jack Paulson Is Nearby" list every day and hadn't had the chance to use it once.

"Bethany!"

I was exhausted, but it was so easy to make Shelby happy. Besides, that morning Coach Sheila had pulled me to the side and said I knew the routines better than anyone else on the squad. The truth was, *Shelby* knew them even better. I just followed her lead. To shake it or not to shake it? That was the question.

"Beth-a-nee!"

I pushed away from the computer screen and walked down the hall. Maybe not like a Polaroid picture, but sure, I'd shake it.

All the next week, Sheila made us shake it again and again. She even scheduled a practice on Saturday. We stayed late, too, although Coach Miller had already let all the boys go home. New Year's Eve was the next day, New Year's Day on Monday. The school would be closed for the holidays. Sheila seemed worried we'd forget every last dance step, hitch-kick, and cheer between now and when school started again.

Moni crossed her eyes. "I can't believe I have to spend New Year's Eve with Monica," she said during the short break Sheila granted us.

I'd already heard this litany twelve times that day, but I nodded. Moni's New Year's would suck even worse than mine. Her mom was going out of town with Starbucks Boy—a development that Moni was still trying to get used to. Her dad's girlfriend was hosting a "soiree" at Moni's father's place. The best Moni could hope for was to escape to the guest bedroom. My New Year's plans might be lame (home, a little Internet surfing), but at least they didn't include Monica—the grown-up version of a gauntlet girl—or pondering my mom's first trip with her boyfriend.

If I'd heard about Moni's New Year's plans a dozen times, I'd heard about the rest of the squad's plans one dozen times infinity. Not that anyone had told me about them directly.

"What are you wearing to Rick's?" Cassidy asked Kaleigh.

"I wanted to wear the patent leather ankle boots I got for Christmas, but Chantal has a pair of those. You know how she gets about people wearing *her* shoes."

"Wear them," said Cassidy. "Chantal went to Aspen for break." Only the way she said "Aspen," it was a lot more *ass* and not so much *pen*. "I can't believe she's missing the party, though. It's almost like—" Cassidy glanced toward us and pulled Kaleigh another ten steps away.

Moni made a face. "Could they make it more obvious we're not invited?"

"Probably not," I whispered. "I bet they've even got a cheer about it. You know, like:

"One, two, three, four,
Don't let the losers in the door!
Five, six, seven, eight,
Party at Mangers, don't be late!"

Moni snorted so loudly that everyone in the lobby looked at us, including Sheila. Moni and I cringed, expecting Sheila to make us run laps or knock out a few push-ups as punishment for disrupting practice. She didn't. Instead she clapped her hands together and said, "Okay, girls, once more through the routine and we'll call it a night."

On the way out, Sheila handed everyone a card. They were handmade, with edging and lace and a personal message. Moni's said: *Add it up for a terrific New Year*, and mine: *Reading, Writing, and a Righteous New Year*.

Not much got past Sheila.

And while she wished everyone a Happy New Year, she made a deliberate stop by Moni and me. "You probably don't believe it now," Sheila said, "but those kinds of parties are never as fun as everyone makes them sound." With a cheery wave, she wished everyone, once more, a Happy New Year, then walked toward the back entrance and staff parking lot.

The lobby doors opened and closed as, one by one, members of the squad left, until it was just Moni and me. The bleak cold of January—already in the air—puckered the skin on my legs beneath my thin yoga pants. All I could think was, *The only way cheerleading is paying off right now is with frostbite.*

Moni stared at the trophy cases and sighed. "I guess we'll have to take Sheila's word for it. But a party at Rick's—" She broke off, that faraway look in her eyes again.

Then, from the gym, came the *thump, thump, thump* of a basketball.

"Oh . . . my . . . God," said Moni in barely a whisper. "It's *Jack*. You got the list?"

I unbuttoned my winter coat and pulled the folded piece of

paper from my pocket. "Always," I said. "But I don't know. It seems kind of—"

I was about to say *hopeless* before Moni interrupted.

"Just talk to him," she said. We heard a car horn, and she peered through the windows at the parking lot. "Oops, Dad's here." She gave me a shove toward the gym and swung open the doors. "You said you wanted a second chance. Well, here it is."

I did say that, didn't I? Maybe not in so many words, but the whole reason the list of "Witty Things to Say" existed was because I couldn't quite give up the idea of Jack. And it wasn't his hot jockness or how popular he was, but what he was doing right now: practicing late on the night before a holiday, after everyone else had left. That sort of thing said a lot about a person.

I took a deep breath, unfolded the paper, and scanned the list. This wouldn't be easy. Many of the things on there were designed for Jack to overhear. Who was I supposed to say these things to now that Moni had left? While I stood pondering, the *thump*, *thump*, *thump* from the gym stopped. A second later Jack peeked through the open double doorway.

"Hey," he said. "You still here?"

I was speechless. So much for the list. I must have given Jack a strange look, because he added, "Uh, yeah, I guess you are." Then I could've sworn he muttered, "Smooth, Paulson, *real* smooth."

"You too," I said.

"My layups need some work."

"Oh, they so do not."

Then he did the most amazing thing. Jack Paulson, *the* Jack Paulson, actually blushed. "You're looking pretty good," he said, and the flush on his cheeks deepened. "I mean, well, everyone on the squad, that new dance. The guys, uh, they really like it." He looked away from me and concentrated on the hallway that led to the locker rooms. "Hang on a sec." With that, he vanished into the gym.

He returned, letter jacket slung over one arm. With the lobby so quiet, I could hear the scrape and clink of quarters in his palm. "All right," he said. "Got enough. Want something to drink?"

"Um," I said. "Sure." So much for witty. I started to cram the list back into my pocket but stopped. I knew it didn't contain any soda-machine-specific advice, but maybe there were a few all-occasion phrases that might work. I had the list poised for a quick glance. Then Jack leaned forward in a crouch.

"Race ya," he said.

And before I could argue he was off, tearing down the hall. I had zero chance of catching up, but I ran after him anyway. Jack tagged the soda machine, and the noise echoed against the walls— too loud in a too quiet school. I skidded to a halt, the note slipping from my hand. It floated to the floor, landing words up. Between the time I'd written the list and now, I'd shadowed all the letters in the title with Day-Glo Sharpies. It didn't take superhuman vision to read "Witty Things to Say When Jack Paulson Is Nearby." Ditto the magenta heart I'd drawn next to his name.

Jack crouched again, poised to scoop up the note. Jock versus geek girl? No contest. He had the skill, the speed, not to mention the whole hand-eye coordination thing in his favor.

But I did have one thing: pride.

I dove for the list.

Jack's fingers skimmed the paper but didn't quite connect. I launched myself forward, slid on my knees, passed the note, then whirled. It wouldn't have surprised me if goofy slo-mo music started playing in the background.

I reached. Jack reached. I tugged. He tugged.

The paper ripped.

Jack came away with a corner, but I had all the words. We sat on the cold tile, each of us panting. "That must be some note," he said at last.

"It's—" It was what? I searched my brain for a way to explain and came up empty. *So long, second chance.* "It's not something a guy like you would understand." I kept my eyes on the floor and tried to will myself into invisibility.

Jack nudged my foot with his and said, "Oh, you mean *smart kid* stuff?" He was being nice. Even if he hadn't read the list, he couldn't have missed his name. Or the heart. But when I looked at him, he just smiled and offered me a hand up.

"So," he said, pulling me to my feet. "Are you a Diet Coke kind of girl?"

I pointed to the Dr Pepper.

"Really?"

"Yeah. Diet gives me a headache."

"Cool," he said. "I mean, not about the headache, but you know."

I did. At least, I thought I knew what he meant. But that didn't matter. What mattered was standing there, while Jack Paulson bought each of us a can of Dr Pepper.

I held on to that can all the way home, long after I finished the last delectable drops. I didn't even let go when Mom and I walked into the house—or when I saw Todd and my father conferring over the innards of Dad's computer.

"It's just some dust," Todd said. "Makes the whole thing heat up."

Dad nodded sagely—no small feat for an old guy who had just been schooled by a seventeen-year-old.

"Todd, you've been so helpful," said Mom. "Stay for dinner? And afterward, we're having family fun night."

Shelby pulled the pom-poms from my hands and launched into a cheer. "Two, four, six, eight, family fun night is really great!"

"It's Scrabble," Mom added, like this was an added enticement. Actually, for Todd, it was.

"Sure, Mrs. Reynolds." Todd glanced at me, then shrugged, as if to say, *If you want me to.*

My body started to make its conditioned response, a nod, a smile. Over the past couple of years, Todd at dinner, Todd playing Scrabble, Todd geeking out with my parents when I wasn't even there, had become normal. Dad hadn't actually said anything, but Moni and I had a bet for when he would pronounce Todd "the son he never had."

I stopped myself mid-nod. Nothing was normal these days, certainly not between me and Todd. I wasn't sure if things ever would be again. Considering the way he'd treated me lately, I wasn't sure I wanted them to be.

Still, when Dad clapped Todd on the shoulder and said, "On to the biscuits!" I smiled. A little dose of normal might be good for all of us.

Dad and Todd continued the computer discussion all through dinner, lapsing into the never-ending debate of PC versus Mac versus Linux. I still wore my practice clothes, still had the "Witty Things" list in my pocket, and still had my eye on the Dr Pepper can. I wanted to make sure Mom didn't toss it in the recycling bin. First chance I got, I was sneaking it up to my room.

After dinner, Shelby set up the Super Scrabble Deluxe Edition she'd gotten for Christmas. *More spaces! More tiles! More points!* The board even rotated so you could view every angle of play. It was a geek's dream come true.

Dad sent me to my room for my functioning laptop, so we could have the Scrabble website and special online dictionary up while we played. I wanted to suggest we simply crack open Todd's skull and use the Oxford English Dictionary he kept in there. Instead I used the opportunity to spirit that empty can of Dr Pepper to my bedroom. No one noticed, except Todd. He gave me a look that said, *I know what you're doing, and why you're doing it, and I think you're totally pathetic.*

I didn't care.

Mom and Shelby played as a team, like they always did. Todd dominated the board, like he always did. We were several plays into the game before I started to pick up on a theme.

I couldn't remember who put down SUPER (seven points), but Todd trumped it by adding FLUOUS (sixteen points and pretty much how I was feeling). Mom and Shelby cheered over the fourteen points they won for DITZ. Todd used the O from SUPERFLUOUS for SELLOUT (seven points), and on his next turn added TRAITOR (fourteen with a double-word score). But when Dad put down AIRHEAD (an extra four points for a double-letter score), I almost left the table. I expected something like this from Todd, sure. My parents, though?

But then Todd surprised me by building onto the D in DITZ, placing each tile on the board with a flourish. He spelled out DARING (eight points), then looked right at me and raised an eyebrow.

I had nothing. No decent letters and no idea what Todd was getting at. I traded three of my tiles, then shuffled the new and the old together on my holder. That G in DARING gave me an idea. With as much fanfare as Todd, I eased each tile onto the board, spelling out my nine-point masterpiece.

G
E
E
K

Trump that, Einstein.

Todd tipped his chair back, crossed his arms over his chest, and shot me a look as cryptic as the ones Jack Paulson gave me. Totally unreadable. Genius or jock, it didn't seem to matter. Boys were born with a gene that kept girls, no matter how smart they might be, from understanding them.

It should have been easy. "Life at Prairie Stone: New Year's Resolutions" was one of those columns that practically wrote itself. I'd collected quotes at school before winter break, but I waited for New Year's Eve to type the actual copy. I'd planned to enter the last word at 11:59 p.m. It was one of those nerdy touches Todd usually drooled over.

But it was already eleven thirty. So far I'd managed the title and the phrase, "This past year at Prairie Stone" and nothing else.

It wasn't like I didn't have material to work with. Even Mr. Carlson, the journalism teacher, was impressed when he listened to the quotes I'd collected on my digital recorder. "Those are outstanding, Bethany," he'd said. "Excellent cross section of the student body. You're really putting yourself out there this year."

I didn't think I was putting myself "out there." Not really. But instead of the usual collection of lines from my "go to" kids—the debate dorks, the band geeks, and the clueless freshmen who still thought being in the newspaper = instant popularity, I had quotations from, well, everyone.

It was weird. And so totally unlike ninth grade. Back then I'd interviewed a senior, who later claimed I'd made up the whole story. Somewhere in between "I have no recollection of talking to you" and "Please, oh please, can I give you a quote for your column?" my social status had apparently shifted. It was as if a pair of pom-poms made people want to talk to you, even when you weren't lugging them around. I found the whole situation bizarre, but—if I were honest with myself—also kind of awesome.

I clicked on the recorder and listened. I had funny quotes, I had heartfelt ones. I had honest, crude, and every other kind of New Year's resolution you could think of.

Karl: Make at least one person laugh each day—without resorting to flinging boogers.

Kelli: Learn to knit.

Elaine: Recycle more. (Hey, Bethany, can I borrow that history paper you turned in last month?)

Whitnee: Work to achieve world peace.

Jarrod: Quit pretending I wear dirty socks because they are lucky.

Brian: Stop responding to my friend's lame jokes with the even lamer LOL.

I even had the one-two punch:

Ryan: My New Year's resolution is to pass Mr. Wilker's Independent Reading class.

Mr. Wilker: My New Year's resolution is for Ryan to pass Independent Reading. I don't want to see him during summer school.

All I had to do was string the quotes together with a few transitions, mix in some "should auld acquaintance be forgot," and e-mail the whole thing to Todd as a belated Christmas present. There was nothing he liked better than tearing apart one of my drafts.

Instead of writing, I logged on to my instant message program. All my friends' icons were grayed out. I picked up the phone, but my fingers stalled on the keypad. Who could I call? Both Moni and Todd were busy with family parties.

I hung up and nudged the can of Dr Pepper, my souvenir. I squeezed my fingertips against the sides, listened to the soft click of aluminum. This year I'd even collected a quote from Jack.

Jack: Making the honor roll, but it's more of a two-year plan.

I wondered where he was tonight. Probably at Rick Mangers's, along with the rest of the Prairie Stone High School royalty. It was an invite that meant you'd made it, socially.

Shelby shifted on my bed, arms clutching the gold and purple pom-poms. She tried so hard to stay up until midnight, and since my parents were out, I'd let her. Yes, even my parents had New Year's Eve plans, a party at another Prairie Stone State professor's house. Claiming I was forced into babysitting duty might make me look less like a dork, wouldn't it?

I could hear the question now: *What did you do for New Year's?*

I had to babysit, I could say. Not that I'd fool anyone, not even myself. A short skirt might get me a few more quotes, but it still wasn't enough to get me invited to parties.

"Those kinds of parties are never as fun as everyone makes them sound," Sheila had said. Was it that obvious that I wasn't on anyone's A-list? True, I could count the number of "those kinds of parties" I'd been invited to on one hand. One finger, even. *That party.* The one that changed everything for Chantal and Traci, and for Dina especially, but for me and Moni, too. I remembered it all, from the moment Ryan Nelson leaned across the counter at Games 'n More last summer to invite us, to when Moni and I left in her mom's car—way before midnight.

Each August the Nelson family threw a Farewell to Summer bash. Ryan was the youngest in a long line of Nelson boys, the last in a long line of hosts to the party that took place on their big farm. Bonfires and hayrides. It was supposed to be good, wholesome fun. A party endorsed by parents, teachers, and even the popular kids. The only difference last August was, this time Moni and I were invited.

"Everyone will be there," Ryan had promised, flyer in hand. He leaned across a glass display case and handed it to me. "And everyone's invited. Directions on the back," he said on his way out the door.

Moni pinched my arm so hard, it left a bruise. I waited until the bell chimed behind Ryan to let out the breath I'd been holding. Moni squealed.

"I bet Jack Paulson will be there," she said. "And you should be too. We all should."

Brian peeked out from behind a display of upcoming video games. "He didn't invite me."

Moni turned on him. "Of course he did. He said everyone."

Brian poked the flyer in my hand. "Naw, he's out inviting girls. Think he cares if another guy shows up?"

"Well, if he doesn't care," Moni countered, "then why not come?"

"You girls go." He gave the life-size stand-up of Lara Croft a leer. "Me and Lara have plans, anyway."

So we went. As soon as we arrived, Moni wandered off to talk horses with Ryan's older sister, leaving me all alone. "Mingle," she'd said. Right.

It's not like I didn't want to. When I saw kids from school heading in my direction, I'd start thinking up something clever to say to them. But by the time I'd settle on a topic, they'd already passed. Or worse, I'd toss out something infinitesimally witty, like, "Hey," only to be answered by blank stares—or no reaction at all. Geek Girl, meet Invisible.

Which is why I felt so grateful when two little girls from Shelby's science camp recognized me. They stopped chasing butterflies long enough to greet me, then ran off again. I called after them out of desperation. "You know, I bet there's a ginkgo tree around here somewhere!"

The last time all three of us had seen one was at the Minnesota Landscape Arboretum. The girls stopped again. They looked at each other like they were weighing their options. I held my breath and prayed I wouldn't get dissed by a couple of nine-year-olds. Lucky for me, they were nine-year-old *geeks*.

We were headed toward a grove of trees when I spotted someone tall, with dark hair, adorably spiked with sweat. I started to turn the girls in the opposite direction, then hesitated. Moni would pound me if I didn't take this chance.

I watched him slip into the trees. I called the girls' attention to a monarch butterfly fluttering past, then ditched my nerd protégées to follow Jack. That was when I found the *real* party.

As I approached the tree line, I saw the elite of Prairie Stone High School duck beneath the branches in groups of twos and threes. Just as one bunch headed in, another would pop out. It seemed almost choreographed—like a changing of the guard. I pushed aside a limb, noting the saw-toothed leaves of the amur maple, and found a path. Once I was under the canopy of trees, not even the piney tang of insect repellent could disguise the thick scent of beer.

I scooted around an outcrop of poison oak and bumped straight into Chantal Simmons. The amber liquid in her cup sloshed over the rim.

"Nice move, Reynolds." She glared at the damp patch of beer-soaked dirt. But then she laughed, loud and long, and handed me the half-full cup. "You spilled it, you drink it."

The evening was turning cool. In the thicket, surrounded by trees, the noise from the parties—both of them—was cut off. It was just Chantal, me, and the buzz of mosquitoes. What harm would it do if I took a few sips?

I brought the cup to my lips. The taste was more plastic than alcohol, more foam than liquid. I made a face. "It's warm."

Chantal laughed again. "Still gets you drunk." She didn't move away, didn't even look on the verge of saying anything mean. She looked almost . . . friendly. I considered asking her what had happened, what changed? How had each of us landed so neatly on separate sides of the popularity fence?

Before I could, Moni broke into the small clearing. At first she looked panicked, but her expression shifted when she saw Chantal—and then the beer in my hand.

"What's going on?" Moni asked.

"Absolutely nothing," said Chantal. She took the cup from me, downed the last drops, and took a few uneven steps down the path—before turning and giving me a nod in the direction of the keg.

Your call, the look seemed to say.

I didn't move. After a few awkward seconds, Chantal staggered off, alone, but probably not for long.

"Whoa. What was that all about?" Moni said.

I shrugged. "She's drunk."

"I got that." Moni peered down the path, her eyes squinting. "Do you think the Nelsons know about this?"

"I doubt it." My eyes followed the trail that Chantal had stumbled down only moments before. "Should we tell?"

"Would it really make a difference?" Moni asked.

"Probably not," I agreed. We were already outcasts as it was. Why make it any worse?

But later that night, long after Moni and I left the party, Chantal and Traci Olson scrunched into the passenger seat, while a drunk Dina slipped behind the wheel of her father's Lexus. A mile from the party, Dina plowed into a guardrail. The car plunged down a small ravine and nearly wrapped itself around an oak.

When I heard about the crash the next morning, a weight settled on my chest. And no matter what I did, I couldn't make it disappear. Would it have made a difference if I had told? Maybe. But, no matter how much I wanted to, I couldn't change history.

Thanks to the accident and Prairie Stone High's zero tolerance policy, Chantal, Traci—and Dina—couldn't cheer this year. Though it had never been intentional, I had Chantal's spot on the squad. I knew, at least intellectually, that none of it—the party, Chantal's drinking, the accident—was my fault.

But that weight in my chest remained. It was like a bruise I'd touch now and then, hoping it had healed, only to find it was just as sore.

6

On Tuesday—our first morning back after winter break—
Moni and I shuffled into the auditorium for a volunteer
awards assembly. We were careful to watch our step
when we passed the rest of the squad. Even though Elaine had
given me a New Year's resolution quote, the hours we'd spent with
her and the other cheerleaders over break hadn't exactly made us
BFFs. An "accidental" foot in the aisle would not have surprised
either of us.

We made it safely through and took the seats Brian had saved for us. Todd shifted away from me, ever so slightly. Must have been afraid he'd catch cheerleader cooties. Our time together over break hadn't done much for our BFF status either. Although something told me he was merely keeping up appearances—even geeks had street cred to think of.

The principal called my name right before Chantal's. Because, you know, Reynolds comes before Simmons—at least in the school directory. Polite applause rippled through the room, and even Todd clapped semi-enthusiastically. The noise doubled, maybe tripled, when Chantal stepped onto the stage. Moni, an alphabet soup of last names away, rocked forward and peered down the row at me. Her face held one question: *What the hell is she doing here?*

Moni wasn't the only one who couldn't picture Chantal Simmons with a presidential award for volunteering. That same question echoed up and down the aisles.

Principal Henderson passed me a certificate and shook my hand. What had started as a one-time-only demonstration at Shelby's science camp had turned into a summerlong project for Moni and me. We'd racked up serious volunteer hours when Moni took over the Math Marvels and I'd catalogued leaves with the Eco-Explorers. It didn't get much geekier than that.

Naturally, we were already signed up to help out next summer.

But Chantal? Who knew she could pencil in volunteering between nail, hair, and tanning sessions?

Besides me, that is.

* * *

After the assembly, students streamed from the auditorium. They stood in groups in the hallway, on the stairwell. They even flowed through the gauntlet. Making a run for it seemed like an option. When the smell of oatmeal wafted over from the cafeteria, it seemed like an even better idea. Jack Paulson might stop by for a to-go bowl before class.

What would I risk for a glimpse of Jack? Just about anything.

But there was something about the gauntlet that made the lockers look taller there. The floor felt slicker too, like the janitor gave it an extra coat of wax. That whole hallway should really have been marked off with yellow tape and traffic cones—CAUTION: DANGER AHEAD. That way you could make an informed decision: Take the long way around and be late for class or push through and hope for minimal damage.

"Check it." Chantal's voice rose above the chatter. "College admissions drool over this kind of thing."

Todd glanced over his shoulder. "Great. Now college is a popularity contest too," he said, his face wrinkling into a sneer. But the gauntlet wasn't just slick, it had a way of amplifying things that were best left unheard, too.

Chantal whirled. She tossed her head, and her blond hair settled against her shoulders. She tugged at her top, stretching the material tighter across her chest. She gave Todd the look she usually reserved for seniors of the male persuasion.

And Todd fell for it. He was instantly rooted to the spot, feet superglued to the once slick floor. Newspaper editor, genius IQ, chess master, and state runner-up debate champion—dissolved into a puddle of boy hormones.

Dork.

"Hey, Emerson," Chantal said sweetly, "you know, it really is too bad."

"Too . . . bad?" His tone held the smallest bit of hope. That he could speak at all was probably a miracle.

Chantal smiled and Todd stood taller. He reached up in a failed attempt to pat his hair into place.

Double dork.

"Too bad money can't buy popularity," she finished. She batted her eyelashes at him. "Or class."

Todd's arms went limp at his sides, and his ears burned bright red. The latest round of cheesy commercials featuring his dad's used car empire had aired constantly over winter break. Todd's dad had money—lots of it. Class? If you think the Emperor of Emerson Motors sounds elegant or sophisticated, then maybe.

"Oh, man." Moni squeezed my arm, her voice a whisper—anything louder was crazy at this point. "She's someone I didn't miss over break."

Neither did I.

"Hey." Where I found the courage to speak, I don't know. But I flashed my own volunteer certificate and said, "Check it. I hear college admissions drool over this sort of thing."

Maybe it was time I told the rest of the world—or at least the rest of Prairie Stone High—the *real* reason Chantal volunteered. It wasn't the community service hours she owed after last August's car accident. It wasn't because her parents made her do it either. And it certainly wasn't for drooling college admissions boards.

Chantal Simmons missed her grandparents. That's right, head gauntlet girl, the queen of cool, hung out with old people on the weekends because she *wanted* to. I'd gone to visit the long-term care facility with her once. Faces lit up when Chantal walked in. Old men flirted with her. She was, oddly enough, a sought-after partner for bridge.

"So the fraud speaks," Chantal said. She turned and looked me over from the top of my head all the way to my toes. "There, but for the grace of a decent shoe store, go I."

Damn. She made me look. I loved my chunky sneakers. They were comfortable and, I thought, cute. But the to-die-for pink leather flats Chantal wore were the stuff of envy, even for a girl like me.

Someone laughed, then everything fell silent. The lockers seemed to loom even taller, the floor felt even slipperier.

"You're such a brain, I'm surprised you and . . . Rah-moan-ah don't get it," Chantal went on, stepping closer. "Hello? Cheerleading camp? Junior varsity squad? Ever do any of those things?"

I already knew the answers. Everybody in the hall did.

"So. For lack of serious competition," she continued, "you get a spot on the squad. And that makes you what? Different? Special?" Chantal snorted. "Hardly."

I swallowed the truth of it. No, Moni and I weren't that good at cheering. I had mastered one jump. One. Since, really, my herkie was hit or miss. And Moni *still* couldn't do the splits.

"You know what that *really* makes you?" Chantal paused for a second, as if either Moni or I might try to speak. "It makes you a joke. A big freakin' joke. The whole school knows it too. It's embarrassing. Seriously, they're *embarrassed.*" With her last words, Chantal pointed. I followed her finger and found a group of seniors from the basketball team.

The instant their eyes met mine, they looked away. A wave of nausea struck me. The notion that the team—that Jack—might be embarrassed made me cringe.

"Oh," Chantal added, "and if you think a short skirt will get you a guy like Jack Paulson, you are so wrong."

Of course she'd bring that up.

All I wanted was to escape, but there was only one way out now—and that was through. I'd have to fight for every inch of it. I tried to imagine Chantal in her underwear, a debate trick Todd had taught me, but that didn't work. Not at first, anyway. In my imagination Chantal had to-die-for underwear, too. Then I imagined her in *my* underwear. When that didn't work, I imagined her in Todd's. I stared at her and her make-believe *Star Wars* Underoos. Incredibly, I found my voice. "And *you're* wrong," I said, "if you think a nose job and three dozen pairs of expensive shoes will make Jack want *you.*"

Something flickered in Chantal's gaze. Hatred? Grudging

admiration? Surprise that I could still speak? I know *I* was surprised.

"Just remember, geek girl—," she started, while Traci Olson coughed and waved her hands. Chantal ignored her. "Jack Paulson is *way* out of your league."

"You know what?" I said, and it was like the entire student body took a collective breath in, stealing all the oxygen in the hall. "He's way out of *your* league too."

"Hey, do ya think you girls could take this outside?" With the kind of ease only a senior could pull off, Rick Mangers parted the crowd.

"I would." Chantal offered him the same smile that had slain Todd. "But Reynolds here and Ramona the Pest—"

Moni gripped my elbow. Her unfortunate nickname—a leftover from the grade-school playground—was a secret she tried desperately to keep.

Rick halted. His gaze slid over Chantal, smile and all, and then over Traci. At last he settled on Moni.

"Ramona, huh?" he said.

Moni nodded, barely.

"That's one sexy name. See ya around, spark plug." He caught one of her curls and let it bounce free before continuing down the hall.

But Chantal wasn't finished. Not yet. "If you . . ." Traci waved again, a frantic look taking over her face. Chantal held up a hand, cutting off her friend. "Think that Jack . . ."

Exhaustion rolled through me then. This was a fight I would

never win. "You know what?" I interrupted. "You're right. He is way out of my league. Go for it, Chantal, he's all yours."

Moni did a double take. Todd raised both eyebrows. I swung around, ready to grab both of them and make a break for it. It happened then.

Jack stepped from behind the cafeteria door. I smashed against his chest.

Behind me, Chantal swore, and Traci apologized, "I was trying to tell you."

"You okay?" Jack steadied my shoulder with one hand and touched my nose with the other. "Nothing broken?"

He smelled warm, like cinnamon or oatmeal. I had no coherent thoughts. And I certainly had no words, but I managed a nod.

"Are you sure?" He surveyed the group behind me, serious game face in place. I turned to look too, relieved, amazed, stunned that Jack picked me over Chantal. Chantal just looked stunned, her mouth open, her icy cool defrosted. Even her hair was less shiny.

"I'm—," I began.

The bell rang.

"Come on," he said. "I'll walk you to class."

That afternoon, winter air sneaked beneath the lobby's double doors and chilled my bare legs, making me wish I'd worn warm-up pants instead of shorts to cheerleading practice. I huddled with Moni, an obvious—if invisible—division between us and the rest of the squad.

It was supposed to be an easy practice, just long enough to assure our coach that we hadn't gone brain-dead and forgotten how to shimmy in the past three days. But Sheila stood in front of us, hands on hips. No sparkle today, no fire. Something had obviously changed.

"I talked to Vice Principal Torrez a few minutes ago," she said, her tone flat.

The girls shifted. Cassidy glared at Moni and me—like we knew what was going on any more than she did.

"I couldn't believe what I heard, couldn't believe no one told me before now," Sheila continued. "You are representatives of the whole school. But you are also representatives of *me*. And even when I can't be there, you still—" She pulled her glossy lips into a tight line. "Your behavior was intolerable." Sheila paused and pinched the bridge of her nose. "*Intolerable,*" she said again, with a deep breath this time. "I'm surprised the squad hasn't been disbanded."

"This isn't about us, is it?" Moni whispered.

I hoped not, but it kind of sounded that way.

"I never expected this from my squad," said Sheila.

Cassidy rolled her eyes.

"You doubt this is my squad, Cassidy Anderson?" Sheila leaned forward and got right into the captain's face. "Without my time, my money, and my sponsorship, there *is* no varsity cheerleading squad. Are we clear on that?"

The freckles on Cassidy's face stood out against her suddenly pale skin.

"Now. Since the boys' basketball team has the gym, everyone will do stairs and run laps through the halls." Sheila cut the groans short with a single look. "I have a stopwatch, and Mrs. Hanson has agreed to stand post on the opposite end." She let her eyes drift across each cheerleader then, inviting dissent. "You'll be running alone. That way you'll have time to think. Because by next Monday"—she pulled a stack of paperbound booklets from her tote—"I expect each of you to review the Prairie Stone High School Athletic Code of Conduct and write a five-hundred-word essay on the duties of a role model."

This time, not even a look from Sheila could stop the groans. She sent each girl off down the hall, one by one, and the pounding of sneakers echoed against the lockers. Kaleigh threw Moni and me a dirty look before taking off. I leaned forward to start my sprint, but crashed into Sheila's outstretched arm.

"The two of you won't need to run," Sheila said.

"But— ?"

"Ms. Torrez told me about the other girls setting you up on the night of the big game. She thought it was unusual that two girls with as little"—Sheila tilted her head—"experience . . . as you would be featured so, uh, prominently. But it wasn't until a board member overheard some girls at the coffee shop that things came to a head. I wish you'd told me yourselves."

With that, she frowned. I thought we might be in worse trouble than the girls who were running laps. But then some of Sheila's sparkle returned.

"Anyway, I always hated getting punished for something I didn't do," she said. "You girls can lift weights with the wrestling team today."

Not an hour earlier, I would've sworn Sheila had been a gauntlet girl in high school. Now I wondered. I looked behind me, then down the recently emptied hallway.

"It's okay," Sheila said. "No one will know."

It was possible, I guessed, that no one would figure it out. But counting on it left me queasy. Moni wasn't nervous at all. She could barely contain her excitement. But then, she was always better at math and had already figured out the obvious:

Weight room + wrestling team = Rick Mangers.

She practically dragged me down the hall and toward the stairwell to the basement. The clank of metal echoed up the stairs. With the first step, the dank smell of earth surrounded us. Weights. Dirt. Rats. *This was better than doing laps?* In this part of the basement the hallway widened, but the ceiling lowered. I always felt like I had to stoop to make it through. What did Jack do when he came down here? Crawl?

The lights above went from fluorescent to bare bulb. "You think Rick's down here?" Moni asked, her voice hushed.

"I guess," I said. "What do you—?" The clanking grew louder, accented by occasional grunts. Boys, definitely. We halted at the same moment and gave each other a look.

"What do I *what*?" asked Moni.

"What do you think the chances are that anyone will find out about this?" I waved a hand toward the light filtering from the end of the hall.

"Who cares?" Moni said, louder now. Her voice echoed down the corridor—if we could hear the boys, then maybe they could hear us. I put my hand on her arm. Moni might think a short skirt and a set of pom-poms made us invincible. I wasn't so sure.

"They deserved it," she said, all defiant, but I caught the flicker of fear in her eyes. "Besides, if they do it again, Sheila will probably kick them off the squad."

We reached the chain-link fence that separated the weight room from the rest of the basement. In a far corner, Coach Donaldson sat at a gray desk. He nodded at us, then went back to his clipboard. When the door clattered behind us, a dozen boys looked up. Then, from nowhere, Rick Mangers appeared at Moni's side.

"Hey, spark plug, I could use someone to spot me. You up for it?"

Moni didn't squeal. At least I had to give her that. But she did squeeze my arm so hard, the circulation was cut off.

"Go," I said.

They really did make a cute couple. Rick was on the short side, and Moni barely skimmed his shoulder. Both of them blond, both with turned-up noses—Moni'd probably already thought up names for a dozen blond-haired, pixie-nosed kids. And Rick? Well, if Rick thought beyond the next wrestling meet, I would be surprised.

I heard the sound of shuffling feet behind me and turned to find five skinny freshmen. One pushed the other so that, domino-style, the boy closest to me stumbled forward. "Hey," he said. "I was wondering, I mean, with—" He pointed toward Moni and Rick. "Do you need a partner?"

I imagined myself crushed beneath the weight of a giant barbell. "Sure," I said. "I kind of lost mine."

"We noticed," one of the other boys said.

"Uh, I'm Andrew." The first boy stuck out his hand so randomly that I had to jump back to avoid being stabbed in the stomach.

"Bethany," I said.

"We know."

Oh. They *knew*? What did that mean?

The other boys jostled one another like kids, but Andrew's face looked serious when he led me to the Nautilus machine.

"Will you guys be at the meet tomorrow?" he asked.

We'd been to all of them so far. Besides, Moni had the book on wrestling memorized; it was her new favorite sport. "Why wouldn't we be?" I asked.

He gave me a grin. "Bench presses?"

I didn't really need his help to do that, and he didn't need mine. Still, it beat lifting alone, I guess, even if his attention made me feel a little awkward. Actually, Andrew was fine; it was the other four boys gawking at us that creeped me out. They laughed when Andrew tripped on his way to the bench, all gangly arms and legs. I tried not to smile. He was sweet, and in a year or two, that boy would drive all the girls crazy with those high cheekbones—he just had to grow into them.

"Why don't you go first?" he said.

That might be safest. I sat on the bench, but before I could adjust the weights, someone spoke on the other side of the room.

Rick sat, an arm braced against his thigh. In one clenched fist he held a weight larger than I could pick up with both hands. "See, spark plug?" he said. "This is the way you do a bicep curl."

It wasn't clear who admired that bicep more—Moni or Rick. I sighed.

Andrew heard Rick too. I could see his expression change, grow harder. He didn't speak, but the way he shifted his posture left me feeling uncomfortable. I leaned back on the bench and grabbed the bar.

After a few up-down clanks, Andrew spoke. "That's too easy. You need to move the setting up. Like this."

Okay. Now *that* was heavy. A burn spread along my arms. Sweat sprouted on my upper lip. That had to be attractive. Between lifts, I fumbled for conversation. As the older woman, it seemed like my responsibility to provide some.

"Ever see a rat down here?" I asked.

Andrew raised his chin, and I saw the baby-smooth underside of his jaw. His gaze focused on something, or someone, across the room.

"Yeah," he said. "I have."

From *The Prairie Stone High*
Varsity Cheerleading Guide:

At away games, you are all ambassadors for Prairie
Stone High. Every move, every cheer, every comment
will be scrutinized. Your behavior represents the
behavior of all Prairie Stone students. Make certain
to present a united front: The squad that cheers
together stays together.

O ver the next few days, I wouldn't say things actually
improved on the cheerleading squad. The invisible
no-geeks-beyond-this-point barrier remained, as did
the attitude, but the rest of the squad hardly got the chance to
put it in practice.

I wondered if maybe Sheila owned a copy of *The Art of War*,
because our coach was a master at countering the mean-girl

tactics of the rest of the squad. At practices, she insisted that every girl treat the others with courtesy to the extreme. If she caught someone give so much as an eye roll, they paid for it in laps and push-ups. She showed up early for every practice—and waited until Moni and I were loaded in our parents' cars before leaving the building.

She even crossed us off the cheer schedule for Thursday's gymnastics meet because she couldn't be there to monitor how the other girls might treat us. We didn't have the heart to tell her that if we didn't show up at gymnastics, *no one would.*

And during those same days, I wouldn't say my standing with Todd, Brian, and the much-missed geek squad improved either. Moni and I were still on the Geek Night e-mail list, but cheerleading took up more hours than I ever thought it could. Between practices, games, and keeping up with homework, there wasn't time for much else. What little headway I'd made with Todd over break vanished the second school started again. I worried my parents had been right. Taking on cheerleading was way more than I'd bargained for.

But Friday of that week, I found myself without Moni and without the mighty Sheila. To make matters worse, I wasn't even in Prairie Stone. I wished cheerleading was on a pass/fail system—or that I could opt for an incomplete. Or that I, like Moni, had opted to use a "skip privilege." Each cheerleader was granted two per season. Because really, cheering was bearable with Moni at my side. And for the past week, when Sheila was there too, keeping the rest of the squad's attitudes in check, it could almost be . . . fun.

But tonight, where was Moni? In Minneapolis, of course, with her dad. And Sheila? Summoned to a hastily arranged school board meeting. And where was I? In cheerleading hell. Alone, at an away game. There was no one in the stands I knew, no one on the squad who didn't hate me.

So it was left to me—and just me—to explain Basketball 101 to Cassidy.

"Think about it," I said, working patience into my voice. "*Panther* territory would be, like, *our* gym. This"—I waved a pom-pom at the entire court—"is *their* gym."

"It's our end of the court," Cassidy said. "*Our* basket."

"But we switch at halftime," I pointed out.

Cassidy frowned for just a second. "I don't see why we can't still do the cheer," she said.

I let my pom-poms drop to the floor. "Cassidy, we can't," I said. "It's a home-court cheer. We'll look like idiots."

"Then don't."

"Don't what?"

Cassidy pointed to the bleachers. "Don't cheer."

Had I just been benched? *All righty, then.* I scooped up my pom-poms and sat, with nothing but the familiar feeling of self-consciousness to keep me company. Wrong place, wrong time, just plain wrong. Really, whoever heard of a benched cheerleader? In front of me, the other girls spread out, arm-distance apart.

"Ready?" Cassidy called. "Okay!"

Together, the squad began to chant, "This is Panther territory. You! Be! Ware!"

A group of loyal fans jumped at the chance to cheer along. If the Panthers won, it would be their fifth in a row; everyone had the regional and state tournament on their minds. But by the second time through the cheer, a murmur of discontent rose up behind me. I turned in time to see the sharper fans give one another puzzled looks. By the third time through, all but the most rabid fans sat down. I was embarrassed—for the squad, for myself.

Someone should stop this. Okay, that someone was me. I stood, uncertain what to do besides tackling Cassidy and silencing her with the pom-poms—although that option was tempting. Definitely tempting.

Cassidy's expression clouded, like she was having an actual thought. "We can't cheer this," she said.

Oh, so *now* we can't cheer it. I reached for my pom-poms, ready to rejoin the squad.

"Stay," said Cassidy, like she was talking to a dog.

"What?"

"You can sit out the rest of the game. And don't even think about going all Miss Tattletale about it. My dad's on the school board."

On the school board? Before I could process that, Cassidy pulled out a copy of Sheila's cheerleading guide from her bag and flipped through the pages.

"Besides," she said, "the captain has the right to, um, to make anyone I want sit out, okay?" She flashed the guide at me. "It says so, right here."

No, it didn't. I would've bet my pom-poms—okay, so pom-poms weren't a biggie—I would have staked Jack's next three free throws that there was nothing in the guide about that. But what could I do? Cassidy was in charge. Her dad was on the school board. And she was reveling in it.

I sat on the sidelines for the rest of the game. Sometimes I called out, "Offense," or "Defense," to clue the rest of the girls in. No one listened.

The Panthers won by a single point, a last-second, center-court shot by Jack that left me breathless. I smiled, even though the rest of the squad still shunned me. After the buzzer, I congratulated the other team's cheerleaders (by myself), slunk off to the restroom (by myself), and headed to the cold, dark bus.

By myself.

The rest of the girls already sat in the back. I found a seat closer to the driver—once a geek, always a geek. It was too dark to read, not that I'd thought to bring a book. Instead, I listened to the whispers and giggles behind me and crushed the pom-poms to my chest.

A few minutes later the boys stomped, high-fived, and laughed their way onto the bus. The seniors headed for the rear, and a squeal went up from the cheerleading squad. It echoed in the narrow aisle and made my ears ache. I swallowed the urge to roll my eyes. Instead I shut them. Maybe I could shut everything out that way.

"Anyone sitting here?"

I opened my eyes to find Jack Paulson grinning down at me. I shook my head and stuffed the pom-poms down by my feet.

He sat, easing his legs into the aisle.

"Good game," I said. *Lame, lame, lame.* But this time it didn't matter. We'd won. "That last shot," I added, my voice sounding as breathless as I'd felt earlier. "Wow."

He shrugged. "I got lucky."

A lone senior, Ryan Nelson, plopped down across the aisle from us. Jack stared at him.

"What?" Ryan cocked his head and peered past Jack, at me. "Oh, I get it," he said. Ryan stood and clamped Jack on the shoulder. He looked back at the squealing mass of cheerleaders and cringed. "I'll take one for the team, man, but you owe me."

I was still trying to translate the exchange between them—from jock-speak to geek—when the doors clanked shut. The lights flickered out. The driver pulled from the parking lot, and darkness filled the bus. A cry rose from the back, prompting Coach Miller to yell, "Pipe down, or I'm separating all of you." He sat in the seat behind the driver and muttered, "Christ almighty."

Jack and I sat in the dark. It was quiet except for the rumble of the bus and the whispered chatter from the back seats. Then Jack leaned forward and grabbed a pom-pom from the floor. "So, this cheerleading thing," he said, "kind of controversial."

"Who knew?" I certainly hadn't.

"I appreciate it." He rattled the fringe and let the pom-pom slide back to the floor. In the dark, his face was all planes and shadows. "I mean, that someone cares enough to actually follow the game."

"I wish I could—I mean, follow it better." I glanced toward the back of the bus and lowered my voice. "I always thought cheerleaders were—" *Were what? Dumb? Brainless? Completely without a clue?* "But it's not that easy to keep track of what's going on when your back is turned." Babbling. Again. Someday I might manage a conversation with Jack without either clamming up or blathering like a total idiot. But that probably wouldn't be tonight.

The bus pulled onto the highway, heading west toward Prairie Stone. An hour's drive. A whole hour sitting next to Jack. And not a thought about what I could say to him or how to sneak my ever-present list of "Witty Things" from my coat pocket and hold it up to the light. What good was having a ginormous brain if it shut down the moment Jack Paulson came within fifteen feet? The drone of wheels against the road lulled everyone, even the rowdiest in the back. Quiet conversations popped up, a word here, a name there. Mine. Jack's. Together. *Did he hear it too?*

"You know," Jack said, "I finished *The Lord of the Rings* over break. Wilker said I might even get that A."

"That's great." More than great, really, if you considered the basketball team's grueling practice schedule. "I'm impressed."

Jack tapped his skull. "Who'd a thunk it, huh?"

I shifted in my seat, enough to face him. Should I go on the offensive? Guys like him understood that, didn't they? "You, Jack

Paulson"—I poked him in the chest—"might be many things, but I've heard you in class. You're no dumb jock."

I didn't mention that I sometimes eavesdropped on his one-on-one sessions with Mr. Wilker. That would have been right up there with admitting I had his address and phone number memorized. Which I did. Cue the scary stalker-girl music.

"It's your fault," he said.

"My fault?"

"Yeah." He looked down at my finger, still poked in his chest. Before I could yank my hand away, he slipped his palm under mine. Our hands dropped so they rested half on his thigh, half on mine. All I could think was: *Jack Paulson is holding my hand.*

Holding.

My hand.

God, I am such a dork.

"I took that class because of you," he said. "I heard you talking to Moni about it. And I—I watch you sometimes when you read."

Oh, yeah, I thought. *Reading as a spectator sport.*

"You get this look," he continued. "It's like you go somewhere else, like reading isn't a colossal pain in the ass."

"It isn't," I said, surprised I could still form words with Jack attached to my hand.

He didn't let go, but something changed in his grip, a new tension, and not the good kind. I needed to say something. Preferably something not stupid, but one good soul-baring confession deserved another.

I drew a breath. "I kind of did the same thing." I couldn't read his face, so I went on touch alone. "Last fall I heard you talking about running, about liking the sound of your own footsteps."

Jack snorted. "I took some major crap for that. You should've heard Mangers."

I was glad I hadn't. "I wanted to know what that was like, so I started jogging. I had to stop with all the snow, but I really liked it."

"Want to help me get in shape for track this spring?" He glanced down. "You got the legs for it, and I already know you're fast."

I gulped a breath, and then another, remembering my dash for the dropped note. "You're a lot faster than me. I'm usually pretty slow."

"Slow's not such a bad thing." His grip tightened on my fingers. "I mean, you got to start somewhere." He gave my hand a squeeze. "Right?"

We rode in silence for a while, but it wasn't the panicked, agonizing silence that generally passed between us. This time the silence was . . . nice. And a dark bus with Jack Paulson holding my hand—that was *really* nice.

"You tired?" Jack asked a few miles later.

"I'm okay."

"Seriously. Are. You. *Tired*?" he said, enunciating each word. He drew his fingers along my face, urging me, just slightly, toward his shoulder.

Oh! Was I *tired*? For a nerdy girl, I was a little slow picking up on the new vocabulary word. "Maybe a little." I sank against him, gingerly at first. He was all lanky muscle and bone through the letter jacket's leather and felt.

"Bethany?" The word brushed against my hair, and his breath sent shivers across my scalp.

"Yes?"

"I . . . never mind. It's—" He laughed softly and pressed his lips to my head. "It's nothing."

Maybe. But that didn't matter. All that mattered was the way Jack said my name and the touch of his lips against my hair.

There were three drawbacks to sitting with Jack on the bus: The sudden stop in the Prairie Stone High School parking lot, the glare of overhead lights, and the shouts that rose up behind us.

"Whoo, Paulson!"

I winced against the brightness and the taunts. By Monday, the entire school would know. I groped for my pom-poms with my free hand and grabbed Jack's ankle instead. Unfazed, he led me into the aisle, his grip still tight on my hand. He scowled toward the back of the bus. "Chill," he said.

And they did.

Wow. If only I could do that.

Outside, a shiver ran through me. Students streamed from the bus behind us, some fanning out through the parking lot while others headed toward the school. I yawned. The cold made me feel stupid. Or maybe it was Jack, who still held my hand. Neither was helping me form words.

"I need to—" I waved the pom-poms at the school. "I mean, my dad."

Jack slung his gym bag over one shoulder. "I can drive you home."

"I don't want to be too much trouble." I couldn't tell. Was Jack just being polite? "I can always—"

"No problem." He led me to a battered Toyota pickup truck. "I mean, if you don't mind the ride. It's not exactly new." He paused and stared at the truck. "It was my dad's, from a long time ago."

"Really? That's cool."

"You think so?"

I nodded. "Yeah, it's like, I don't know, a legacy."

"He drove it when he first started dating my mom."

His words, spoken so low, almost escaped me. I stared up at Jack while he turned his attention to his shoes. "Then it really is a legacy," I said.

He didn't speak, didn't smile, but something in his expression changed. It was another one of those unfathomable looks, the kind I still couldn't read. But he unlocked the truck door and held it open.

When he slammed his own door, the truck rocked. I clutched the armrest.

"Sorry, it sticks. And that." He jerked a thumb over his shoulder at the gym bag on the flatbed. "Stinks. And—" He shifted in his seat and turned the ignition. The engine whined and sputtered, clearly not happy about the cold. "I've got to let her warm up for about five minutes. Didn't know what you were getting into, did you?"

"I d-don't m-mind," I said, but the chattering of my teeth gave me away.

"Oh, man." Jack took my hands in his. "You're freezing."

"My fault. I am the one wearing the miniskirt." Really, there should be some kind of exception for cheerleaders in Minnesota.

"Yeah, well." An incredible smile lit his face. "I really like that skirt."

Jack scooted closer. My teeth chattered even harder. Cold? Nerves? I wasn't sure. I was alone. With Jack. In his truck. He leaned closer. His fingertips came to rest along my cheekbone. He tilted my chin with his thumb. Then Jack Paulson kissed me.

Kissed.

Me.

The feel of strange lips against mine surprised me, and I forgot to close my eyes.

Jack eased away. "You know, you gotta kiss back. There's this whole guy ego thing tied up in that."

"Oh." I shut my eyes then, trying to block the sudden tears. "It's just, I never—" Oh God. Did I really just admit that?

"What? No way." Jack looked shocked, then leaned forward, all earnest.

"I'm sorry—," I began.

"For what? Don't be sorry," Jack said. "I just—I mean, you're so—and then there's Todd."

Todd? Did people actually think Todd . . . and me? No wonder I didn't have a social life. "It's not like that, if that's what you mean," I said.

"I don't know what I mean." Jack fiddled with the Toyota's heater. "Look, you're smart, you're pretty, and that intimidates the hell out of most guys."

"Even guys like you?"

He turned so our faces were even. "Especially guys like me."

His mouth was only a breath or two from mine. For once, he looked vulnerable. So maybe I didn't know the rules to this game, or maybe any games that guys like Jack played. Did it matter?

We met halfway, and kissing back was so much better. Air from the heater flowed through the small pocket between my face and his, tickled my nose, and roared in my ears—or maybe that was my pulse. I couldn't say for sure.

"Now I know why you're on the honor roll," Jack said, his lips still against my mouth. "You learn fast." He eased back and reached for his seat belt, fingers fumbling with the strap. "I should get you home, but I—can you believe it? We're practicing tomorrow, otherwise—would you?" He shook his head. "Never mind."

"What?"

"We have a break on Saturdays from twelve to one." His hands came to rest on the steering wheel. He stared straight ahead as though he were talking to the windshield instead of me. "I thought maybe you could stop by and we could—I don't know—go get some lunch?"

Okay. This I understood. Maybe it wasn't a date, but Jack Paulson was asking me to lunch. "Sure."

Jack put the truck in gear. When it leaped forward, he gave me that little-boy grin.

From *The Prairie Stone High
Varsity Cheerleading Guide*:

When you cheer for our Prairie Stone athletes,
friendships and bonds will develop. Make certain
you don't favor one friend, one team, one sport over
another. Remember, they all need our support.

Twenty questions greeted me when I got home: *Who drove
you? Why didn't you call first? Do we know him?* They came
at me so rapid-fire that I couldn't answer, all I could do
was swivel from one parent to the other.

But when Mom said, "I'm not sure you know what you're doing
anymore, Bee."

And Dad followed with, "Todd said something about strange
boys, and we're concerned that—" I had to make it stop.

"What?" I said. I think the outrage in my voice surprised all three of us. "In the first place, who says I *ever* knew what I was doing?" I paused to make sure they were going to hear me out before they decided to ground me permanently. "In the second place, I thought you wanted me to try new things. Or maybe there was something in all those lectures about being 'well rounded' that I didn't understand. In the third place—"

"Hold on there, young lady," said Dad. "I think your mother has a point. First you try out for cheerleading, then you're riding around with strange boys. Who knows what could happen next?"

Who knows what could happen next.

Two hours earlier I would have disagreed with them. I would have explained the Distributive Property of High School Popularity: You can take the girl out of the geeks, but you can't take the geek out of the girl.

Then Jack Paulson kissed me.

Jack Paulson kissed *me.*

And I had to admit, "You're right."

Not only had Jack kissed me, but I had a date to meet him for lunch. *Anything* could happen next. That is, if I wasn't grounded times forever. What was it that *Art of War* guy had to say? Something about "He who can modify his tactics in relation to his opponent . . ." That was it.

"I should have called first," I told them. "I should have asked your permission. I can tell that you were really worried about me and I'm sorry that I made you worry." Things changed, I thought. I remembered that interview I did for my Life at Prairie Stone column. *We were talking about change and how we resist it, even when something good happens to us.*

I could almost hear Dad say those words. And when I used them in my column, Todd hadn't edited them, which meant he was impressed.

"I guess some things *are* changing," I said out loud. But I couldn't follow it up with anything beyond that.

Still, I wondered if Dad heard the echo of his own words. His anger melted, and then he offered up a slight smile. "We'll talk about this in the morning," he said.

I nodded, shrugged off my coat, unlaced my shoes, and stowed everything where it belonged—in the closet, instead of on the hall bench where I usually dropped things.

"G'night," I said before climbing the stairs to head for the bedroom hallway. "Oh, and Dad?" When I turned back I found him still standing, openmouthed, staring up at me. "That boy who drove me home, Jack Paulson? He's a lot less strange than Todd."

Oh, the handyman's son, that nice Paulson boy. I could see the recognition settle on their faces.

Something about the name "Jack Paulson" and a good night's sleep mellowed my parents considerably. It didn't hurt that I got up early and made breakfast.

"Keep us informed," Dad said over maple syrup and pancakes.

"You don't suppose she needs a cell phone?" Mom mused.

I nearly broke into a spontaneous cheer but played it cool. The phone was still up for debate, but otherwise, things were kind of/

sort of back to normal, which meant, late Saturday morning, I studied the two kinds of bread we had in our pantry like I was about to make the most important decision of my life.

Multigrain or sourdough? Ham and cheese or the old standby, peanut butter and jelly? Both? The smell of warm brownies filled the kitchen, but nerves kept me from trying one. One careful spreading of peanut butter later, I felt I'd reached a compromise—good, but casual. *Casual* sandwiches? I let my head rest against the refrigerator. I had totally lost it.

I wished Moni would answer her phone. I needed help dissecting Jack's every word and move last night. I needed someone to tell me that what I was about to do wasn't socially or romantically stupid.

I was shrugging on my coat when the phone rang in my room. I almost dropped the lunch in my rush down the hall. Bag in one hand, I launched across the bed and grabbed the receiver.

"Good, you're home," Moni said.

"I almost wasn't."

"What?"

"I'm having lunch with Jack Paulson." In anticipation of her reaction, I held the phone away from my ear.

"You're *what*?" Moni squealed. "Tell me everything."

"No time. When I get back. I'm meeting him at noon."

"Oh God. Call. If you don't, I won't tell you who I talked to last night."

"Brian?" I guessed. She'd been ignoring him since winter break and even switched partners in the Math League. Maybe he'd stopped taking Todd's advice and offered that Party Quest wand to Moni on a more permanent basis? That would be big news.

"What?" she said. "No way."

"Then who?" I needed to leave, like five minutes ago, but even over a phone line I could sense that Moni was smiling.

I waited for Jack in the school lobby, thinking. Thinking about Jack, about the nerd quotient of multigrain bread. About Moni.

She'd refused to say much, just that Rick Mangers had called her. That he was the reason her phone had rolled into voice mail until two a.m. last night. They'd talked for hours, she said, and he was calling again. Tonight. Nice. Maybe Moni could pencil me in for a chat before Geek Night at Todd's.

Finally basketball players started streaming from the locker room. The scent of warm boy sweat overpowered the smell of the brownies. Jack broke from the group, stuffed his hands in his pockets, and stopped in front of me.

"Hey," he said, then added, "You're here."

The surprise in his voice made me wonder if he'd really meant it. Maybe "meet me for lunch" was one of those standard—yet insincere—lines the popular boy always said to the loser girl.

"What's that?" Jack asked.

I contemplated saying "Nothing," but come on, it was a grocery sack. Even geeks don't randomly carry around large paper bags for no reason.

"I brought food."

The line of Jack's jaw tightened and he tilted his chin, the start of his game face settled around his eyes.

Oh, no. Bringing lunch was a bad idea. I clutched the paper handles and racked my brain for a way to recover. I settled on, "Ham and cheese or peanut butter and jelly?" I was doomed.

Jack's face softened. He eyed the bag and then me. "Can I have both?"

Before I knew it, we were sitting in the first-floor stairwell, serious gauntlet-girl territory. With the way Jack tore through the sandwiches, I was glad I'd done the math at home. Even without Moni's help: Teenage boy + athlete = a megaton of food.

By the third brownie, he graduated from inhaling food to chewing it (sort of). He paused long enough to speak. "Bethany."

I loved the way he said my name. I was pondering the deliciousness of it when I realized the word held an edge to it. I pushed a lump of peanut butter past my throat and waited.

"I can afford to buy you a hamburger, you know," he said. "Or a salad, whatever."

"Cheeseburger?"

"Yeah, I can even swing a slice of cheese." No smile, but some of the sharpness left his voice. "Look, I know you're not the kind of girl who'd order surf and turf—"

"They have that at McDonald's?"

"Big Mac and a Filet-O-Fish." He seemed determined not to smile. "Thing is, if we're going out—"

If we're *what*? I set the sandwich down. If Jack was saying what I thought he was saying, I might have to save that PB&J, enshrine it with my Dr Pepper can, and treasure them both forever. "We're going *out*?"

"That's up to you."

At some point I must have said, "Yes," or "Okay," or at the very least, I nodded. It was the only explanation for Jack's quick, brownie-laced kiss, his wide grin, and my own somewhat hysterical laughter.

When he bit into another brownie, I calmed down. Some. "I'm sorry. I shouldn't have—"

"No. It's cool. Really," Jack said. "I mean, some girls wouldn't get it."

Some girls. Like those who specialized in expensive shoes?

I couldn't say how long we sat there. Maybe five minutes. Maybe fifteen. I asked about his truck. Jack leaned forward, and his big shoe knocked the last brownie down the steps. He lurched after it—and ate it.

"Five-second rule," he said.

Teenage boy + food = kind of gross.

But cute.

After launching into a monologue about carburetors, engines, and brake pads, Jack sat back. "Sorry," he said. "I get carried away."

I was about to say something about loving carburetors, although that would have sounded totally weird. Thank God the whoosh of the front doors cut off my reply. The rest of the varsity basketball squad returned from lunch, stomping snow from their shoes, their voices echoing in the lobby.

"I better—" Jack stood.

"Yeah, I know."

"Next time," he said, "we'll talk books."

Next time? Books? I wasn't sure which to believe. "We don't have to do that."

"No, really. We could talk about . . ." He walked toward the locker room while he spoke. "I don't know, *Pride and Prejudice*, maybe?"

Oh, of *course*. "I'm sure Wilker's essay test has nothing to do with it."

"Not a thing." From his jacket pocket, he pulled my copy of the book. "See? I carry it with me everywhere I go."

"I got the DVD for Christmas," I said. "We should probably watch it," and when I realized what I was suggesting, I rushed to explain. "You know, so we can do a compare and contrast for Wilker." Which, of course, made me sound even more like a dork.

Jack raised his eyebrows while I fought to keep from smacking my forehead.

"That's not cheating?" he asked.

"Not if you read the book."

"Yeah. That."

When we got to the gym, Ryan Nelson and a few other senior boys were running through layups; basketballs thumped against the floor. Jack reached for one, then simultaneously slipped off his jacket and shot at the basket.

"Wow."

He glanced back at me. "Lunch was . . ." He gave me that wide grin, the one that made him look like a little boy. "Great."

"Thanks."

"Thank *you*." He kissed me—quick—and Ryan shouted something that ended in "dawg." Translating it was impossible with the feel of Jack's kiss still on my lips. "I'll call you tonight?" he said.

I blinked, unable to communicate by normal, human means. Jack laughed before turning to jog across the gym. Wait! How could he call? He didn't have my number. "Jack!"

He skidded to a halt and spun.

"Do you, I mean, my—" I swear, my IQ dropped a hundred points every time I was near that boy. "My phone number," I finally stammered.

That grin again. Jack didn't say word. Instead he tapped his forehead with his index finger, once, twice, before scooping up a ball and shooting it from midcourt.

"Wow."

I'd gone to my room that evening, determined to start on my homework. For the last half hour, I'd looked out my window and contemplated the dark street and the ghostly snow instead. Lunch.

Jack. Way more interesting than the extra-credit history report I was supposed to be doing with Todd, "Dictators through the Ages."

I couldn't help noticing how quiet it was, both outside and in. I'd left Moni a voice mail and sent a detailed e-mail describing my "date" with Jack, but I still hadn't heard from her. Nothing from Todd, either, not even a nudge about the report, or a reminder about Geek Night. I would've been glad to see spam in my in-box, and I almost e-mailed myself, just to see if the program still worked.

Saturday night *was* Geek Night. I weighed the pros and cons—again—about skipping. It was a standing tradition with the debate dorks, the chess team, the symphonic band, plus me and Moni. Video games, anime, trivia contests, and the occasional replay of *Jeopardy!* shows. It was how the brainy bunch bonded.

I missed those boys; I even missed Todd. Despite what he might think, I wasn't avoiding him on purpose. I wasn't avoiding Geek Night, either. Not really. Ever since Moni and I had started cheering, we hadn't done much of anything that didn't involve schoolwork or a referee. Maybe cheerleaders weren't really so stuck-up; maybe they didn't have time to talk to anyone.

I had just opened a book about Mussolini when the phone rang. My heart skipped a beat, and for a second, I hoped it was Jack on the other end, but I knew better. It was prime Moni-calling time. The hour when Moni's dad and Monica bonded over creating bacon-wrapped sea scallops and saffron rice, and Moni retreated to the guest room until dinner. "About time you called." My words came out in a huff.

"I said I would."

Not Moni, not even Todd, although he usually IM'd me. No, it was Jack on the other end of the phone line. I groped for words and came up empty.

Jack laughed.

"I thought you were Moni," I managed to say.

"So I figured."

But then he grew quiet, and I wondered if we were destined for one of those awful phone calls that contained more silence and static than actual conversation.

"So," Jack said. "What are you doing?"

I glanced at the book in front of me. I almost hated to admit it. "Homework."

"That's what I'm doing too." A shrill whistle interrupted Jack, and he swore. "Sorry, I'm also listening to the radio. The T-wolves are playing."

Instead of my throat clamping up, I relaxed. "Really?" I said. "They have basketball on the radio?"

"Yeah." He said it like it was the most normal thing ever. "I can see the game in my head."

Even though I was really glad it was Jack on the line, I didn't want to miss talking to Moni. I reached for my laptop and logged on to IM, thinking she might try to message me.

"That sounded lame," said Jack.

What sounded lame? Had I managed to say something stupid, without even knowing it? I wound back through the conversation.

Oh. "Seeing the game in your head doesn't sound lame at all," I told him. "That's how reading is for me. Kind of like watching a movie, but in your brain."

My IM program flashed. QT_Pi (aka Moni) wanted to chat.

QT_Pi: Wassup? Phone. Busy.

Book_Grrl: I know.

QT_Pi: And? And?

Book_Grrl: And what?

Yeah. I was teasing her. On the phone, Jack said, "You wouldn't want to help a dumb jock with his homework, would you?"

I laughed. "What's the subject?"

"Pretty much all of them."

QT_Pi: Tell. Me. NOW!

Book_Grrl: Phone = Jack.

Instead of typing actual words, Moni filled her entire message space with exclamation points, followed by one word: *DEEETAILS*. In all caps.

QT_Pi: OMG! *My* phone.

Book_Grrl: Who?

Nothing. I tried again.

Book_Grrl: Who?

QT_Pi: Rick, rick, rick, rick!!!1

Her IM icon went gray. So long, Moni. Hello, Jack. For a while, we discussed his Grammar and Comp class, which frustrated him. And trig, which frustrated us both. Math was always Moni's subject, not mine.

"Oh, man," he said as I heard the ref's whistle blow again. "T-wolves suck—and so do I. This stuff is too hard. College—what was I thinking?"

"Where do you want to go?" I asked.

"U of M, but I have to get a scholarship first."

"Basketball, right?"

"I'm hoping," he said.

"You'll look good in maroon and gold."

"It's not a sure thing."

Wasn't it? "Okay, so I don't know a lot about basketball," I said, "but I know talent when I see it. You have talent, Jack Paulson. Any Big Ten school would want you."

"They'd want you, too, along with Harvard, Yale . . . all the rest."

"Right," I said. "That's Todd's thing."

With the mention of Todd, Jack went so quiet that I could hear the game's play-by-play in the background. I'd learned enough about basketball to know the T-wolves really were sucking—and so was our conversation.

"What?" I asked.

"He's—" Jack paused. "Really smart."

"So?" But I got it. Hard to believe *the* Jack Paulson might be jealous of Todd Emerson, dork extraordinaire. "You're smart too," I said.

"Not like . . . that. Not like . . . you."

"There's different kinds of smart," I said. "There's smart in your head and then there's—" *Smart in your heart,* I wanted to say, but just thinking it made me blush.

"There's . . . ?" Jack prompted.

"There's, uh—" I scrambled to come up with something that didn't make me sound like I was doing a commercial for Lifetime TV. Got it. "Who's the guy talking on the phone, doing homework, and seeing a basketball game in his head? You're still doing all of that, right?"

"Yeah."

"So, that's smart," I said. "Hey, you want an easy way to raise your history grade?"

"Can I still listen to the game?"

I laughed, then explained the ins and outs of World History extra-credit projects. "You could do basketball through the ages," I suggested. "Did you know the ancient Mayans played a game that's kind of a cross between basketball and soccer? Of course, the losers were sacrificed."

Jack burst out laughing. "Good thing those weren't the rules when I played freshman year."

After a while, we simply talked, low and quiet. No more shrill whistle in the background, no more ancient Mayans, no regrets about skipping Geek Night. No more sacrifices, either. The pauses weren't torturous. They just were. I simply was. With Jack. In a weekend of amazing things, that was the most amazing.

9

I'd really hoped to see Jack before first bell on Monday. Hoped
it, and dreaded it too. What if he acted like nothing was
different? I scanned the space above the students crowding
the hall. That was the best way to spot Jack.

But not Moni. She barreled into me, out of breath, her curls
flying. She pulled me against an empty spot along the bank of
lockers.

"I hate to say I told you so," she said, "but—"

"I know. I know. This cheerleading thing is paying off. Big-time."

"Say it like you mean it. Come on." Moni bent her head toward mine. "Jack Paulson and Rick Mangers?"

Okay, so Moni had a point.

"It's way more than just the cheerleading thing with Rick," Moni added. "We have so much in common. His parents are divorced too. *Finally*, someone who gets it." She leaned against the lockers and sighed. "You have no idea."

Moni didn't say it to be mean, but her words still caused my stomach to lurch. Hadn't I been there for Moni *the whole time*? But Rick Mangers comes along, and after a couple of phone calls, now *he's* the one who totally gets it?

Before I could say anything or change the subject, Rick Mangers slid in front of us.

"Hey, spark plug. We got ten minutes until the bell. Wanna split a doughnut?"

Moni played it cooler than I could've imagined. She took Rick's arm and they glided down the hall, making a way cute couple—her smarts for his strength. I thought about following them. Maybe Jack was in the cafeteria, shoveling down spoonfuls of oatmeal.

But that meant a trip through the gauntlet. It meant chatting with Moni, which was fine, but it also meant seeing Jack—at school, with everyone around. If he blew me off? Well, I wasn't sure I could take it.

I turned toward honors history instead, then stopped. I might be even less popular in there, especially since I'd neglected Mussolini in favor of the Mayans. I stood between my two choices, each of them uncertain territory, until the bell rang.

What I didn't realize until I walked the halls to third-period Independent Reading was this: Every single tile on the school floor, every classroom, every encounter was uncertain territory—and I didn't have a map.

I slipped into my chair, one of the first people in class. I went through all the motions—books tucked under my desk, notebook, novel, pen and pencil ready. I waited for Jack to walk through the door. When someone tall, with dark hair, sauntered in, my heart landed in my throat. I couldn't choke out a single word.

Not that I needed to. It was Ryan Nelson. I'm not sure how I looked: disappointed, relieved, insane? All I knew was he burst out laughing—but not before he winked at me.

I opened my book and reread the opening line to *Pride and Prejudice*. "It is a truth universally acknowledged, that a single man in possession of a good fortune must be in want of a . . ." I closed my eyes and crossed all my fingers under the desk. *Oh, please*, I thought, *don't let Jack Paulson be as girlproof as I once imagined*. I'd only glanced away for a second or two, but when I turned back, Jack stood at his desk, staring at it rather than me.

The bell rang.

Jack still stood there.

"Well, Mr. Paulson." Mr. Wilker paused in writing Regency-era vocabulary on the whiteboard. "Plan to join the rest of us?"

More laughter, from Ryan—who hadn't really stopped—and the rest of the class. Jack slumped in his seat. His books landed on the desk with a thump. From the corner of my eye, I could see the neat pile, his hand gripping the edge of the desk. I was almost too afraid to look, but I had to know. Was I about to get majorly dissed?

I turned.

He turned.

I smiled.

He—*thank God*—smiled.

I floated for the rest of Independent Reading. Mr. Wilker called on me. I gave answers. Since no one laughed (again), I assumed I hadn't substituted Jack's name for Mr. Darcy's. Something told me that was the result of pure luck.

I floated all the way to lunch, too. When Jack landed in line behind me, my feet barely touched the floor.

"Hey," he said.

I craned my neck to peer into his face. "Hey."

Scintillating conversation would have to wait, especially with the way Jack piled his tray with food. I felt my eyes grow wide. If he shoveled it in every second between the time he sat down and the bell for sixth period, could he eat it all? Maybe. Did jocks eat that much all the time?

Jack's gaze went from my face, to his tray, and back again. "Carbo-loading. For tomorrow's game."

"Wow," I said, "you're dedicated."

We waited in line for the cashier together. We picked up forks, napkins, and ketchup together. We even took the first few steps down the middle aisle of the cafeteria together. Then Jack turned one way. And I went the other.

He froze. I froze.

Moni sat at the geek table, a hand clasped over her mouth. Clearly, she saw the problem. Todd looked at the soda machine, the ceiling, and even ducked his head under the table like he'd dropped something. Clearly, he didn't care about the problem.

Opposite the geeks, in a corner near the door, was the jock table, with one chair empty. True, no one had stenciled PAULSON across the back. But it was Jack's chair. And there certainly wasn't one beside it marked AND HIS GEEKY NEW GIRLFRIEND.

I stood there, wondering why every awful thing in the universe had to happen right in the middle of the cafeteria.

"Actually," I said, "I need to go over some German notes with Moni. So, you know, pretty boring. If you want to . . ." There I was, in full-on babble mode.

"Yeah. I mean, Mangers and me, we have . . . notes too."

"Hey, Paulson!" The voice boomed across the cafeteria. Rick Mangers, of course. "You gonna sit?"

Maybe I was used to getting laughed at in the cafeteria, but Jack wasn't. The laughter wasn't even all that mean (and I knew the difference), but it brought more pink to his cheeks—and mine, judging by how hot they felt.

"I'd better—," Jack began.

"Yeah. Me too." I resigned myself and turned for the geek table. Three things happened then, almost simultaneously:

Jack's hand jostled my elbow. My milk carton pitched forward and landed—*splat*—on the floor. And in front of the entire cafeteria, Jack Paulson kissed my cheek.

A collective gasp went out before all the hooting and foot stomping. My head spun. And I spun, taking everything in at once. Jack's retreating back, the quick grin over his shoulder, Moni's expression of amazement, Todd's raised eyebrow, and Chantal Simmons's flowing hair as she marched from the cafeteria.

It couldn't be happening. Except. It did. Moni sprang up and led me to the geek table, talking nonstop the whole time.

"Oh, my God, I can't believe it. He kissed you. In the middle of the caf." She planted her elbows on the table and leaned forward. "I'm going to need more details. Seriously."

"Yes. Please share," Todd said. "Perhaps you two have a grab and grope penciled in before the next bell?"

Moni spared him a sniff and a glare. "Ignore him. Oh, oh, don't look."

And so, of course, I tried to.

"I said don't look." She aimed a little finger wave at the jock table. "That was Rick. I think he's giving Jack a hard time—but in a good way."

The screech of chair legs against linoleum stopped all conversation at our table. Brian stood, shoving his sack lunch, books, scientific calculator, and some Dungeons & Dragons dice into his backpack.

"Brian, don't—," I started, but it was too late. He stormed from the cafeteria. Todd, with a long-suffering sigh, gathered his own things and followed.

"Brian's really upset about Rick," I said once they'd both left.

"Then maybe he can *do* something about it," Moni countered.

I'd have to amend my theory. Maybe for every awful thing that happened in the cafeteria, something wonderful happened for someone else, until it all evened out. Cafeteria karma. Good or bad, you didn't get a choice. It just happened.

The doors to the gym were closed when Moni and I arrived in the lobby for practice. I could barely hear the thump of basketballs, or catch a glimpse of Jack through the small windows as he drove for a layup. And that wasn't all that was different. Sheila stood in the center of the space, inspecting a broken fingernail. A rogue lock of hair stood apart from its perfectly coiffed brethren. Her lips were dull, as if she'd chewed all the gloss off of them.

Six folding chairs lined the wall in front of the trophy case. Six women, in various states of daintiness, sat upon them.

Moni lifted her eyebrows at me, then shrugged. Most of the others on the squad fidgeted, pulled threads from their T-shirts, and stared at the floor. Only Kaleigh and Cassidy seemed at ease.

Sheila clapped her hands. "Girls!" she shouted.

We took what had become our usual spots in the formation,

two rows of five and one with just two. Except in classes where everyone sat alphabetically, Moni and I always took spots near the front. But here, in cheerleading land, we knew our place—the rear.

"As you might have noticed," Sheila began, "we have some visitors with us today." She adjusted a bra strap. "Our little group has come to the, um, attention of the school board, and they—" She paused to inspect her manicure again. "They would like to see, firsthand, how hard you all are working. I know you won't disappoint them." With that, Sheila looked at each of us, holding her gaze for a split second longer than was comfortable.

She gestured to the chairs. "You all know Ms. Torrez, Mrs. Hanson."

The vice principal and guidance counselor half-waved from their chairs. "And Ms. Bailey." The consumer and family sciences teacher nodded from hers.

"Some of you may know our other guests, Mrs. Dunne . . ." The wrestling mom, seated next to Mrs. Hanson, smiled at the entire squad. When she got to the back row, she winked at Moni and me.

"Mrs. Bartell and Mrs. Anderson," Sheila finished.

Of course. Mrs. Bartell was Kaleigh's mom, though I couldn't spot a resemblance. Cassidy and her mother, on the other hand, looked like they could be clones.

Moni shuffled closer to me and whispered, "Shit. This can't be good."

I might've whispered my agreement back, if Mrs. Bartell,

Sheila, and Ms. Torrez hadn't all cleared their throats at once. *Shit, indeed*, I thought.

Sheila clapped her hands one more time. "Stretches," she said.

And we stretched. Except for occasional murmurs from our "audience," most of practice continued as usual. We'd worked through stretches, into stunts, then chants, before Sheila called out sharply, "Cassidy!"

We all froze in place when Cassidy spun, not in the direction of our coach, but toward her mother. She had a *See, I told you so* look on her face. Mrs. Anderson went rigid.

Sheila walked over and held a hand in front of Cassidy's pouting mouth. There was nothing so unusual about that, either. At least three times a week our captain forgot to spit out her gum before practice. But this time, instead of complying with her normal grudging eye roll, she blew a bubble.

It was as if we really were a collective of cheerleaders then; every one of us drew in a breath, even Kaleigh. Sheila barely flinched. Without moving her hand, she turned toward Mrs. Anderson, tilted her chin up, just a notch, and waited.

She didn't have to wait long. Mrs. Anderson left her seat in a flash. She reached her daughter in a few long (yet dainty) strides, grabbed Cassidy by the wrist, and marched her down the hall and around the corner. Whoa.

"Let's work on the dance routine now," Sheila said. She hit the on button and turned up the volume on the CD player. It wasn't *quite* enough to drown out Cassidy's plaintive, "But Mom . . ."

After practice ended, I waited by the lobby doors. Most everyone had left, even Moni, but Sheila still stood in the center of the lobby, her back to me. She took a few deep breaths, then tucked her hair beneath a knit hat.

"Sheila?" I said, when she'd gathered her stuff and approached the exit.

"Yes?"

"I—I was wondering." The rest of the words came out in a rush. "Was this because of me and Moni?"

"Oh, Bethany, sweetie, no."

"Then . . . what?"

Sheila sighed. "Let's just say that, for some people, high school never really ends." I must have grimaced, because she added, "It does get better, though, I promise."

"Is there anything I can do?" I asked.

She tilted her head to the side and rearranged the tote bag on her shoulder. "Are you giving it your best effort?"

I started to nod, but really, I thought, was I? Moni and I had started this thing as a joke—at least I had. Then it all became real, and I did try. But somewhere along the way I'd settled for just surviving the season. That wasn't fair to the rest of the squad. And it certainly wasn't fair to Sheila.

"I will," I vowed. "I will."

Moni and I agreed to make good on that vow. Just *how* we would do it stumped us at first. It wasn't like we could ask the other girls on the squad for help. Over the next few days, any time we didn't have a game or a meet, we met at my house to practice. We worked on stretches (Moni *still* couldn't do the splits) and the dances (Shelby shimmied and kicked along with us), but it still wasn't enough.

On Thursday I said, "Remember that cheerleading website, the one with the wrestling cheers? Do you think there's more cheerleading stuff online?"

It turned out there were thousands of cheerleaders on the web, and they all wanted to share their knowledge with us. They didn't seem to mind that we were newbies and dorks—probably because we weren't *their* school's newbies and dorks. Whatever. They added us to e-mail lists and sent us links to instructional videos.

"Don't you think it's a little weird?" I said to Moni. "You could become a cheerleader and not even have to leave your house."

She snorted but continued scrolling through the videos. "This is it!"

"What?"

"A shoulder sit. It's a two-person stunt; we can do it on our own. How's that sound?"

"Dangerous?"

"Only if you mean dangerously close to perfect."

Shoulder sit? A lot harder than it looks. Especially when you're the base (the sittee in cheerleading-speak) and not the flyer (the sitter).

"Think of it, Bee," said Moni, and I swear, her eyes got all misty. "We could do this at the next wrestling meet." Where, oh by the way, Rick Mangers was bound to be.

I huffed about it a little, but I went along. She had a point. Being the school's cheerleading joke (at worst) or just mediocre (at best) wasn't sitting well with either of us. We were honor-roll girls; we were used to collecting gold stars for our efforts.

By late Saturday afternoon, my thigh was imprinted with the sole of Moni's Skecher and my shoulders ached. Even after we recruited Shelby as a spotter, I still dumped Moni on my bed at least ten times.

Then we got it. Moni locked her legs behind my back. She raised her arms in a V, and I stuck my fists on my hips. We held it there for one . . . two . . . three seconds.

Shelby let out a congratulatory whoop just as the phone rang.

And Moni and I still held it.

Shelby grabbed the phone. "Hello, Bethany's room," she said.

Moni started to shake with laughter.

"Is it Todd?" I asked.

Shelby's eyes were huge. "No, it's a *boy*!"

Moni shook harder and tumbled from my shoulders to the bed. Shelby pushed the phone at me. Before I could say hello, Jack's voice filled my ear.

"It's not Moni," he said, "or Todd."

"I guessed." I glanced at Moni and mouthed, *It's Jack.*

"Whatcha doing?" he asked.

"Moni and I were . . ." Did I admit to Jack Paulson that we were striving to become better cheerleaders? "Hanging out," I finished.

"Oh, 'cause I was thinking," he said, "if you wanted, you could maybe come over for dinner. You know, as thanks for lunch last week."

"You don't—"

"Nothing fancy," Jack added, his voice sounding rushed. "Me and my dad, and then a Timberwolves game."

"More basketball?" Just what I needed.

"Do you mind?"

Actually, I didn't. "I don't have to cheer through the whole thing, do I?"

Jack laughed but then fell silent, waiting for me to answer.

I held my hand over the receiver and whispered to Moni, "He wants me to come over for dinner."

"Are you crazy?" She practically spat the words. "Say yes already!"

Shelby bounced with excitement.

"I could pick you up," said Jack. "And bring you home."

"I—I have to talk to my parents," I said. There was no way around that, even if it did sound middle school. Geek Night was one thing. Dinner at Jack's? Maybe some kids could get away with going wherever they pleased, but especially after last weekend, my parents would completely freak if I said I'd go without getting permission first.

Shelby turned toward the door. "Mo-o-o-m! Da-a-a-d!" I

grabbed her and covered her mouth. I tried to hand her off to Moni, but she squirmed free. The two of us raced for the living room.

"There's-a-boy-on-Bethany's-phone." Shelby stopped to take a breath. "And-he-wants-to—"

My parents looked up. At that same moment I heard Jack laugh and say, "Hang on a sec."

"What's going on?" both Mom and Dad asked.

I shot Shelby a glance that said, *If your fingers ever want to touch pom-poms again . . .* And miraculously, she grew still.

"Uh, hold on," I said. I strained to decipher the muted noises coming from Jack's house. From my room, I heard Moni giggling.

"Bethany? This is Dale Paulson."

"Uh, hi, Mr. Paulson."

"Please, call me Dale. Can I speak to your mom or dad?"

"Sure." Since Dad was closest, I handed him the phone. "It's Mr. Paulson," I said.

He looked from the phone to Mom, who raised an eyebrow. He spoke to Jack's dad for a moment. "It's more than fine."

Whew, that sounded positive.

"We had the contractors in, and they said they couldn't have done a better job themselves."

Oh, the basement. Of course. What else would they talk about? Then my dad looked toward me and blinked. "I wouldn't expect anything less," he said, then handed the phone back to me.

"Hey." It was Jack.

"Hi."

"So, can you be ready in about twenty minutes?"

My mind catalogued the contents of my closet and dresser drawers. Twenty minutes? There were those cute jeans I got for Christmas. And the chunky knit sweater that matched my black sneakers. I was a little sweaty from practicing with Moni—and from racing Shelby—but nothing a little deodorant, face powder, and lip gloss wouldn't fix.

"Bethany?" said Jack.

"Oh. Sorry. I was . . . I was . . . " Then I gave up and admitted, "I was thinking about what to wear."

"Will that take more than twenty minutes?"

"Nope."

Jack laughed. "Gotta love a low-maintenance girl. So we're on?"

I looked at my mom and dad. "I—I think so." I held my hand over the receiver again and asked my parents, "Please?"

Shelby echoed, "Please, please?"

"What about Moni?" Mom asked.

"Moni's going home!" came the cry from my bedroom. Even Mom's lips twitched at that.

"We don't really know Jack," Mom said, then added, "that well."

I couldn't exactly plead with them while Jack was on the other end of the phone, Moni was down the hall, and while Shelby was still threatening to spontaneously combust at my side. Besides, I understood their concern. This wasn't Todd or Brian. This was Jack Paulson, the star of the basketball team, the boy who could have any girl he wanted.

In my mom and dad's world, life was like a ginormous graph, where everything was neatly plotted out. My trajectory and Jack's should never intersect. But that was on paper. Chalk one up to variable C—otherwise known as cheerleading.

"Dale says he'll chaperone," Dad said. "I think it's okay."

"Don't you usually go to Todd's on Saturdays?" asked Mom.

Yeah. I did. If I wanted things to get better with Todd, I really *should* go to Geek Night. But, I justified, it had always been an open invitation. No one held it against you when you couldn't make it. It might not work that way with Todd, though. Not now. Not if he found out about Jack. Was I really the sort of girl who would blow off her friends for some guy?

Todd would call me a sellout (or worse) if I ditched him for Jack. Moni would call me an imbecile (or worse) if I didn't. I couldn't win. Then I thought of Jack, with my copy of *Pride and Prejudice* tucked in the pocket of his letter jacket.

"Todd will understand," I said. Or not, as the case might be. I'd deal with that on Monday. But tonight?

Mom pulled at a snarl in her needlepoint, then nodded.

Tonight I was headed to Jack's.

When I got back to my room, Moni sat on my bed, scrolling through the display on her cell phone. Shelby had my sophomore yearbook open to the boys' basketball page.

"Him?" She pointed to Jack. "You're going out with him?"

"Looks that way," I said.

"Didn't he come to our house once?"

I nodded.

"Wow."

"Uh, wow," I said, nudging Moni's foot with mine.

"Huh?" Moni tucked her phone into her pocket, then stood. "Have fun at Jack's."

This was so unlike her. Five minutes ago, she nearly went through the roof.

"Moni, what's wrong?"

She shook her head. "Nothing. Why would anything be wrong? You're going out with Jack Paulson. I get to go home and watch my mom and Starbucks Boy rehearse before they take off for a poetry slam."

Oh, so that was it. "You want me to cancel?"

"Don't you dare." Her voice went fierce. "One of us"—she waved a hand at my laptop, where the video cheerleaders were frozen in a shoulder sit—"should get something out of this."

She left. I heard her chirp good-bye to my parents. A minute later her mom's car was crunching snow in the driveway. I considered calling Todd. I could try to force him to play nice, ask him to extend a special Geek Night invitation to Moni. That probably wouldn't work. If Todd and I had hit a rocky patch in our friendship, the space between Todd and Moni was strewn with boulders.

Maybe I could get ahold of Brian. But that might be even worse. He'd buried his nose in *Gamers' World* magazines at our lunch table all week, refusing to even look at Moni (at least when Moni was looking back). I had less than twenty minutes to get ready for Jack, and something told me the only phone number Moni wanted to see on her cell was Rick's.

The doorbell rang while I was still pulling the sweater over my head. I peeked out the window. The battered red Toyota sat in our driveway, exhaust billowing, forming a thin cloud over the snow-covered lawn. I raced downstairs in time to see Jack shake Dad's hand, smile at my mom, and wink at Shelby.

"After the game?" Jack said.

They were discussing curfews. Oh. Great.

Dad nodded. "Sounds fair, but call if it goes into overtime."

Since when did Dad know about basketball and overtime? Had he been studying too?

"You ready?" asked Jack.

I nodded, possibly a bit too emphatically. I grabbed my coat and struggled into it on the way out the door—the faster we left, the better.

"Sorry," I said.

"For what?"

I nodded toward the house.

"That?" He gave me his little-boy grin. "You forget. We're having dinner with my dad." With that cryptic remark, he led me to the Toyota.

Apparently, Jack could cook.

Outside, the Paulsons' old Victorian sported two basketball hoops. Inside, a wood stove warmed the house, and the tangy scent of tomato sauce and basil made my stomach growl. Spaghetti swirled in a pot of boiling water. It was the sort they served in the cafeteria at school, the thick kind that stuck to your insides. No spinach-colored angel-hair pasta in this house.

"Do you do all the cooking?" I leaned against the kitchen counter.

"Since eighth grade. My dad"—Jack lowered his voice—"really can't cook."

"I heard that!" The response came from the living room. Jack made a face, and I giggled.

"At first all I wanted to do was figure out my mom's recipe for spaghetti sauce." He chased the noodles around the pot, the steam from them making his skin glow. "She was one of those people who kept it all up here." He tapped his head.

"Looks pretty impressive," I said.

"You think?"

"Yeah, I do," I added, but I was talking so softly, the steam absorbed my words.

Jack smiled. "The secret ingredient is sugar," he said. "It cuts the acid from the tomatoes. Here, taste." He gave the sauce a quick stir, then stepped close to me and held the spoon to my mouth.

"Mmmmm, delicious," I said. And it was. In more ways than one.

"Are you sure? Usually I put more garlic in it, but since . . ." Jack's voice trailed off.

"Since what?" We stood so close that speaking above a whisper seemed weird.

"Since . . . ," Jack whispered back. He looked up at the ceiling for a second, then grinned back down at me. "Since you were coming over."

What did that have to do with . . . ? Oh.

Jack still held the spoon. His other hand still cradled the space beneath it, guarding against spills. But he leaned in anyway, and I closed my eyes. Our lips met in a not-so-garlicky kiss.

Just then Jack's dad shouted from the living room, "How're things coming along in there? You need any help from me?"

My eyes flew back open.

Jack kept his lips on mine, and my mouth buzzed with his words as he said, "What do you think? Are we doing okay? Or should I call for reinforcements?"

I pushed him away, and we both laughed.

Mr. Paulson set the table while Jack pulled garlic bread from the oven. I was reduced to carrying three glasses of water. *Please*, I thought, *let me make it to the table without tripping*. Mr. Paulson grinned at the two of us as I twirled spaghetti on my fork, conscious of every move. It was the wrong thing to eat when you were under scrutiny.

Jack's dad excused himself. "Forgot the drinks," he said.

I pointed to the water glasses, but my protest died when a rattle came from the kitchen. Mr. Paulson returned, tossing a can across the table to Jack.

"There you go, Jackie."

In a blur of red, white, and blue, Jack popped the tab and took a long swallow—of beer. Then he froze, his eyes meeting mine above the rim of the can.

"Oh, Bethany, honey, I'm sorry," Mr. Paulson said. "Would you—?"

Would I what? *Like a can of beer?* I tried to hide my shock while I gave my head a quick shake. So yeah, my parents drank once in a while, wine at Christmas, that sort of thing. When they came home from their New Year's party, they even opened a small bottle of champagne and poured a glass for me. But they didn't pop cans of Bud at the dinner table. And they never offered one to me.

"I'm fine with water, thank you." Gah, my voice sounded so prissy.

"You know, Jack's mom used to like a glass of wine with spaghetti, didn't she, Jackie?"

Jack unclenched the beer can and set it on the table. "She did."

"But I guess you're stuck with us two bachelors," said Mr. Paulson. "Not a drop of vino in the house." And then he stared, obviously expecting an answer.

I ducked my head and studied my plate, but the garlic bread wasn't giving up any clever small talk. At last I said, "Well, it could be worse." Oh sure, even the garlic bread could have come up with something better than that.

Mr. Paulson laughed, and the tension eased from Jack's face. His hand flirted with the beer can, back and forth between it and his plate, until at last I nodded. He gave me a grateful look before taking another swallow.

During the rest of dinner, I stole glances at the photograph of Jack's mother that hung on the opposite wall. Jack was tall and lanky like his father, but he had the dark hair and eyes of his mom. That was where the true resemblance was. I kept up my compare-and-contrast until Jack caught me midlook. If he minded, I couldn't tell.

The moment Mr. Paulson excused himself, I sprang up and collected the dirty plates, only to have Jack protest.

"What are you doing?" he asked.

"The dishes?"

He reached for the plates, and we ended up in a tug-of-war over them.

"You really want to help?" he asked.

I nodded.

"We got twenty minutes before tip-off. Think we can do it?"

"You've never seen me load a dishwasher."

He stared down at the dining table. "It's just a sink."

How could I be so stupid? In a world where "everyone" had a cell phone—except me—I should've known better. "Well," I said, after swallowing hard, "you've never seen me sterilize dishes with only a single pot and a campfire."

He raised an eyebrow.

"Girl Scouts," I said. "I can also fry an egg in a paper bag and start a pretty good one-match fire, if you're interested."

He scowled at the wood stove. "You can?"

"I'm better at it than I am at cheerleading."

"No, no, you're a good cheerleader," he said. "I mean, at least I can tell you care." If he said I let my school spirit shine, I was going to collapse and sob. "And that you like the game," he finished.

I let out a long breath. "I do."

"Then we better—" He looked at my hands, at the crumbs of garlic bread, the sauce and noodles that painted my fingertips. "Oh, man. I'm sorry."

"Dinner was so great, I thought I'd wear it."

His gaze went from my face, to my hands, and back again. Then he grinned. "Come on," he said. "Let's get started."

Seconds before the game's tip-off, Jack tugged me to the couch, telling me to forget the pot with its strands of spaghetti glued to the sides.

And seconds after tip-off, Jack's dad pushed himself up from his tattered recliner and left the living room. Before I could ask, he returned, loaded down with chips, dip, and a fresh six-pack of Budweiser. He tossed a can to Jack.

"Hey, Jackie, did you ask Bethany what she thinks of our Christmas present?"

Jack caught the beer and nodded toward the television set—a small flat-screen.

"It's nice," I said.

"We decided on it instead of socks and underwear." Jack stuck out a foot and turned it, revealing the underside of his tube sock, held together by—*was that duct tape?* "Care to see my boxers?"

I blushed. I'm not sure whether it was from the mention of underwear or the idea that Jack couldn't afford socks.

"No, not really," he said, holding back a grin. "I'm just way behind on laundry." Like I said, teenage boys = gross.

When his dad turned away, Jack set the beer—unopened—on the coffee table.

Watching basketball with Jack was a learning experience. He explained rules, calls, and strategies, things about the game that I didn't even know existed. After halftime, the instruction slowed down. Jack leaned forward, almost in a crouch, hands on knees, his game face on. When the Timberwolves scored, he punched his fists in the air and fell back on the sofa, jostling me. When a referee made a bad call, he'd turn to me and say, "Oh, man. Do you believe that?"

"No, man," I answered, deadpan. "I don't." Then he'd laugh, ruffle my hair, and maybe give my cheek a quick kiss. I found myself wishing the game would last forever.

But way too soon, I'd thanked Mr. Paulson—who made me promise to come back—and stood outside in the January night, the air sharp in my lungs. Jack started the truck but didn't get inside it. He leaned against the door, arms crossed, and tilted his head toward the stars.

"He doesn't always drink like that," he said.

"I—I don't . . . ," I started to say, but Mr. Paulson had finished off the entire six-pack during the game, with no help from "Jackie," and we both knew it.

"Since my mom died, it's . . . he's . . ." He paused. "And then, of course, tonight he was nervous."

"Nervous?"

Jack glanced away from the stars to look at me. "About meeting you."

"No way. I'm the one who was nervous." Try on the verge of a breakdown. I remembered Mr. Paulson's remark about having only bachelors in the house. It made me realize that Jack never brought girls home. I wondered if he'd invited *anyone* to his house recently.

"I warned him he had to be on his best behavior." He looked at the sky again. "Still didn't help."

"Your dad was fine."

Jack winced. "He hasn't been all together since my mom died. Sometimes I think a part of him died when she did. Not that he was ever any good at cooking." He smiled for just a second, then looked at me like he was measuring something. In the clear, cold night I shifted from one foot to the other.

"I started driving when I was twelve," he began. "Well, not legally," he corrected himself. "I was tall enough to reach the pedals, and I'd help my dad on jobs. Then one day after I turned fourteen, we'd been doing some concrete job from hell, and he tossed me a beer. I know it sounds—weird." Jack shrugged. "But it's just the way things are now. I'm not always sure anymore who's the dad and who's the kid."

I held out my hand, and Jack took my thick wool mitten in his worn leather glove. He tugged me closer. I stepped forward.

Neither of us saw the patch of ice until it was too late. His foot skidded. My arms flailed, but he caught me, snagged my waist. I dangled in his embrace, with my head tipped back, almost like we were ballroom dancers.

Except ballroom dancers—or cheerleaders—weren't usually so graceless. I looked up at him and laughed. It beat crying.

"Testing my reflexes?" he asked.

"Oh, yes. That's it exactly."

"Good thing I caught you. You get sidelined with an injury and I might lose that bet with Mangers." He said it with a smile, his eyes warm with humor.

"That bet," I echoed. "Were you guys really serious about that?" Maybe a hundred bucks didn't mean much to Rick Mangers. But the boy standing across from me? Well, that was a different story.

Instead of answering, Jack nodded at the truck. "I think she's warm enough to drive." He gave the Toyota a pat on the hood. "And you're probably cold enough for hypothermia."

"I'm fine." But the words came out soft, lost in a cloud of my own breath.

Jack went through the motions of adjusting the heater and defrosting the windshield, but he didn't put the truck in gear. Instead he cupped my cheek with an icy glove. The mention of Rick Mangers and the bet had frozen me stiff, but Jack's warm kiss stole all my thoughts.

And we kissed for a very long time.

"Warm enough now?" he asked, his lips still against mine.

"Oh. Yeah."

"Me too." He eased away from me, then he dove back in for another kiss. "I gotta get you home. Or else."

Or else what, he didn't say, and I didn't ask. The quiet drive felt right. The silent walk to my door didn't bother me. Neither did Jack's quick hand squeeze good night. I didn't think of Rick Mangers, how he hadn't called Moni, or the bet. I didn't think of Geek Night, either. At least, not until I reached my room and found my voice mail and in-box empty.

10

From *The Prairie Stone High Varsity Cheerleading Guide*:

Alcohol and drug use will not be tolerated on the Prairie Stone High School varsity cheerleading squad. Unlike other infractions, breaking this rule will result in immediate dismissal from the squad. No exceptions!

I spent a quiet Sunday with Jack, my telephone, and a really sore left ear. I tried calling Moni early in the day but ended up in voice mail. I tried e-mail and had to be satisfied with a short response of, *No, really, I'm okay.*

That Monday morning at school, I looked for her first. I didn't need to. She sprang on me from behind.

"Just. Saw. Rick." She bounced up and down, cheerleader-style.

"Deep breath." I waved a hand in front of her face. "Are you hyperventilating?"

"Get this," she said between gasps. "I told him if he won his match on Thursday, we'd have a surprise for him."

"We will?"

She punched my arm. "The shoulder sit. We'll debut it then."

Oh, *great*.

For a second, I thought Moni would insist we practice—right there in the hall. If Todd hadn't marched up to us, stony-faced, she might have.

"We've been missing you at Geek Nights," he said to me.

"What about me?" asked Moni. "Don't you miss me, too?"

Todd swiveled to stare straight at her. "No, but Brian does." He dismissed her without another word and turned back to me. "Meet me in the Little Theater, Reynolds. Sixth period."

Dork domain—it wouldn't surprise me if Todd had recruited the entire debate team to ambush me. Their extemporaneous topic? "Reasons Not to be a Cheerleader." He spun away from us without waiting for my response. Not that I apparently had a choice in the matter.

"Well." Moni shook her curls. "That was rude. But then, that was also Todd." She rolled her eyes. "Are you going to go?"

I shrugged. "I guess. What would you do?"

"After everything? Probably blow him off. He's really being a jerk."

It was just like Todd to go all drama king on me. He could

have IM'd me over the weekend. Or he could tell me during first-period honors history. But no, not Todd. Jerk or not, I still considered him one of my best friends. I might regret it later but, yeah, I'd meet him.

Inside the Little Theater a single spotlight lit an empty chair at center stage. It made the surrounding dark seem even darker—and creepier.

"Take a seat," a voice launched from the dark.

I let my eyes adjust and searched the room for a form to match the voice. This was too much, even for Todd.

"Come on," I said. "Turn on the lights."

Silence. This was stupid. I should turn around, head to the library, and spend my free period with Moni like always. Instead I took a step, then another, down the stairs that led to the main floor. Then I found myself climbing up, stage right.

My footfalls echoed in the space, and I was glad it wasn't a cheer day. No way would I be up there in a miniskirt. The metal folding chair glinted under the light. No way was I sitting on that, either.

"Sit." Todd's voice held a commanding tone, but I crossed my arms over my chest and tapped my foot.

"Okay, okay," he said. The spotlight flooded me with a soft pink hue, and the stage floor appeared to glitter. I was almost afraid to move. With a click, the door to the control room opened and shut. Someone—or something—clattered down the steps and across the floor. I squinted in the direction of the approaching sound. Only when he reached the stage did I recognize the mass of bed-head hair and those dork-a-rific glasses.

Todd leaned against the stage and propped an elbow on its edge. Chin on his fist, he scrutinized me.

"I take it you wanted to talk," I said.

"Yes . . . and no. There's something I've been meaning to tell you for a while now. It's just . . . I haven't"—he raised his eyes heavenward—"figured out how to say it."

This could not be good. Why now? Was it because Jack had started paying attention to me? If this was one of those guy competition things, I might have to break down and cry. Todd had always claimed to be above all that.

"Todd, I don't think—"

He held up a hand. "Please, just let me get it over with."

I cringed, but nodded.

"I have discovered something about you," he said.

All the synapses in my brain aligned themselves into fight-or-flight sequence. If he said one word about hooking up . . .

"You," he said, pointing to me, "are a muse."

I blinked. "I'm amused?"

"No, no. You." Todd pointed at me. "Are my muse. You know, a daughter of Zeus. A poetic inspiration."

My arms went slack, and I groped for the back of the chair. The metal was cool, sturdy, and real—while everything else was *so* not. "Maybe you could explain," I said. "How exactly am I your muse?" If the job description for a Daughter of Zeus required hand holding and kissing, I was out of there.

"Sit. Come on, Reynolds. I'm not going to bite." He laughed. "I'm not going to ask you out, either."

"You're . . . not?" I felt my way around to the front of the chair and settled onto it.

"Sure, I considered it," he said. "I mean, it's not fair that guys like Paulson get all the cute chicks. And you are almost my intellectual equal. That should make us compatible."

"In your dreams, Emerson."

"Well, yeah," he said without a trace of embarrassment. "Sometimes."

I hid my face in my hands. Someone really needed to teach him the meaning of TMI.

"Then I thought about it," Todd continued. "Really thought about it. And you. And this whole cheerleader thing. At first I was pissed."

"Yeah, I noticed," I mumbled into my palms.

"I couldn't believe you'd actually try out."

I peeked at him through the V of my fingers. "Moni made me do it."

Todd rolled his eyes. "Figures. But then you stuck with it. And it occurred to me." He glanced behind him. I think he wanted to rush upstairs and adjust the lighting for dramatic effect.

"We don't have to wait," he said.

O-kay. "Wait for what?"

"For anything. We're always talking. Can't wait for the week-end, can't wait for summer, for graduation. For anything that doesn't involve high school. I mean, I wouldn't have picked cheerleading—"

"You don't have the legs for it."

He held up both hands to shush me. "But there you are, embrac-ing the here and now, making the most of high school."

Oh, so that was what I was doing? And I thought all I'd been trying to do was keep most of the school from seeing my purple-clad butt.

"And why the hell shouldn't we?" Todd smacked his fist against his palm. "Who says you've got to be popular to be a cheerleader?"

Certainly not me.

"Or . . ." He peered at me over the top of his glasses. "Student body president."

Wow. I sure didn't see that coming. But in that case, popularity probably helped. For a moment I studied him: the untamed hair, oversize glasses, the misbuttoned plaid shirt that covered his "I Did It All for the Wookie" tee. There was no way.

Or was there? Todd certainly had the brains to be student body president. He had leadership ability too. And, with his superior debate skills, he might even be able to actually secure the often-promised, but never realized, coffee shop next to the school store. At the very least, he could probably talk the administration into upgrades for the school newspaper. Was that enough to win the election? No. Todd would have to look the part.

I gave him another once-over. Despite its present condition, his hair had a decent cut. I knew his mom still took him to get it trimmed. Maybe switch out the nerd-screaming glasses for an updated pair? Or contacts, even. The plaid shirt would have to go, of course. Ditto anything even vaguely Wookie-ish.

Todd wasn't cute, not in a boy band sort of way, but his features were strong—presidential, even. Moni and I could take turns dressing him.

I eased off the chair and inched across the stage until I knelt above him. "Are you serious?"

"Come on, Reynolds. We both know Chess Club president is a bullshit extracurricular. I'm aiming for the Ivy League. I got the grades. The SATs will be a snap, but I need more."

"You're no slouch at debate," I said, "and the paper—"

"It's expected," he said. "And so typical, it's boring. The genius kid excels at chess and debate. And runs the school newspaper. Big freaking deal."

"It takes more than brains to be student body president, you know," I said.

"That's why I came to you."

I hopped off the stage and headed for the door. "Come on."

I waited while Todd dashed up the stairs to shut down all the lights. The bell hadn't rung for seventh period yet, and the halls were quiet. I didn't have what Todd so desperately needed, but Moni did. I dialed the combo to her locker and swung it open.

"Mr. President," I said, handing him a green and pink plastic bottle, "I'd like you to meet Mr. Hair Gel."

Moni kept her promise to Rick. We choreographed a more complicated two-person routine, including the shoulder sit with a snazzy dismount. When the referee held Rick's hand high in the air, declaring him the winner in his weight category at Thursday's meet, we got to it. Whistles from the boys, cheers from the stands. Rick blew Moni a kiss. From the stands, Jack gave us a thumbs-up. After the meet, Andrew and his freshmen teammates came up to us.

"Wow, you guys are really getting good," Andrew said. "You should compete."

In cheerleading? The boys were sweet, but we weren't *that* good and probably never would be. We weren't bad, though. I doubted if even Chantal still thought we were the school joke.

At the thought of jokes, my mind went to that bet between Rick and Jack. It still struck me as odd. I turned to Moni. "Has Rick ever said anything about the bet?"

"What bet?"

"The one they had, about us cheering for wrestling all season."

Recognition flickered in Moni's eyes. "Oh, that. I thought it was a joke, that they were just . . . flirting with us. No biggie."

"Jack said something the other night. . . ."

"What'd he say?"

"That if I got sidelined, he'd lose the bet with Mangers."

"So?"

Jack can't afford to lose a hundred dollars. I couldn't say it out loud. Sure, the whole school knew, but saying it felt like betraying Jack.

"Rick bet against us," I added.

"They're jocks. They compete. It's what they do. Bet or not." She pointed at herself and then me. "Who're the real winners here? Cheerleading. Payoff. Big-time. Remember?"

I turned toward the bleachers and found Jack grinning at me, and I had to wonder what I was worried about. Moni and I would show up for every meet. Jack would win. Nothing else mattered.

Friday afternoon Jack caught me around the waist after the last bell. No one stared at us, not anymore. We'd been deemed an official Prairie Stone High couple. And now that we were? Old news. No one cared. Well, almost no one. I'd felt Chantal's icy glare more than once while walking through the halls, either on my own or hand in hand with Jack. It was like she couldn't look away, even though I thought that maybe she wanted to. Call me petty, but after everything that had happened—especially what happened in the gauntlet—I was kind of glad she couldn't.

I wouldn't say being with Jack elevated my status on the cheerleading squad, but it didn't hurt it either. What seemed clear was this: No one wanted to upset me, because that might upset Jack. Behold the power of the A-list jock. It was weird—and a little disconcerting—that Moni and I couldn't hash out a compromise with the squad on our own. But after what had gone down with the school board and Sheila, it was a relief.

Jack swung me in circles. Then, while I was still dizzy, he asked, "Want to go to a party tonight?"

"Sure!" I said without giving it a thought, without wondering where the party might be, or whether my parents would let me go. It was one of the few Fridays we didn't have a varsity basketball game. The Panthers had coasted to a win on Tuesday, and Jack was still coasting on that high. Saying yes was easy.

"It's at Mangers's," he said, almost as an afterthought.

Oh. One of Rick's parties. It wasn't the sort of thing I thought I'd ever be invited to—or Moni, for that matter. And now, we were. Or at least, I was. Moni had left school halfway through German to meet her dad. Monica, it seemed, had planned a night at the opera for the three of them.

"Opera?" I'd said when she told me.

"Yeah, I'm sure the fun will be over way before the fat lady sings."

I'd seen Moni before school and at lunch. We'd been partners for *Gesprächsaustausch* ("conversation exchange"), and she hadn't said a word about Rick throwing a party.

A few hours later a twinge of guilt hit me when Jack pulled the Toyota through the main entrance of Prairie Stone's only gated community. This was Todd's neighborhood and I knew the area, if only for that reason. Just as I knew that right now, he was hosting a *Star Wars*–themed campaign kickoff meeting. And yeah, I'd been invited. And yeah, at the last minute I'd sent him a cop-out e-mail saying I couldn't come. And with Shelby at a sleepover, my parents were headed to a movie. I'd mentioned Jack, and going out, and only got a reminder of my curfew. Technically not lying didn't make me feel any better about it.

We came to a stop at a T. Valley View Estates was at least as pretentious as it sounded. To the right, it was even more so. Large, conspicuous, hey-look-at-me mansions lined the lane in that direction. The one on the crest belonged to the Emerson family. The sight of the Death Star (as Todd called it) made me duck my head. I leaned forward, pretending to adjust the hem on my jeans.

We turned left, where slightly smaller houses stood, their land-scaping creating sculpted mounds beneath the snow. It was nothing like the area where I lived—student housing mixed with families, close enough so Dad could walk to campus when the weather was nice. It was even less like Jack's neighborhood, in the old part of Prairie Stone.

I glanced behind me just as Todd's house slipped from view. "Guess the tractor beam is off tonight," I said.

"What?"

I shook my head. "Never mind."

Jack rounded the last curve before Rick's house—"house" being one of those relative terms. I guessed you could fit two of mine inside it, and still have room for Rick's ego.

In the basement, I added my coat to the lump of outerwear that was growing in the center of a spare bed. Jack kept his letter jacket on.

After the cold of outside, the first thing I noticed was the hot, sharp scent of alcohol. It was too dark to see much of the basement beyond lots of leather, lots of chrome, lots of polished wood. The place was huge, with one main room and several smaller ones down a long hallway. The music was turned down low, in what I thought was more of a "make-out" vibe than a "drink until you puke" one. Maybe this wouldn't be so bad?

A long bar ran nearly the entire length of one wall. Rick stood behind it, playing bartender. He spotted us—or at least Jack—and waved us over.

"Paulson." He tossed Jack a Heineken. Then Rick turned to me. "Beer?"

When I shook my head, he made a show of searching behind the bar, clattering glassware. "You know, I think I have some milk and a bottle, I mean glass, right here."

Oh, ha-ha. Hilarious.

"I'll just have water," I said.

"Water?"

"It's that stuff that falls from the sky when it's raining. And when it's really cold," I pointed to the patio doors and the snow outside, "it looks like that."

Jack laughed and gave my waist a squeeze. "She got you, man."

"Score one for the quiet chick." With equal amounts of humor and condescension, Rick pulled a petite bottle of Evian from the fridge and handed it to me. I cupped it in my hands. I used to think the tiny bottles were cute. That was before Rick Mangers handed me one.

Rick moved on to serve someone else, even though most everyone was already serving themselves—from a keg by the patio.

Jack tucked the unopened Heineken into the pocket of his letter jacket. "For my dad."

What was he going to do? Walk into the house and say, "Hey, Dad, just got back from a party and thought you'd like a souvenir beer?" Of course, with Jack and Mr. Paulson, that scenario was entirely possible.

Jack's hand lingered at my waist. Standing apart from him was something he didn't seem to want me to do. So I stayed there, safe and content in the crook of his arm. The room was filling up with high school royalty, the anyone-who-was-anyone jocks, and the seniors from the cheerleading squad, every last one, including the captain.

Cassidy's high-pitched laugh cut off when her eyes met mine. She gripped the beer she was holding even tighter, and her face drained of color. We stared at each other. For once Cassidy didn't appear hateful. She gave me a small smile of conspiracy and sipped her beer. *I won't tell if you won't,* her look said.

So much for Prairie Stone High's zero tolerance policy. All I could think was: I *so* didn't belong here.

Track star R.J. Schmidt wandered past, then backtracked and parked himself right in front of us. If there was a poll for that kind of thing, R.J. would be voted Fastest Boy in the senior class. That "honor" would have nothing to do with his record-breaking hundred-yard dash.

"Nice manners, Paulson," R.J. said. "Aren't you going to introduce us?"

Jack's eyes narrowed. "This is Bethany," he said. But by his tone of voice he might as well have been saying, "This is mine."

"Gotcha," R.J. said, and laughed. "See you around." He winked at me and headed for the keg.

Jack shoved his free hand deep into his letter-jacket pocket, but he kept the other one on me. Judging by his scowl, he could've been on the basketball court, not standing in the middle of Rick Mangers's basement.

Someone clamped us both on the shoulder. I yelped. Next to me, Jack tensed. Rick wheeled us around. We were apart for a second, then Jack tugged me close again, and this time slipped his hand into my back jeans pocket.

It was a little too fast, a little too strange, a little too intimate. I jumped, and Jack got his fingers caught in my belt loop.

"Got yourself a live one there, Paulson."

Rick's grin said it all. I not only embarrassed myself, but I was bringing Jack along for the all-expense-paid trip to Dorkland. He stepped apart from me and crossed his arms over his chest.

"Hey, I was just talking to Amanda." Rick tugged a tall, blond, obviously older girl over. "She goes to Prairie Stone State. Doesn't your dad teach there?"

I nodded, reluctant. Anything to do with my parents at a Rick Mangers party could not be good.

"Really?" Amanda said in between snapping her gum. "What's your dad's name?"

"Professor Reynolds," I said, and a second later realized how snooty that sounded. "He teaches psychology."

"No way!" Amanda squealed. "Intro to Psychology?"

"Yeah, and a couple of other classes."

"Oh, that's great, that's just great," she said, but a moment later she burst out laughing. I thought about the senior I'd interviewed for my Life at Prairie Stone column. He'd made Dad's class sound cool. But he'd also mentioned how many times my dad talked about me in class. Amanda whispered in Rick's ear, then laughed again. Rick smirked.

"Small world, isn't it?" With an arm around Amanda's waist, he swaggered away.

Jack watched them leave. "She's probably failing," he said. "Not the sharpest stick in the . . . er, whatever sticks come in." He sighed. "But then, that's the way Mangers likes them."

Then why does he like Moni? The question nearly left my mouth, but I swallowed it back because the answer had already occurred to me. *Maybe he doesn't.*

A few minutes later Rick was back, this time pulling Jack away from me. "Come on, man, I gotta show you something." When Jack balked, he added, "It'll take what? A whole friggin' minute? Come on."

"I'll—" Jack threw an annoyed look at Rick, then turned back to me. "I'll be right back, okay?"

It was the last thing I wanted, but I nodded. And then, in a room filled with people, I was alone. I hugged myself, but that looked desperate and defensive, so I dropped my arms. I found myself inching from the center of the room, away from people I didn't know. Well, I knew *them*. They just weren't the sort who wanted to know *me*.

I backed into a wall and pressed my palms against the paneling. I wished I could blend into the woodwork. So this was a coveted, infamous, if-you-have-to-ask-you-weren't-invited Rick Mangers party?

God, it sucked.

Then, from a room down a hallway, came the whiz and pop of guns along with cries of dismay. It sounded just like . . . Geek Night?

I should have stayed where I was; Jack had promised to come right back. But the lure of the familiar was too much. A bunch of guys playing video games? That I could deal with.

A door opened, and the glow from a television spilled into the hallway. Inside the room, a group of jocks packed a couch. The overflow testosterone took seats on the floor. A beach scene filled the TV screen, where a game character was trying to push past a squad of soldiers. He wasn't having much success.

Oh! I knew this one! I crept toward the couch. "Go toward the shoreline," I said.

A few of the boys turned, gave me a weird look.

"If you go in the water, you can walk underneath without

drowning and get by the soldiers." I shrugged. "It's a glitch in the game." One of many things guys at Geek Night had discovered, catalogued, and assigned a weighted rank based on usefulness to overall strategy.

"Hey!" the boy with the controller shouted. "That works. Move over, Peterson." With this, the boy named Peterson landed on the floor. "Come here," the boy said without looking at me. "You know any more tricks?"

"A few." I took a tentative perch on the edge of a cushion, my fingers pressed against a coffee table loaded with soda cans, beer glasses, deflated bags of chips, and an empty bottle of vodka.

The boy next to me beamed with each trick I fed him. "Cool," he said. "I've never gotten past this level."

I got so caught up in the game that I barely noticed the boy on my other side leave. Only when R.J. Schmidt slid into the open spot did I sense a change in the room, a tension. R.J. leaned forward, tucked a strand of hair behind my ear.

"Paulson shouldn't leave a girl like you all alone. So, when'd you move to Prairie Stone, Beth?"

"It's Bethany, and I've lived here almost three years now." Not that someone like R.J. would've noticed. I tried to scoot away from him, but there wasn't any room. "I really need to—"

"Pretty girl like you doesn't need to do anything. Just relax and let R.J. take care of everything."

I looked to the boy next to me for help. He sat like a statue, face forward. In fact, every set of eyes but R.J.'s were glued to the television screen. If I'd sprouted horns right then, I don't think anyone would have stirred. R.J. slipped an arm around my shoulder.

"Hey," I said, squirming away. Then, "Please, I'd really rather—," I started, but he didn't seem to understand a polite refusal. Instead he pulled me a little closer.

"Stop!" I felt the kid next to me stiffen, but despite his bravado in the video game, he didn't have the kind of courage it apparently took to stand up to someone like R.J.

I snaked my hand into R.J.'s rib cage and pushed as hard as I could. He stopped, blinked, then smiled.

"You look like you could use a beer," he said. "Hey, Peterson, help a girl out, huh?"

When Peterson turned to me, I shook my head. "No, I don't. I'd really—"

"Want a joint instead?" R.J. asked.

All I wanted was to get out of that room. The door opened briefly, and I took advantage of the shift in everyone's attention. I stood. "Jack's looking for me," I said, hoping it was true.

R.J. reached for my wrist. "Stay," he said. "You wouldn't want to miss all the fun." The crazy thing was, he sounded sincere. Like making out with a total stranger was the same kind of fun as the latest shoot-'em-up game.

"Let go."

The voice wasn't mine. And it wasn't Jack's. Ryan Nelson leaned over the couch and grabbed R.J.'s arm.

"Screw you, Nelson."

Ryan frowned. "She's Paulson's girl. You want to get into it with him, just keep on pushing. But I wouldn't recommend it." It sounded like a warning—or maybe a threat.

R.J. snorted, but he glanced away. His grip loosened. I pulled free.

Go, Ryan mouthed, then gestured toward the door. My hand fumbled with the knob, and when I finally plunged into the dark hall, I took three steps and crashed into someone. Lukewarm beer soaked my jeans.

"Oh, my God," said the voice that went with the beer. "I'm so sor—"

I looked down. The first thing I saw were pink and silver leather flats, a three-hundred-dollar pair that could only belong to one person.

Chantal Simmons.

Chantal never finished apologizing. She looked from her beer cup, now only a quarter full, to my jeans, to my face, and laughed. The hall was crowded, too loud, and now it smelled like beer and musky perfume, the sort that always stung my eyes. I blinked a couple of times.

All I wanted was to go home. Since I reeked of Miller Lite, I couldn't do that, either. The door swung open again and R.J. burst out, followed closely by Ryan. Chantal tossed her head and acted like she hadn't just dumped most of her drink on me. R.J.'s gaze flickered from her to me and back again.

"So," he said. "You friendlier than she is?" R.J. nodded toward me.

Chantal did that move that made her hair shimmer. "I'm *very* friendly."

R.J. slipped an arm around Chantal's waist and steered her across the hall. He opened the door to a dark room.

"Chantal, you don't—," I started.

She spun and nearly lost her balance. "Don't what?" she said, and though I could tell she meant to focus on me, it was clear that her eyes weren't cooperating. God, she was so drunk.

"Jack and me—I mean, if you need a ride home."

Chantal laughed. Then she smiled up at R.J. "Who's Jack?"

"Now that's what I like to hear."

He pulled her into the room and shut the door behind them. Just like that.

"Should we—?" Should we what? I didn't have an answer for that, and I darted a glance at Ryan.

He gave the closed door a disgusted look, although whether that was for R.J., Chantal, or the situation in general, I couldn't tell. "It's not like it's the first time," he said. "Come on. I'll help you find Paulson."

11

From *The Prairie Stone High
Varsity Cheerleading Guide*:

Cheering for our Prairie Stone High School athletes
makes it easy to get attached to them. Affairs of
the heart will happen. I won't warn you away from
that special football or basketball player. **But I will
caution you—as your friend and "big sister": While
all our Prairie Stone High athletes are talented,
make certain the one you choose is special.**

Nothing could be worse than that party. Absolutely
nothing. I was convinced of that—right up until the
moment I stepped outside and the subzero temperature
iced my jeans. I'd worn my pink pea coat, and the entire length of
my legs was exposed to the wind's chill.

Jack started the truck but didn't wait for it to warm up.

The pickup sputtered and choked its way through Valley View Estates. We couldn't look more out of place. On top of that, I reeked of beer. And Jack had a bottle of it tucked in his pocket. If a police car decided to stop us . . . I couldn't finish that thought. I squirmed in the seat and tried to pluck the frozen jeans away from my skin.

"It wasn't supposed to be that kind of party," Jack said when we turned onto the main road.

"What kind of party was it supposed to be?"

"Quieter. You know . . . a couples' party."

A couples' party? "You mean a make-out party?"

"No," said Jack. "I mean, not really."

He fell silent, which was just as well. I needed to figure out what to say to my parents when he dropped me off.

Hi, Mom, Dad, just back from a party I didn't tell you about, where I wasn't supposed to be, and where I wish I'd never been. That wouldn't work.

When we reached the turn for my street, my nerves were a bundle in my stomach. I didn't need Moni's help to do the math. The probability of me racing through the house and into my room without Mom or Dad noticing either my soaked jeans or the scent of beer was easy to calculate: Zero.

Jack drove past the turn. I opened my mouth, then shut it. He was taking me home, all right. His home.

How Jack's dad knew to meet us at the door, I don't know. I'd never been so relieved to see anyone's parent in my entire life. "Oh,

Bethany, honey," Mr. Paulson said, "inside, quick." He turned to Jack. "You have the heater on during the drive?"

"Full blast."

He'd directed all the vents toward me as well. Kids in Minnesota learn about frostbite early. Mr. Paulson found a pair of Jack's sweatpants for me to wear. I was glad the beer hadn't soaked my underwear. Things were bad enough without that added humiliation.

By the time I'd changed, dropped my jeans down the laundry chute, and entered the kitchen, a mug of hot chocolate waited for me. Instant, with bobbing little marshmallows. I sipped, convinced nothing had ever tasted so good. It warmed me from the inside out.

Jack's dad sat at the kitchen table, the now open bottle of Heineken next to him. "No white spots on your skin?" he asked.

I shook my head. "No. Just pink." Little pinpricks ran along my thighs. It felt almost like burning, but that was good. That was normal. No frostbite.

"I was telling Jackie how this reminded me of something that happened to me and his mom, back when we were in high school. Only I was the one who spilled the beer, on myself." Mr. Paulson chuckled, and his face grew tender. "I was supposed to meet her parents that night too. You might not believe this"—he pointed the beer bottle at me—"but I was kind of a screwup in high school."

I wasn't sure what the proper response should be, so I just raised my eyebrows.

"We ended up at a laundromat," said Mr. Paulson. "I wore some stranger's towel while my clothes went through a wash and dry. In the end we were only ten minutes late. But you know what happened?" He didn't wait for an answer. "That night Jack's mom broke up with me."

"Really?"

Mr. Paulson nodded. "I didn't have sports to keep me grounded, like Jackie does, and his mom—she was pretty serious about school."

I looked at Jack. His back was turned, so I couldn't see his face or gauge his reaction. But Mr. Paulson seemed to want to tell this story, to relive the details with a fresh audience. Could that hurt? "What happened?" I said.

"I asked her out every week. And every week she turned me down. Finally, to get me to stop, she agreed to go to prom with me."

"And did you go?"

Mr. Paulson nodded.

"And then?" I asked.

"And the rest is pretty much history." Mr. Paulson grinned at me. "I'd better go check on the laundry, so we can get you home before your parents start to worry."

What? *My* parents? *Worry?* I'd waltz in smelling like dryer sheets instead of beer. It was all good. I relaxed against the kitchen chair. But Jack still had his back toward me.

After I tugged on my still-warm jeans and laced my boots,

and after we climbed into Jack's truck, he might as well have *still* had his back turned. The drive home was dark and silent. He left the truck running when he walked me to the door. It seemed ridiculous to say, *I had a nice time,* so I settled for, "Thank you, and tell your dad thanks too."

Jack nodded. Then, without a kiss good night, without even a squeeze of my hand, he headed down the porch stairs and back to his truck. By the time I turned to close the door behind me, his headlights had vanished from the driveway.

I stepped back into the night and stared up at the stars, brilliant and clear in the frigid air.

"It wasn't supposed to be that kind of party," Jack had said.

Whether that was true or not, I didn't know. It wasn't supposed to be that way last August, either. I thought about bumping into Chantal Simmons in the hallway tonight, and months ago, on the crooked path to the keg in the woods. She was no better at holding her beer inside than she was outdoors.

I thought about Dina's Lexus wrapped around that tree, too. It really might have made a difference if I had spoken up last summer. If I could wish upon a star, I would take it all back. But maybe it would have just delayed the inevitable.

At some time, at some point, at some other party, Chantal would get drunk again. She'd get into someone else's car, or wander into a dark room with someone she barely knew.

Like tonight.

And then there was Jack. I drew in a breath—to hold back the start of a sob—and the cold assaulted my lungs. Tears blurred my view of his brake lights, still waiting at the corner. Should I run to him? Try to explain the differences between girls like me and boys like him? My boots stayed frozen to the spot while Jack's lights tapped once, twice, then disappeared. *No risk, no reward*, I thought. The stars blinked their agreement.

I pulled open the storm door and stood behind it until my breath crystallized on the glass.

The safest place to spend a cold winter Saturday was the Internet. I wouldn't have to talk. I wouldn't have to explain. I wouldn't even have to think. All I had to do was point and click. I sat on my bed, fired up the laptop, and took advantage of the wireless network Dad had asked Todd to install for us at Christmas. With a pile of pillows around me, I felt something I hadn't felt in a long time: almost invisible. Right up until the IM program flashed, letting me know I had a new friend request.

No matter what I did, I couldn't convince myself that it wasn't Jack—even if that made zero sense. One, he didn't have a computer. Two, if he wanted to talk, he wouldn't schlep through minus-five-degree temperatures to the library or coffee shop for free Internet. He'd use the phone.

The IM program flashed again.

Moni? Was that better or worse than not hearing from Jack? I'd called her cell earlier that morning. I'd let my thumb hover over the talk button, half-ready to hang up. I didn't have to make that choice, though. Moni's phone rang and rang while I considered how much to tell her about the party. Should I mention Chantal? R.J.? The beer? What about Rick and the blonde who was probably failing my dad's class? Voice mail seemed like the wrong place for all that. I hung up without leaving a message.

The IM program flashed at me again. I clicked the icon, and the new friend request appeared on the screen: Prez_Emerson.

I should've known. Todd discarded screen names like Chantal went through shoes. I approved the contact, and Todd's message popped up.

Prez_Emerson: Do you want to talk about last night?

Did he mean my nonappearance at the campaign kickoff or Rick's party? I was so not going there, not in IM anyway. I scooted farther into the pillows and tried to change the subject.

Book_Grrl: Getting a little ahead of ourselves, aren't we, El Presidente?
Prez_Emerson: Positive visualization.
Book_Grrl: oic
Prez_Emerson: You know I hate that.

Oh, he did, with a passion. Maybe it was the speed chess, or the notes he took for debate, whatever. Todd could type normal, grammatically perfect sentences faster than IM junkies could whip out shorthand. As editor of the school paper, he tore into my Life at Prairie Stone columns with a glee most kids reserved for a snow day.

Prez_Emerson: So, forget last night. What about tonight?

Good question. The way Jack had hustled me out of Rick's, his silence both at his house and on the ride—the missing good night kiss—did it mean things had changed? I couldn't really blame him. In less than one hour, I'd dissed his friend, antagonized both Chantal and R.J., and gotten a beer bath. What good was a girlfriend if you couldn't take her anywhere?

Prez_Emerson: Look, before you answer, let me say I know about the beer, and that you guys left early.

He did? My fingers trembled on the keyboard while I typed my response.

Book_Grrl: I'm afraid to ask. How do you know?
Prez_Emerson: Networking.
Book_Grrl: What?
Prez_Emerson: Wrestlers.
Book_Grrl: You know wrestlers?
Prez_Emerson: *Freshman* wrestlers. Think about it. They're members of the tribe.

He had a point; they were. So now Todd knew. Freshman wrestlers knew. By Monday, everyone at school would know.

Prez_Emerson: So, about tonight. We always have room for the prodigal daughter at Geek Night. We can watch Firefly *and* Serenity. If you want, I'll let you beat me at Scrabble. You can even play with my light saber.

I choked back a laugh.

Book_Grrl: That's not a euphemism, is it?
Prez_Emerson: Euphemism? Big word for a cheer-leader. But no, it's not a euphemism . . . unless . . . *waggles eyebrows suavely*
Book_Grrl: NO!
Prez_Emerson: About tonight?
Book_Grrl: About the light saber part. I'm still thinking about the rest.
Prez_Emerson: Look, if you want, you can forward your calls to my cell.

Todd would do that for me?

Prez_Emerson: I just want you here.

Oh. Wow. I sank into the pillows, only to jolt forward when the phone rang. The laptop teetered and nearly slipped from my knees. The phone rang again. What if it was Jack? Gah. I really had to get my parents on board with caller ID.

Book_Grrl: vev

My fingers fumbled on the keyboard.

Book_Grrl: bly

I needed to catch the phone before it flipped into voice mail. One more time. I took a breath, found the keys, and wondered if maybe Todd had a point about Internet shorthand.

Book_Grrl: brb

I managed to pick up on the fourth ring. My "hello" came out in a rush of breath and heartbeats. And for three seconds, all I heard was silence.

"It's me," he said finally. "Jack."

"Oh." I eased the laptop from my legs and caught a flash of messages scrolling down the screen. Surely the boy genius could figure out what *brb* meant. I inched the laptop screen lower to block the abuse Todd was no doubt hurling at me.

And then, over the phone, that awful, excruciating silence fell. It was like the past two weeks had been erased—all those talks, dinner at Jack's. I was as tongue-tied as I'd been on that first day of Independent Reading. Now that we couldn't talk to each other, I finally realized that we had been.

"I was wondering," Jack said at last, "if you're not busy, you could maybe come over. The T-wolves are playing again, and—"

"I have plans," I blurted out, startling myself.

"Right. I mean, I figured you probably—"

"It's just this thing . . . we do. . . . Everyone's invited," I added, softer now.

"Everyone?" he asked.

Well, everyone who wasn't anyone.

"Even a guy like me?"

A jock at Geek Night? Talk about messing with the natural order of things.

"Even a guy like you." I paused. "At least, I think. Can you hang on a minute?"

I'd seen how the other half lived. Now it was Jack's turn—if I could get Todd to agree. With my free hand, I eased the computer onto my lap. I set the phone down gently on the nightstand and then lifted open the laptop.

Prez_Emerson: What the hell?
Prez_Emerson: Oh. Be right back. Got it. Okay. I'll wait.

Prez_Emerson: Here I am. Waiting.

Prez_ Emerson: Amazingly, I am still waiting.

Prez_Emerson: Like I don't have better things to do.

Prez_Emerson: Actually, I don't.

I snorted and scrolled through the remaining messages.

Prez_Emerson: About my whole thing against shorthand. It reduces complex thoughts to single letters and muddies communication in the process, and that's *before* you add the gender gap to the equation. And by the way, I'm still waiting.

Prez_Emerson: Okay, Reynolds, I'm giving you one more minute, starting . . . now.

I rushed to type before he logged off, but another message stopped me midsentence.

Prez_Emerson: So I lied. I can see you're still logged on. Look, forget Geek Night, you don't have to come, but will you at least talk to me?

Book_Grrl: Yes.

Prez_Emerson: Yes, you'll talk to me, or yes, you'll come to Geek Night?

Book_Grrl: Both.

Before he could respond, and before I lost my nerve, I closed my eyes, typed four words, and hit enter. If it came out coherent, it was meant to be.

Book_Grrl: Can I bring someone?

No response. Part of me itched to pick up the phone, to check to see if Jack was still there. But I sat motionless, afraid to upset the balance between the silence on the phone and the silence on the screen. The cursor blinked. Todd hadn't logged out. Maybe he was e-mailing Brian or wired into some multiplayer game while chatting with me. But probably not. I thought to type the message again, in case it hadn't shown up on his side. But I could see it. Probably he could too. Whatever happened was meant to be. Then Todd's icon dimmed. I stared for several seconds before realizing he'd sent a message at the very last moment:

Prez_Emerson: Sure.

Jack didn't kiss me, but he did come inside to shake Dad's hand again. When we left, he held open the door to his truck. Even better, he didn't freak out when we reached Valley View Estates and turned right—at least not until I told him to pull over in front of the Death Star.

"You're kidding," Jack said. "Can I park around back or something?"

"Nope. Here's fine."

"I'm going to get towed."

In front of any other house in this part of Valley View Estates, I would've agreed. Some of the residents might even call the police to check for "undesirables" in the neighborhood. But in front of Todd's house? Not going to happen.

We stood in the cold, staring up at the mansion.

"Don't worry about it," I said. Jack's Adam's apple bobbed, but he didn't respond. He didn't take a step toward the house, either.

"We could always do something else," I said. "Are you sure you're okay with this?"

"You think *they* are?"

I really wasn't sure how the geek squad would react, but I was pretty sure they wouldn't riot just because a jock entered their inner sanctum. Besides, Jack's letter jacket felt thin through my mittens. He couldn't possibly be warm, especially since the temperature had dropped ten degrees with the sunset. "Come on," I said. "Let's go."

No one met us at the door. I just opened it and walked right in, but that was standard operating procedure for Geek Night. Jack balked at the threshold, and I had to tug him inside.

"It's okay." I slipped off my coat and slung it over one arm. "I swear."

Whizzes, bangs, and pops came from the basement, along with canned laughter from the Cartoon Network. I caught the scent of brownies—fresh baked—and caramel corn, and looked at Jack. He blinked, that little-boy grin spread across his face. A coil of tension inside me loosened. Things really would be okay.

The clomp of hard-soled shoes rang through the hall. Todd's dad, Charlie Emerson, roared into the space. His tie was still on, but it was loose at his neck. He worked late a lot, cutting last-minute deals, in between passing out free hot dogs, soda, and balloons. Last summer I'd earned extra cash by helping kids in and out of the inflatable super jump (shaped like a castle for the Emperor of Emerson Motors, of course).

"Who owns that red Toyota out front?" Mr. Emerson bellowed.

And if Jack had attended as many Geek Nights as I had, he would have known: Bellowing was Mr. Emerson's standard operating procedure. But Jack had never attended any Geek . . . anythings. His smile vanished. He raised a hand halfway. With his other hand, he fished around in his pocket for his keys. Mr. Emerson raced past us and flung open the door.

"My God! Would you look at that!"

"I'm sorry, sir. It's mine. I can move it."

"What?" Mr. Emerson shut the door with an emphatic click. "Don't you dare. I was just admiring her. She's a beaut!"

Now Jack really was fazed. He cast me a look, but all I could do was shrug.

"What year is it?" asked Mr. Emerson. "Early eighties?"

Jack nodded.

"Whatcha been doing for upkeep?"

And then they were off. Words like brake pads and fan belts

left Jack's mouth and entered Mr. Emerson's ears. Quite possibly two happier people never existed.

"Impressive," Mr. Emerson said.

"I'm hoping to get another hundred thousand miles out of her," Jack added.

Her? Who decided that trucks were girls?

"Hey, Dad?" Todd stood halfway up the basement stairs.

"It's so unusual," Mr. Emerson continued as if he hadn't heard Todd, "for a boy these days to know something about automotives. Grown men come into my dealership, can't even change the oil in their own cars."

Todd rolled his eyes, then sent me a "here we go again" look—a look Mr. E. noticed.

"Bethany!" Todd's dad called out. "Why, I didn't see you standing there."

What? With all the car talk? That wasn't surprising.

"We've really missed you at Todd's . . ." Mr. Emerson glanced over his shoulder at Todd. "What is it you call these things?"

"Geek Night, Dad," said Todd.

Mr. Emerson shook his head, and a short sigh escaped his lips. "You know what, son?" He said this to Jack. "I didn't get your name."

"Oh, I'm sorry," I said. "This is my—"

Jack flashed me a smile.

"My friend," I finished, flustered. "Jack Paulson."

"Well, of course!" Mr. Emerson waved a hand, indicating Jack's height. "Who else could you be?" Before Jack could answer, Mr. Emerson pumped his hand. "You're having a great season. Think you boys will make it to the state tourney this year?"

"We're trying," Jack said.

"Pleasure to meet you. Real pleasure," Todd's dad said. He headed up the stairs, but he paused halfway. "Hey, you wouldn't be up for a little one-on-one, would you?"

A little . . . what? I glanced at Todd, who looked like he wanted to throw up, and then at Jack, who shrugged.

"Hey, son," Mr. Emerson said, and this time he was actually talking to Todd. "Go get your old basketball."

That Todd owned a basketball, old or otherwise, was strange enough. That he hadn't taken a knife to it and left it to rot in some landfill was downright bizarre.

"Dad, I don't think—"

"Go on," said Mr. Emerson. "It'll be fun."

If fun involved throwing the patio doors wide open, shoving grills, and heaving frozen iron patio furniture around so Jack, Mr. Emerson, and a handful of skinny freshman wrestlers could go three on three—then, yeah, I guess we had fun. But as much as I loved watching Jack play, the frigid air drove me back inside. I hugged myself and shivered.

"Oh, look," Todd said, his tone dry. "It's the son he never had." He turned from the pulse of the basketball and left the room.

I found him sitting on the stairs that led to the basement and took a seat one step below him. "I'm sorry," I said.

"For what?" Todd asked.

For bringing Jack, I almost said, but I owed him the truth. I wasn't sorry about that. Not really. I was sorry Todd's dad could be so . . . so . . . I tried to think of the right word, but could only say, "Everything?"

"It's okay," said Todd. "Besides, when people come over, my dad can make believe I'm popular." He leaned back and peered up the stairs. "This must be a dream come true for him." He sat up and examined me over the edge of his glasses. "And when you show up, it reassures him I'm not gay."

I didn't know whether to giggle or blush, so I did both.

The *thump, thump, thump* of the basketball reached us in the stairwell. From the cadence, I guessed Jack had the ball—the rhythm, the control, it was all his. I listened, intent on the sound. I didn't realize I'd tipped my head back and closed my eyes until Todd laughed.

"You really like him," he said.

"I do." It felt good to confess. "And I think, at least I hope—"

"He does," Todd said.

I looked at him.

"Like you," he finished. "You think he'd be playing basketball with the Emperor of Emerson Motors if he didn't?"

Probably not. The notion of it, of Jack liking me—really, truly liking me—gave me goose bumps. I smiled and shivered. I caught Todd rolling his eyes. "Oh jeez, Todd, I'm—"

"It's okay," he said. "It would be really stupid to get upset about the outcome when you were never in the race to begin with."

"What?" Sometimes Todd went off on tangents that mystified me.

"Do I have to spell it out for you, Reynolds?" he said.

Uh, yeah.

"You know those teen movies, the ones where there's a girl and these two guys, the popular jock and the dork?"

So much for tangents. I knew exactly where this was going.

"The whole audience knows she's supposed to end up with the other guy," he said. "You know, the dork?"

I gave the slightest of nods.

"Well, this isn't the movies."

No, it wasn't.

"And I'm not that guy."

"You're not that guy," I echoed, buying a little time to think. Was Todd giving me the green light where Jack was concerned? Did I really need him to? Maybe not. But until that moment, I hadn't realized how much I'd wanted his okay.

"Then who are you?" A pair of red high-top sneakers appeared on the landing. Jack moved to take a seat on the top stair, but Todd nearly tumbled down three steps making room for him.

"So, man," Jack said, in mock seriousness. "Really. Who the hell are you then?"

"Damn, I didn't—I mean, I'm—," Todd began.

"The future student body president of Prairie Stone High?" I suggested.

"You thinking about running?" asked Jack.

"Bethany's my campaign manager."

His *what*? "I thought I was your stylist."

Todd brushed away my comment. "That too."

"It might be nice for a change," Jack said, "you know, having someone who's smart and not just pop—" He broke off and looked away. An embarrassed Jack Paulson was cute.

Really, really cute.

But the word he didn't speak stayed with us. Jack inspected his shoes. I shifted. Todd stared into space.

"You know," said Todd, "it wouldn't hurt to have a celebrity endorsement."

"Me?" Jack touched his chest with his fingertips.

"Yeah, you. An inroad to the jock vote." Todd nodded way too vigorously. I was surprised he didn't rub his hands together like an evil genius. "I'm starting to really like this idea."

"He's going to have to do something about this, though." I lifted a strand of Todd's hair between two fingers, then let it drop. "Tell him, Jack, being president is all about the hair."

Jack grinned at me. Todd tried not to.

"You might as well come all the way downstairs." Todd gave the stairwell a fleeting glance. "The hard part is over."

"For you, maybe," Jack said. "But I gotta go where no jock's gone before."

Todd pursed his lips, then smiled. "Why didn't you tell me he was funny?" he said to me. "Come on. Let's go."

* * *

We headed downstairs, into the glow of Geek Night, the video games, the neon signs.

"Whoa." Jack halted, and I bumped into him. He remained rooted, steadying me with one hand, but his attention was clearly on something else, something that took up most of one wall. The plasma-screen television. If any inanimate object was assigned a gender, it shouldn't be a truck. Instead it should be Todd's ginormous television. I had yet to see a boy pass by without getting snared in all *her* high-definition glory.

"Christmas," Todd said. He continued through the room with barely a glance at the TV.

And Jack was the first—the only—boy I'd seen turn away from it. I remembered the tiny flat-screen in the place of honor in Jack's living room and gave his hand a squeeze.

Like the Mangers's basement, the Emersons' also had a wet bar that took up one entire side of the room. Only this one featured every designer caffeine known to man. Brian was playing bartender—a friendlier, far more likeable option than Rick.

Except when we approached, Brian flung open the mini-fridge and pulled out a Red Bull. He shot Todd a death glare, then stomped past me, past Jack, all without acknowledgment.

"What the—?" Todd pointed to the bar, but Brian ignored him. "Whatever." Todd jumped up with one hand on the granite countertop, swung his legs over, and landed on the other side. It was a smooth move. Of course, I'd seen him practice—and wipe out—at least a hundred times before.

Drinks led to light sabers, or did for Todd and Jack. Sadly, this was the sort of thing that happened at Geek Night. As a rule, I stayed away from light sabers, although when Todd said things like, "Luke, I am your father," I sometimes wished I had a blaster.

The boys dueled, and the light sabers clashed. Jack looked pleased by the authentic, straight-from-the-movies whiz and hum. He had natural athletic ability, but Todd had more Jedi training time. *Clash, whiz, hum. Clash, whiz, hum.* It continued until, light sabers crossed, the special effects silent, a voice rose from the other side of the room.

"She wants to date a prick? Well, *I* can be a prick!"

Ahh. So that explained why Brian was being such a jerk. Part of me wanted to mention the wand incident. It put him in close second when it came to the prick contest. But I heard the hurt and regret in Brian's voice.

Todd stepped back, shut his eyes for a moment. "I'm going to have to cut off his Red Bull supply," he said.

Todd's distraction was too much for Jack. The competitor in him took over. He lunged forward, ready to take Todd down. Todd parried, took a step to the left, and sank his light saber into Jack's chest.

They stood like that for several seconds. Jack held both hands in the air, a startled expression on his face. Maybe I should've told him about Todd's three years of fencing lessons—the compromise between him and his father over sports.

Then Jack threw his head back and laughed. The boys shook

hands and did a punch, slap, shove thing that I chalked up to male bonding. Todd secured the light sabers above the bar, then turned to Jack.

"Isn't there a T-wolves game on tonight?"

Jack shrugged. "No biggie. We're not having the greatest season."

"Come on." Todd pointed to the television and the group that surrounded it. "Like any of these guys need to see this episode of *Naruto* for the hundredth time."

The boys walked off together, leaving me behind, forgotten. I pulled my legs up so I sat cross-legged on the granite countertop. I planted my elbows on my thighs and watched them. It looked like the start of a beautiful friendship.

We need to talk!

That was all Moni's e-mail said, but I knew the code by heart. Weekends with her dad were jam-packed and hectic. Sure, she could chat on the eighty-mile drive south to Prairie Stone, but the code also meant whatever she had to say wasn't for parental ears.

I could hardly wait for her call.

In fact, I cleared off everything in anticipation. Homework, done. Dishes from Sunday night dinner, done. A long conversation with Jack, done. We'd even talked about the party at Rick's.

"We don't always have to go to those," he said.

I felt the last bit of leftover tension from the party slip away. "We don't always have to go to Geek Night."

"Hey, I'll go wherever there's a game on." Which was exactly what he was doing now, watching some sports thing on ESPN with his dad.

As a bribe, I even let Shelby have full, unsupervised access to the pom-poms. I snuggled into the pillows on my bed and waited for the phone to ring.

I didn't have to wait long. "Guess who I had brunch with?" were the first words from Moni's mouth, not even a "hello" to get things rolling. In the background, I could hear a car door slamming and the crunch of tires, and I guessed she'd already said good-bye to her dad.

"Wait," I said. "I know this one. Orlando Bloom."

"Better than Orlando Bloom."

There was better than Orlando Bloom in Moni's world? The actor had always been Moni's ultimate brunch—or anything—date. She'd watched the Lord of the Rings trilogy so many times that she could finish any of Orlando's lines. It was fantasy life on an epic scale—and Moni knew how to dream big.

And how to fall hard. That was why I'd planned to listen first before telling Moni about Rick's party. It could wait. And the blonde—Amanda—the one who dissed me and my dad's class? Maybe that should wait forever.

I heard her keys drop, then the scrape as she opened the front door. Moni was a barely contained bundle of news and nerves, so, to give her an opening, I said, "What's better than Bloom?"

"Two words: Rick. Mangers."

"Not Rick the—"

Moni drew in a breath. "You can't say it, because it's not true."

I wished it weren't. Or that it was all just a case of mistaken identity. That there were two Rick Mangers, the nice one Moni was crushing on, and his evil, party-throwing twin.

"He called Saturday," Moni continued. "When I told him I wouldn't be back until tonight, he said—get this—that it was 'too long to go without seeing his spark plug.' You did notice the *his*, right?"

Rick Mangers was even smoother than I had guessed possible.

"And then he drove all the way to Minneapolis this morning just to meet us for brunch. Can you believe it?"

Actually, I couldn't. But I couldn't doubt it either. Despite Moni's enthusiastic fantasy life, she could tell reality from fiction, and dream dates from real boys. Even if the idea of Rick Mangers driving to Minneapolis sounded like something from a romance novel.

"Really," I said, hoping Moni wouldn't hear the tightness in my voice.

"It was the best. We went to this place Monica wanted to go to, of course." Moni made gagging noises. "But it wasn't that bad. And get this. Rick totally distracted Monica so I could, you know, have an actual conversation with my dad."

Moni drew in another breath. "Then we went to the Walker Art Center, and while Monica was going on and on about modern art, Rick did this thing—" Moni broke off. It sounded like she was stifling giggles. "This thing," she tried again, but the giggles returned in force. "Never mind, you had to be there."

I was glad I hadn't been.

"And then he drove me home!" she ended with a squeal.

An awful realization hit me. That was Rick Mangers's car I'd heard in the background, not her dad's. He'd been right there, only moments before. With Moni.

"Was he . . . just now—?" I began.

"Yes!"

"Wow," I said. *He didn't happen to mention Friday night's party on the drive back, did he?* I wanted to add, but couldn't. Moni's voice was beyond ecstatic. Beyond brunch with Bloom, even. And it was real.

At least I hoped so.

"So," said Moni. "How are you and Jack?"

"Things are, you know, good."

"The kissing?"

"That's good too."

Moni laughed. "So, what happened after you guys left the party?"

"The party," I said, my words flat. *Moni knew about the party?* How could she? Unless Rick told her. I didn't like that option at all. It was one thing for Todd to hear secondhand accounts from skinny freshman wrestlers. It was a whole different thing to have Rick the Prick Mangers feeding his version of the story to my best friend.

"Rick says next time it won't be so last-minute—that way I can come too."

"Oh. Of course." I wasn't sure Moni heard me, because she barely paused before her next words.

"Can you believe Chantal?" she asked. "Oh, my God. Rick told me she was totally wasted. Some people never learn, you know?"

Despite my relief that Moni apparently hadn't heard some of the more horrid details, I felt kind of sad. All of it, Rick and the blonde, the encounter with R.J., the beer, and Chantal. I wished none of it had ever happened.

"We went to Todd's on Saturday," I said to change the subject.

"Please don't tell me you took Jack Paulson to Geek Night?"

"Well, yeah. Why not?"

"I'd never take Rick there."

"Is there something wrong with it?"

Silence from the other end. I waited, worried that somehow Moni and I had started speaking different languages. Then, over the line, came the *whoosh* of the refrigerator door.

"Of course there's nothing wrong with it," Moni said around a bite of something. It's just . . . you know."

"No. I don't know." I didn't mean to say it sharply, but there it was. "Jack and Todd got along great," I added.

"Whatever. I just can't see Rick there."

"Well, hey," I said, "at least we agree about that." You could probably poll the entire student body of Prairie Stone High, and they'd all agree about that.

"You really don't know him," she said after another bite. "He makes jokes about his mom trading up and all that. I know he's a jerk at school sometimes. But on the way home, we talked forever, about everything. And I think this is it, the real thing."

"You really like him," I said, echoing Todd's words to me.

"God, yes. Even though people say he's a—"

"Prick?" I suggested.

Moni laughed, and I relaxed a little.

"Yeah, that. Except he's not." Her voice went quiet and dreamy. Of everything I'd heard during the conversation, this scared me the most.

"He's not," Moni said again. "Not with me, anyway."

12

From *The Prairie Stone High
Varsity Cheerleading Guide*:

It's a fact of cheerleading: our players can't win them
all, no matter how much we want that, no matter how
hard we cheer. Be there for our Prairie Stone athletes
during the downtimes and defeats. Now, more than
ever, you must let your school spirit shine.

I stared at my clock until one thirty in the morning, when
I couldn't stand it any longer and turned over. Monday I
arrived at school bleary-eyed. Cheerleading practice was
going to kick my butt.

"So what do you think?" Moni whispered. We were standing
by my locker, talking behind the door. "I mean," she continued, "the
whole drive up to Minneapolis and back again? You can't call that
anything but serious."

Actually, I wanted to call it a lot of things. "Unreal" was at the top of my list. But during my midnight tossing and turning, I'd decided to follow Todd's example. After all, I brought a jock to Geek Night. The least I could do was give Rick Mangers a chance.

"Hey, spark plug!"

It looked like I had my chance right then. The two of us peered from behind my locker door. At the entrance to the cafeteria, Rick stood and waved Moni down the hall. She took a few steps before turning to me. "Come on. Jack might be there."

He might. But then, so would Rick. And I wasn't in the mood to deal with that. "You go. I've got to finish up some notes before history."

But I stayed at my locker, hand on the door, and watched Moni half glide, half bounce down the corridor, straight past Chantal and company without a glance or bump in her stride. Rick's protective arm around Moni's waist didn't bother me, and neither did the condescending tug to her curls. But then he leaned back and flashed a look at me.

What was that about? It felt like he was laying down a challenge. Like when it came to Moni, it was either him or me. Couldn't we go for one of those peaceful coexistence things? But Rick was a jock. "Peace" and "coexist" weren't in his vocabulary. Of course, words of more than two syllables weren't either.

Moni likes him. A lot. Be nice. Think nice thoughts, I told myself.

I pulled a stack of note cards from my backpack. I'd written them the day before, while on the phone with Jack. Should I go see if my oatmeal-loving boy was busy shoveling in breakfast? Prepare for honors history and avoid the inevitable lecture from Todd?

Or stand here like an idiot with a stack of note cards in my hand?

The bell rang. Decision made.

According to Sun Tzu and *The Art of War*, "The worst calamities that befall an army arise from hesitation."

I hoped he was wrong.

The way a guy said your name meant something. I came to that conclusion after Jack started saying mine. I'd also come to the conclusion that cheerleading took up more time and dedication than anyone would ever suspect. Really, before people talked trash about cheerleaders, they should walk a mile in their Skechers.

By the time the last bell rang, I was exhausted. I still needed to push through the students pouring from classrooms, stop by the library to pick out a new book for Independent Reading, drop off a draft of the abstract for my chemistry project, change for cheerleading practice, and then spend a couple of hours in the newspaper office.

Between now and then, I hoped to devise a reasonable excuse for why my next Life at Prairie Stone column—"Life as a Cheerleading Coach"—still wasn't finished. I had all the material for it and had even listened to the interview with Sheila during sixth period. After the school board fiasco, I felt I owed her. Besides, it was way better than Todd's proposed column idea. But other than the title, I couldn't get a single word on the page.

I checked the big clock in the hall and calculated the minutes and seconds it would take to race to the locker room. If I didn't swap shirts, I might still make it on time. I couldn't force myself to leave, though. Even with the halls so crowded, the jock-talk from where Rick Mangers stood in the middle of a bunch of seniors was all I could hear.

The way a guy said your name meant something. And the way Rick said Moni's gave me the shivers. Especially when the response to her name included laughter. And grunting.

I pretended to flip through my notebook while I tried to listen. I couldn't pick out many words, but everything I needed to hear was there in Rick's tone. It was there in the way a couple of the boys stole looks at me. Ryan Nelson even blushed.

"Hey, Bethany!"

That was another way to say someone's name. I turned and stepped out of the way just as Andrew nearly crashed into me.

"Hey," he said again, out of breath. "You and Moni cheering for wrestling this week?"

"Weren't we there last week?" I teased. "And the week before?"

"Yeah, but you know." Andrew gave his shoes thorough consideration. "The guys wanted me to check." He looked up at me and started to say something more, but raunchy laughter came from Rick's group.

"He's such an ass," Andrew said.

"I thought he was a prick."

"That too."

"I'm going to do it," I said out loud. I wasn't certain what "it" was, but I took a step forward anyway.

"Wait." Andrew touched my sleeve.

I teetered slightly. "What?"

"I can—we can, you know, keep our ears open in the locker room." He eyed Rick. "Make sure everything's okay."

"Doesn't that go against some kind of secret guy code or something?"

Andrew rubbed his shoulder in a way that made me wonder what exactly went on in the boys' locker room. "Technically," he said, "you need two human beings for that. Mangers—he doesn't count."

Did all guys have to be jerks? At least Jack wasn't. And neither was this skinny freshman wrestler standing in front of me.

"I'm still going to talk to him," I said.

"I'm still going to listen." He turned from me and headed down the hall.

I called after him. "Hey, Andrew."

He spun, almost losing his balance, and I bit back a grin.

"When you're a senior, promise me you'll remember all this."

"I'm never going to forget." He vanished into the crowd of students—not tall enough yet to track, not large enough to cause a ripple in the mass of high school humanity.

By now the jocks had closed ranks; the group seemed tighter, more solid than before. I marched up to them anyway, still not sure what I'd say to Rick. Of course, that was assuming he'd let me say anything at all.

"Excuse me? Rick?"

The group shifted, all at once. And damn if it wasn't intimidating. Rick stared.

"Can I talk to you?"

He shrugged, palms outward. Nice time to go all dumb jock on me.

"Alone?" I added.

He slapped one of his palms against his forehead. "Oh, alone." He turned to the other boys and winked. "You gentlemen will excuse me? Duty calls."

A snicker ran through the crowd, but I ignored it—or tried to. And when Rick grabbed my elbow, I tried not to flinch—but I did. "Ooh, Paulson's got himself a live one," he said.

Moni likes him. A lot. Be nice. Think nice thoughts.

I couldn't. The only thing that came to mind was Rick's nickname. He truly was a part of the male anatomy. We stood for a moment, silent.

"This is the part where you talk," said Rick.

Okay. I knew that. "Moni's my best friend," I said.

"I know. She talks about you. All the time."

I could tell he was positively thrilled about that. "She's been through a lot of stuff lately, especially with her parents, you know," I said. At least he *should* know. If Rick even half listened to anything Moni said, that should've been obvious.

The divorce was way less friendly than everyone liked to pretend. Moni's dad had gauntlet-girl-all-grown-up Monica. Her mom drowned her sorrows in poetry readings and now Starbucks Boy. But when Moni's schedule put them all on a collision course, there were usually no survivors.

I had been along for one of those once, and it wasn't the insults or the anger or even anything the four "adults" *did* that got to me. It was Moni, the way she stood stock-still, waves of sadness rolling off her. I'd tugged on her arm. Together we'd walked away from the group, found a coffee shop, and ordered white chocolate mochas, the large size, with extra whip. And no one, *no one*, bothered to find us.

Rick needed to understand that. Instead he checked his cell phone. "Anything else?"

"I don't want to see her hurt," I said.

"And what makes you think I'd do that?"

"Oh, I don't know." I didn't. Not right away. "Maybe . . . that bet?"

But Rick only laughed. "Yep, a live one."

Oh, SHUT up. "Moni deserves the best," I said. "And you need to prove that's what you are."

He stepped back, surprise erasing the smugness on his face. I didn't really get him with that, did I? It didn't seem possible.

"You think Paulson's all that perfect?"

"This isn't about Jack."

"If he doesn't win that bet, do you think he can even afford to take you to prom?"

That was low. "I don't care about prom."

Rick gave me a look, one that said, *All girls care about prom*. "I've got a stretch Hummer lined up already."

Of course he did. A more perfect vehicle for Rick Mangers did not exist—a real prickmobile.

"Maybe spark plug and I can give you two a ride," he added.

"I don't care about prom," I repeated. What was the big deal, anyway? "I care about Jack." My mouth clamped shut, but it was too late. I couldn't believe I'd just said that. Out loud. To Rick Mangers.

"Oh? You *care* about Paulson?" he asked, gloating in his voice. "Well, here's a tip for you. Paulson doesn't like uptight chicks."

"I am not uptight."

Rick laughed again, louder this time, longer. "You're wound so tight, you're about to spring a leak."

I blinked, trying to imagine what that would look like. "That's a mixed metaphor," I said.

"A what?"

"A mixed metaphor," I said again. "I'm tutoring English this spring." Actually, I was signed up to start as soon as cheerleading ended. And yeah, it was snarky, but I added, "You might want to stop by and—"

"You think you're pretty smart," he interrupted, "but you don't know everything that you think you know, you know?"

"What's that supposed to mean?"

"You're the one with all the brains. *You* figure it out."

I climbed the stairs, wondering—not for the first time—why the newspaper office had to be on the top floor. My legs trembled, and I used the handrail to pull myself up. Sheila had been brutal in practice that afternoon.

I collapsed at a desk in the journalism classroom. A few feet away, Todd gave me a salute with the blue pencil he was using to mark up some poor freshman's attempt at a feature article.

"So," Todd said. "Life at Prairie Stone?"

Sucks. "Working on it," is what I said out loud. "I modified your suggestion."

Todd arched an eyebrow. "So no 'Life as a Cheerleader'?"

I didn't want to go there, not in print, anyway. "'Life as a Cheerleading *Coach*.'" Todd opened his mouth, but I rushed to speak before he could say anything. "I have a ton of material. For instance . . ." I dug through my bag and brought out the notes and the digital recorder I'd used during my interview. "Did you know Sheila's had articles published in *American Cheerleader*?"

"I didn't know there was such a thing."

I ignored him. "And she published her own book." Okay, so it was *The Prairie Stone High Varsity Cheerleading Guide*, but that counted, right?

"I was hoping for something meatier," Todd said. "An exposé. A first-person account. A look at the high-stakes world of varsity cheerleading from the inside. A little scandal. Personality conflicts." He paused. "Catfights. You know, the good stuff."

Oh, please. "Well, you know, today, at practice . . ." I leaned across the desk and made my voice all breathless. "Somebody stole Kaleigh's lip gloss, but it turned out she just left it in her locker."

Todd closed his eyes.

Before I could say anything else, Jack rapped on the door frame, then strolled in. His hair was still damp from the showers, skin still flushed from basketball practice. He collapsed, much like I had, into the desk next to mine. I was surprised that he'd found me. Sure, I mentioned something about the newspaper during Independent Reading, but nothing about when I'd be there or for how long.

"Look," I added. "No one wants to read about my life as a cheerleader."

"I would," Jack said. "I like reading all your columns."

"Then tell her to write one," said Todd.

"Right," I said.

"And if you could get her to lose the one-word sentences . . . ," Todd continued.

"Those are my favorite," Jack said. "Hey, I'm a jock." He shrugged. "We're all about the one-word sentences."

I giggled. Todd scowled. Jack grinned, looking rather pleased with himself.

"Listen, Reynolds." Todd reached out to touch my hand. "You're a columnist, not some freshman flunky churning out copy. You have real clips, ones that matter."

"Like I said, right." The *Purple Pride* was hardly the *New Yorker*, but I didn't dare tell Todd that.

"Think about college applications. Clips, combined with your academics, and now this cheerleading thing. Colleges will be begging you to apply." Todd turned to Jack. "You get it, right?" he said. "I mean, with that recruiter coming—"

"What? Wait. Whoa." I swiveled in my seat to look at Jack. "A recruiter?"

"According to this article." Todd tapped the papers in front of him, the ones covered in blue marks. "Basketball, swimming. We have a couple recruiters coming in."

"That's great," I said, then, "Who? I mean, where? And when?"

"University of Minnesota," Jack said. "This Friday. Hey, newspaper girl, I think you forgot the What and the Why." He tried to hide a smile.

"Wait," said Todd.

"That's not one of the five Ws, newspaper boy," I said, and grinned at Jack.

"No, seriously." Todd pressed his fingertips against his temples. "I'm about to be brilliant."

Oh, God, no. Todd's last "brilliant" newspaper idea was my Life at Prairie Stone column. I braced myself for the worst.

"You." He pointed his blue pencil at Jack. "How would you like to be sports editor?"

Sports editor? Was he kidding?

"Why hasn't anyone thought of this before?" Todd asked. "A new perspective. Sports from the inside out."

I had to admit it wasn't such a bad idea. Still. "It's hard to report on a game when you're in the middle of it," I pointed out.

"She's right, bro," said Jack.

"A guest column, then, like Bethany does." Todd stood and stepped around the desk, tucking his pencil behind his ear. "We could call it, As the Ball Bounces. Or wait! The Thinking Man's Jock."

Jack looked appalled, although whether it was from the title suggestions or the notion that he'd actually have to write something, I couldn't tell.

"Just imagine it." Todd sat on the desk across from Jack. "Recruiters see something like that in your file, along with everything else? You'll be golden."

"I can help," I offered. "And we don't have to call it the Thinking Man's Jock." Really, we should call it anything but that.

"Can it wait until after the game on Friday?" Jack asked.

"Of course." Todd spread his hands wide, the picture of the easygoing, kindhearted editor.

Ha. I knew better.

"So, Reynolds." Todd swung on me. "Your column?"

What? Like it had magically written itself while we'd been talking? "Actually—"

"Actually . . ." Jack stood, then started gathering my notes, pencils, and recorder. "I need Bethany's help." He pulled *Pride and Prejudice* from its home in the pocket of his letter jacket. "Too many big words. But I'll make sure she finishes her column. I promise."

"Go. Go." Todd waved us from the room. "Why you can't be a normal couple and simply disgust everyone with PDA is beyond me."

By "everyone" he meant himself, of course. But I figured we should leave before hearing his lecture on public displays of affection. We were silent until we reached the hall. Then I let out a long breath.

"Thank you," I said.

Jack grinned. "Not a problem. It looked like you wanted to escape."

I sighed. "I'll do the column tonight." Assuming I could find the words to write. Suddenly I felt like I'd used them all up by talking—words wasted on Rick, words shouted at cheerleading practice; I didn't have any left in reserve.

"Was he serious about . . . ?" Jack asked.

I nodded. "He gets crazy ideas, but he generally means all of them. And this one isn't too terrible."

Jack gave me a wary look. "And were you serious? About helping?"

I stopped and planted myself right in front of him. "You have to ask?"

"No." He leaned close, let the backpack slip from his arm. It hit the floor with a clump of books and the whisper of canvas. "But I wanted to." Then he kissed me.

I came up for air and caught a blur of movement at the other end of the hall by the yearbook office. A flash of teal and lemon, with footwear to match, and the unmistakable flip of magazine-worthy long, blond hair. My eyes focused just as Chantal turned on the corked heel of her patent leather pumps and stomped around the corner. Then Jack reeled me in for another long kiss.

Serious PDA, I thought. *Todd should see us now.*

The second half of Friday's game had just started, and already I knew. Jack was playing his worst game ever, and it wasn't going to get any better. Coach Miller called a time out and herded the boys into a circle.

No one on the cheerleading squad—not even Cassidy—saw the point of rushing midcourt for a pyramid, or even the "fun" of tossing Moni in the air. Instead we stood at the sidelines waiting for the game to resume, waiting for the final, pathetic verdict.

"God, what's wrong with him?" Moni whispered. "Is he sick or something?"

"I don't know." I scanned the crowd, then looked at Jack for the billionth time that night. During the first quarter, I'd given up trying to figure out which fan was the mysterious recruiter. It looked like the usual Prairie Stone crowd—some dads in ties, some in John Deere caps, some of them in both.

"Coach Miller might even bench him," said Moni.

And then, as if Moni had telepathed the suggestion, Coach Miller did just that. He replaced Jack with Ryan Nelson, who had racked up less court time in four years than Jack had in one.

"We're going to lose," Moni predicted.

Jack sat on the bench and dropped his head into his hands. He didn't slump his shoulders, though. They remained a straight, hard line. Somehow, that made me feel even worse.

"Do you want to sit?"

I jerked. The pom-poms slipped in my hands. I turned to see Cassidy at my side. I was being benched, again. *What did I do this time?* It took a minute for me to realize Cassidy was asking, not ordering. Together we looked at Jack. Sit out, in solidarity with him? If that would help, I would.

"It's okay," I said. "I'll cheer." I'd been in the world of jocks long enough to know sitting out wouldn't help, and that Jack wouldn't want me to. Besides, it gave me something else to do, someone else to look at other than Jack. Every time I turned, though, every time I spun, or looked over my shoulder, Jack was still there, unmoving.

By the end of the fourth quarter, the Panthers were barely holding it together. At least we scored well enough that the loss wasn't spectacularly embarrassing.

"From one sucky thing to the next," Moni said, with a nod toward her dad and the infamous Monica. "She wants us to do 'girl stuff' this weekend. So I was like, '*Cool*—I'll bring the calculus.'"

In spite of everything, I laughed. "Don't torture her too much."

Moni rolled her eyes. "Call me."

"Like I ever forget."

I watched the three of them leave, Moni on one side of her dad and the tall, überstylish Monica on the other. No doubt about it, she wore great shoes. And no doubt about it, back in high school, Monica had been a gauntlet girl. Chantal Simmons all grown up and a potential stepmom? It was enough to give a geek girl the heebies.

The crowd around me thinned. With no dance tonight, everyone headed elsewhere. Earlier I'd overheard Cassidy whispering something about a party at Rick Mangers's. I'd darted a look at Moni, but if she knew—or heard—she wasn't saying. Jack hadn't mentioned it either, not that I blamed him.

The line for the pay phone dwindled. Still no Jack.

It wasn't like we'd made plans for after the game. Not exactly. I thought about calling my dad, but I wanted to do something to help Jack. How, I wasn't sure. Stuff that cheered Moni up wouldn't work on a boy. Not unless Jack had a secret thing for Orlando Bloom.

Three guys from the basketball team slunk out of the locker room. A minute later, a few more passed me. Then one more, and another. Not one of them looked my way. Ryan Nelson walked out alone. He veered toward me while still managing to avert his eyes.

"Paulson said to tell you that you'd better call your dad. He won't be able to drive you home."

"Where is he?"

"He's . . ." Ryan glanced over his shoulder. "Busy."

Sure he was. "Where?"

He shook his head. "He's—"

"Please?" I begged.

He looked at me then and nodded toward the locker-room hallway—and the school's back entrance.

"Thanks," I said, and jogged down the hall.

"Hey," Ryan called after me. "Maybe you shouldn't."

I halted, my shoes squeaking. "Shouldn't?"

"Just don't say I didn't warn you, okay?" He shrugged and turned for the doors.

Outside, lamplight cast a yellow haze on the asphalt. Teachers parked behind the school. Across the lot was the annex building, where students took woodworking, electronics, and auto mechanics. A single basketball net was attached to the building's side.

The *whoosh* and *clunk* of slam dunks filled the air. I saw the blur of orange, heard the clink of the chain-link hoop. The cold air sneaked through my winter coat, froze my bare legs. My teeth were already chattering.

Jack wore only basketball pants and a Prairie Stone High Athletics sweatshirt—no jacket, no hat, no gloves. He chucked the ball through the metal hoop with relentless precision, never missing a shot. God, he was good—really good. Talent. Hard work. He had it all. What had happened tonight?

"Jack?"

"Go home." He dribbled the ball and lunged for the hoop, not looking at me once. "Call your dad."

"I'm not leaving until you talk to me."

He swore. "What would you like me to say?" At least he stopped moving. He tucked the ball under one arm and approached me. When he got close, I could see the grim expression in his eyes.

"I'm sorry about tonight," I said.

"Not as sorry as I am."

My mind searched for something to reassure him. "Maybe it was just a rumor about the recruiter." A rumor. That was good, and possibly true. "Does anyone know if he was really here?"

"Doesn't matter if he wasn't. I *thought* he was." He started to spin the ball on his index finger, then stopped. "When it really counted, I choked. No one wants a player who can't handle pressure."

"You had one bad game. It happens. Everyone, even a recruiter, knows that. They'll look at your record—"

"What do you know about it? What do you know about *anything*?" He slammed the ball against the pavement and nabbed it on the rebound. "You got money for college?"

"I—"

"Yeah. Like your mom and your dad the professor, aren't saving up."

I sighed. My parents had been putting money away for college since I was little—that didn't mean cost wasn't a consideration. It wasn't like I could pick any school I wanted. But, yeah, I could go. I knew it was different for Jack.

"There'll be other games," I said. "Other recruiters. What about Prairie Stone State? I bet—"

"Podunk State? No one gives a shit about Division II schools."

Podunk State. Nice. "Uh, my dad might. They have a decent team, and it's a good school."

"Would you go there?"

"I'll apply."

"Not the same thing."

It was true. Prairie Stone State was my backup school, my *extreme* backup school. I didn't expect to end up there.

"Thing is," Jack said, "this was it—my one chance."

"You get more than one—"

"Who says? I'm not like you. Okay? I know I'm not smart. This . . ." He cupped the ball between both hands and shook it at me. "It's my only shot, and I blew it."

He threw the ball, and it smacked against the metal wall of the annex and bounced a few times before winding its way back to us. Jack picked it up and rolled it from hand to hand. "Remember that party last summer?" he asked. "You know, the one where . . ."

He didn't have to elaborate. When I thought about it, I used the same phrase. *That party*. I nodded, but then I said, "I don't understand what that has to do with this—"

"I saw Dina the other day," he said.

I still didn't understand, but I waited, quietly, in the cold. Whatever Jack had to say, it was serious.

The basketball flew across the court, and Jack followed. It was as though he and the ball were one, working together to make the basket. The chain links jingled, and his sneakers pounded the asphalt. "I don't have to think to do that," he said.

In two steps he crossed to me. He wound a hand around the back of my head and pushed his mouth hard against mine. It was a kiss full of desperation, full of regret. He let go so suddenly that I stumbled backward.

"I don't have to think to do that, either," he said. "But Dina. Dina has to think just to walk across the room." He looked right at me, but I doubted he saw me. "I was supposed to be in the car that night."

The cold that threatened me before took hold. My whole body shook. Fringe rattled. I let the pom-poms drop to the ground and hugged myself, tight.

"The brakes on the Toyota were acting up," Jack went on, "and Dina offered me a ride home. Of course, Traci and Chantal came along with the deal." He shook his head. "Earlier that day, my dad got a delivery of"—his eyes searched the sky—"junk. For free. He was so damn proud of it too. But there it was, all this . . . shit . . . spread across our front lawn."

Soft clouds of breath came out with his words. Tiny snowflakes speckled the air around us. It was strange how a moment could be both beautiful and heartbreaking.

"You know how those girls are, especially when they're together," he said, giving me a significant look. *Oh, yeah. I knew.* I waited for him to continue.

"If it was just me," he said, "I wouldn't have really cared. But I didn't want them making fun of my dad, even if I wasn't there to hear it. So I walked home."

Pride again, I thought, and I longed to say something, anything.

"I saw the accident, or what was left of it. Dina's Lexus in the ravine, the tow truck, a few cop cars, the ambulance pulling away. It made me . . ." He paused, rolling the basketball between his palms again. "It made me think about things, you know? Like, I could do something with my life, or I could just keep going on, letting it all slip by."

He dribbled the ball. It thumped against the ground, then spun from his hands and crashed against the wall of the annex again. "And there it went. Tonight? *That* was my second chance." He looked at me like he'd just noticed I was still there. "You don't need a guy like that, a guy who's going to peak in high school."

"I don't know—," I started to say.

"Of course you do. Mangers is right. A girl like you and a guy like me? What a joke."

A joke? Somehow it always came back to Rick Mangers, and my thoughts went to that stupid bet.

"Is that all this is? A joke?" I hadn't meant to say it out loud. And I was pretty sure I didn't want to hear the answer. But now that it was out there, I had to know. "So what do you really have to do to get that hundred bucks?" I asked.

"What?" he said, and his face turned stony.

"You and Mangers? Is this all some kind of . . ." What? My mind clicked through endless possibilities for humiliation. What had Rick said? *You think you're pretty smart, but you don't know everything that you think you know, you know?*

Okay, I'd suspected there was something I didn't know—or at least didn't *want* to know—since the very start.

You're the one with all the brains. You figure it out.

These were boys; more important, they were jocks. What did jocks do, other than compete? My mind, still spinning with all those possibilities, stuck on one.

"Is this a race?" I watched Jack's expression for clues to the truth. His lip twitched. "To see who could get . . . the furthest the fastest?" Jack's lip twitched again, and he glanced away.

Bingo.

In the seconds it took to sink in, I calculated the spiraling levels of humiliation. "So. Who's winning?"

Jack stared at the ground. "Who do you think?"

Oh, God. Moni. Moni and Rick. According to Moni, all they'd done so far was kiss. She wouldn't do something like . . . *that* . . . without telling me. Would she? I shook my head to clear it. Under the spell of the great Rick Mangers? She just might.

"Listen," Jack said. "It might have started—"

"No. You listen. I may not be prom queen material, but I'm a real person. Moni is a *real person*." I paused, just long enough to catch my breath, but I wasn't through. "And your dad? Isn't he real too? Or was dinner at your house just a joke? Is he a joke?"

Jack looked up sharply. Oh, yeah, I knew his dad was totally off limits, but I didn't care. "It's funny," I said. "Because I don't think it was a joke to him."

Jack took a step forward, but I held my ground.

"You don't get it at all," he said.

"That's just it. I do." I scooped the pom-poms from the ground. They rustled, the sound loud in the frigid air. I walked toward the back entrance, willing myself not to give Jack another look.

"Bethany." The way a guy said your name meant something, but all I heard in Jack's voice was pity. The pom-poms quivered in my hands.

"It's not what you—," he began. "I mean, I'm sorry," he said.

"Not as sorry as I am." Tears clogged my throat. I hurried to the back doors, half hoping he would follow me.

He didn't.

13

From *The Prairie Stone High
Varsity Cheerleading Guide*:

Resignation is a serious step. Not only won't you be
able to come back if you change your mind, you put the
possibility of cheering on future squads in jeopardy. Give
it serious thought before you turn in your pom-poms.

Even the best squads have their ups and downs.
Remember, I am your first line of defense. If you
can't solve a problem on your own, please bring me
into the loop.

I gave up.

For most of two days, either Moni's cell phone rang
and rang, or it rolled into voice mail. I had left three
messages already—three frantic, urgent messages, complete with

all the embarrassing details. Then I wrote the whole thing out and e-mailed it to her. Whoever said writing was therapeutic was wrong—I felt even worse afterward.

I ignored all communication from Todd, especially the e-mailed invites to Geek Night with "Bring Paulson, Too" in the subject line. IM? I didn't even bother to log on.

Instead I did homework. I tucked it in my folders, then double-checked it hours later. I had no memory of filling in the blanks, writing out essay questions, or even reading chapters for honors history. Great. I had a broken mind to go along with my broken heart. I shoved everything into my backpack and crushed something at the bottom of it.

I reached in, my fingers finding a crumpled piece of paper. I knew before smoothing the crinkles what it said: "Witty Things to Say When Jack Paulson Is Nearby."

I took it and the Dr Pepper can and tossed them both in the trash. Three seconds later I dug them both out. I pressed the can against my temple, the aluminum cool, one soft click sounding in my ear. I couldn't throw it away, but I couldn't stand to look at it either. At last I put both in my bottom desk drawer—a compromise between letting go and holding on.

By three on Sunday afternoon, I'd abandoned everything: the phone, homework, the computer. I stared at my ceiling, willing the world to go away. When Shelby came into my room without knocking, and then asked about Jack, I snapped.

"Leave! Me! Alone!" I shouted. I chased her out of the room and slammed my door. But seconds later, when I heard sobbing in the hall, I peeked out the door.

"Hey," I said. "I'm sorry."

She wiped away her tears, sniffed. "It's okay." But her quivering lip said it wasn't.

"You want to learn the new dance?" I offered.

With a squeal, Shelby grabbed the pom-poms and headed for the living room. Soon "Get Ready for This" was screaming from the stereo, and we were step-shimmy-kicking it like never before. Even Mom joined in. It made me happier, and sadder, in an odd way. After three dances, Mom and I collapsed on the couch while Shelby continued moving through the routine.

"I'm going to have to buy her a set when it's time for you to turn those things in," Mom said, and laughed.

When I turn those things in, I thought, and my brain offered up images I would have rather not considered. Like, cheering on the sidelines with Jack out there on the court. I reached up to hold my head. *How did I ever let myself get so stupid?* Geek girls and cheerleading, geek girl and Jack Paulson, those things were like oil and water. Impossible to combine.

"Honey, do you want to talk about what's been bothering you all weekend?"

"I—" *How did Mom even know?* I hadn't said a word about the breakup. If you could call it that. Then I thought, of course, no phones, no visits, no Geek Night. Hard not to know that something was wrong. I shook my head, but when a tear escaped down my cheek, Mom moved closer.

"I'm sorry this had to happen, but maybe it's better this way." My mom groaned. "Sorry. That sounds like something a grown-up would say. What I mean is, I never really dated in high school. And I certainly wasn't a cheerleader."

"I'm not much of one either."

"Oh, honey, but you *are*." She stroked my hair. "I'm amazed at what you've done. Madame Wolsinski should see you now. You know," Mom continued, "when I was your age, you could pretty much call me a nerd."

Like mother, like daughter.

"Then, when I got to college," she continued, "I was so overwhelmed by it all. Someday I'll tell you about the frat party from hell."

That sounded like something Rick Mangers would host.

"This way, maybe you'll be more ready than I was. Dating, boys, all of it," she said. "Think of this experience as a big social experiment."

"And the hypothesis is: I suck at it."

"Everybody does at first." My mom squeezed my hand. "Doesn't make it easier, though."

The song ended. Instead of hitting replay, Shelby dropped the pom-poms and plopped down next to me on the couch, her eyes huge and sad. She squeezed me tight around the waist. I didn't think—what with the music going at full blast—she'd overheard Mom and me. I hugged her back, just as tight, and wished I was nine again.

"So, Reynolds, tell me about this deal between Paulson and Rick Mangers."

I whirled from my locker Monday morning, jostling the door. It rattled shut. My head felt thick, my fingers stupid. I had to run the combination twice to open it again. I felt the flush start along my jaw. It seemed to simmer there for a moment before spreading across the rest of my face. So. Todd knew about the bet. How on earth . . . oh, freshman wrestlers, *of course*. So if they knew, and Todd knew, then the whole damn school must know.

"Sure, Paulson's got that black eye," he said, "but I still say Mangers ended up with the worst of it."

"Jack's got a what?"

"Black eye," said Todd. "Uh, you've seen it, right?"

I tried to piece together what he was saying. "Jack and me—"

"Jack and I," Todd corrected, then concern clouded his face. "Hey, Bethany, is everything okay?" Again I was reminded—the way a guy said your name meant something.

"Everything is—" *So not okay*, I thought. But I didn't know how to start that conversation, or whether I wanted to. "I guess . . . I don't know what you're talking about," I said. "How did Jack get a black eye?"

"All I know is Saturday, Paulson and Mangers got into it in

the boys' locker room. It took five seniors to pull them apart."

"A fight?"

"A bad one too. Pretty-boy Mangers is looking rough this morning."

"Over what?" I asked.

"That's just it. No one knows." Todd shrugged. "I figured you'd have the inside scoop on that."

"I'm not on the inside of anything." I turned back to my locker and pretended to look for a pencil. So Todd *didn't* know about the breakup—or the bet—which meant maybe no one else did either. I should've felt relieved, but the weight of it hung over me. It was like waiting for the other Skecher to drop.

Todd touched my shoulder. "What's going on?" he asked.

"Nothing." I shrugged.

"Really?"

"There's nothing going on. At least not anymore, not between me and Jack."

"No way," Todd said. "Since when?"

"Since Friday." I swallowed a breath. "After the game."

"Well, that explains Geek Night. You should've come anyway."

"Wasn't in the mood." Still, it was nice to know I was welcome somewhere.

"Damn." Todd leaned against the next locker and stared at the ceiling. "This sucks."

His concern was actually touching.

"You don't suppose he'll still support my campaign, do you?"

Todd pushed the hair away from his glasses. "I admit it might be a little awkward at first, but with time—" He broke off at the look on my face.

"What one usually says at this point is, 'Gee, Bethany, I'm sorry.' Or 'Gosh, Bethany, that's too bad.' You do not wonder if it will hurt you in the electoral college."

"Look, Reynolds—"

My jaw was so tight, it hurt. "So if it was a choice, between him and me?"

Todd opened his mouth, but nothing came out.

"Wrong answer." I slammed the locker door, not caring if I had everything I needed or not. I marched, head down, toward history, the opposite direction of Todd, the cafeteria, the gauntlet, Jack, Rick, and even Moni—the opposite direction of everything.

The classroom was empty. I sat at our table and considered sprinkling Todd's chair with pushpins from the bulletin board. I stared at the map of the world and thought about hearts: how Todd's was two sizes too small, how much mine hurt, and how Jack's was a mystery.

Except . . . it was no mystery. I'd seen him with his dad. Jack's was one of the best hearts I had ever known. That I never really had a spot in it—well, that was what hurt the most.

I stood down the hall from the cafeteria door, at the spot where I usually met Moni for lunch. I hadn't seen her all morning. My throat felt rough—from tears, from not talking, from holding everything in while Jack Paulson sat across from me in Independent Reading. God, I needed Moni, and I needed her *now*.

Chantal and the gauntlet girls filed past. Each of them gave me a long, hard stare. It was their standard intimidation tactic—guaranteed to work on freshmen, sophomores, and the occasional esteem-challenged upperclassman. Once upon a time, it would have worked on me, too. But even in my current state, I knew I looked fine, or as fine as anyone coming off a weekend-long crying jag could look.

Todd gave me a mock two-finger salute when he passed by. Brian and most of the debate team shuffled past in his wake, careful not to look me in the face. So. Todd was mad that I was mad? *Oh, grow up,* I wanted to shout.

There was no sign of Moni. Or Jack. But Rick Mangers skulked past. His nose was swollen. Bruises colored his forehead and one cheekbone. He didn't glance my way. But Todd had been right: Pretty-boy Mangers looked rough today.

I spotted Moni at the far end of the hall. When I realized she was flanked by Anna and Kaleigh, a strange fight-or-flight impulse kicked in. "I'll catch up with you guys," Moni said when they reached my spot in the hall. Kaleigh and Anna exchanged looks. I swore they laughed once they were inside.

"Hey," I said. "What's up?" But Moni didn't stop, just slowed a little, and I hurried to catch her.

"I almost lost my boyfriend thanks to you. That's what's up."

"Moni. Didn't you listen to my messages? We—"

"Look, it's not my fault you screwed things up with Jack." Moni's words were shrill. "Rick is the best thing that's ever happened to me, and I swear, if you try anything else, I'll—"

I shook my head, but what I really wanted was to shake some sense into my friend. "This whole thing is a joke. *We're* a joke, to both of them. This isn't real."

She turned to me when she reached the cafeteria door. "You're the one who needs to get real. We make the cheerleading squad and a bunch of good stuff happens, but all you can do is bitch about it." Moni's eyes were small and fierce behind her glasses. I'd never seen her like this.

"I don't know what I did, but—," I started. Except . . . I did know. This was Rick's work. He'd taken my words, mixed up some metaphors, and fed them to Moni.

"You messed up everything. Don't you get it?" She leaned close and spoke her next words slowly. "You almost ruined my life."

"I didn't—"

"Don't get me started. You don't even want to know what Rick said about you."

She was probably right about that.

"Why can't you just chill? Even my mom isn't this uptight."

Uptight? Okay, she was definitely right—I didn't want to know what Rick said, but I could guess: *Paulson doesn't like uptight chicks.*

"Just because you can't stop being a loser doesn't mean I have to do the same thing."

Maybe Moni's voice rose in volume, or maybe the chatter in

the cafeteria had hit a natural low point. Either way, her words rang out across the space. People turned and stared at us. A few kids smirked. Several more giggled nervously. And she wasn't done yet. "Do me a favor, Bethany," she said. "From now on, stay out of my life." Moni spun away from me and headed inside the cafeteria.

I stood on the threshold. Fight? Or flight? With the gauntlet girls at lunch, the path to the bathroom was clear, but that was the coward's way out. I forced down the lump in my throat and stepped through the door.

Mechanically I filed through the food line. Then there it was, the sea of cafeteria tables before me. I thought about the first day of freshman year, how nothing could be worse than that. Then I thought, *Maybe I was wrong.* The First Law of Cafeteria Karma = Things can always get worse.

No one waved me over. Moni sat with Rick, Anna, and Kaleigh, at a table centered between the jocks, senior class royalty, and the gauntlet girls. Chantal did her best to preside over all four tables at once. She leaned across and said something in Moni's direction, and a ripple of laughter floated above the noise. I whirled around, and my tray connected with someone else's, someone with dark, spiky hair. Someone who was pretty much the last person I wanted to see—who also happened to be the only person I wanted to see.

Jack raised his gaze from the mingled mess of our lunches. I saw the black eye then, purple and painful-looking.

"I'm sorry," I said. And I was. Sorry about everything. This mess, the one on Friday, the fight with Rick, Moni. You name it, I was sorry for it.

"My fault." Jack walked away, dropping his tray into a trash can, dumping it all in—food, milk, tray, silverware, all of it.

And still, I just stood there, while Jack's chocolate pudding oozed into my applesauce.

The acoustics in the cafeteria would never match those in the Little Theater, or in the gauntlet for that matter, but from the far corner, I heard a distinct "Ahem."

Todd and Brian, the members of the debate team, the Chess Club, and a few freshman wrestlers—all stared at me. Todd's expression held a hint of apology. The tip of his head said, *Come on, you know you want to.* But I couldn't.

I wasn't embracing the here and now, or whatever it was he thought I was doing. I dumped my food, untouched, into the garbage, just like Jack had, and headed for the exit. When I passed the last table by the door, someone laughed.

Todd cornered me after school. I was standing at my locker, ignoring the stares and whispers of those passing by—or trying to. I wished I could simply go home and stay there. But first I had to make it through cheerleading practice, then I was due back at the gym for the last wrestling meet before sectionals.

"Look, Reynolds," Todd said. He leaned against the closed locker next to mine and offered up a smile. "I know I can be pretty stupid for a smart kid sometimes. And you probably don't even care what I have to say anymore, but for the record, I wouldn't think any less of you if you gave this up."

"This?" I asked.

He waved a hand at the cheerleading uniform. "Nothing wrong with a strategic retreat." With that, he gave my arm an awkward pat and left before I could say anything.

I'd thought about resigning. Sure. Even more so during practice that afternoon. It seemed stupid to stick with cheering when everyone else on the squad hated me. Moni and Kaleigh huddled together and never looked my way. Even when the entire squad lined up for a cheer or routine, there was this perceptible distance between all of them and me—like I was contagious.

I avoided both my mom and Shelby once I got home. Up in my room, I pulled the cheerleading handbook from my backpack and flipped through until I found Sheila's phone number. Ready? *Okay,* I told myself, *just do this.* After today's practice, I figured Sheila might even understand. But when the call rolled into voice mail, I felt a strange sense of relief. I hung up without leaving a message. I'd tell her tomorrow.

That night, a wrestling meet was the last place I wanted to be. I stood outside Prairie Stone High, in the cold, my feet itching to run toward my mom's ancient Volvo that was pulling up the hill and away from the school. I dashed up the school steps, more to escape the cold than from some great desire to let my school spirit shine. I'd barely made it through the double doors when I was surrounded.

"There she is!"

It was Andrew and the rest of the freshman wrestlers, all decked out in purple singlets, Prairie Stone High hoodies, and funny wrestling shoes. "You're here," one of them said. He added an, "Ow," when two of his teammates nudged him.

"I said I would be, didn't I?" I tried for enthusiastic and hoped my voice didn't give away my true feelings. "Which one of you is up first tonight?"

"Tyler is," Andrew said. "He's been spitting into trash cans to make weight."

Eww. I wrinkled my nose, and Tyler blushed. Then all conversation stopped. After an uncomfortable silence, I asked, "You guys all warmed up?"

They looked at one another and shrugged. No, they hadn't warmed up. They'd been hanging around the lobby.

Waiting.

For me.

"So," I said. "Anyone care to walk a girl inside?"

That got them going. They yelled and jumped, all arms and legs. At the entrance to the gym, Andrew let the others bounce ahead while he hung back. His shy smile faded. "He isn't here," he said.

I didn't have to ask who "he" was. Moni's speech in the cafeteria pretty much guaranteed the whole school knew it was over between Jack and me. But it was only after Andrew mentioned it that I realized I'd been hoping Jack would show up tonight. I squelched a sigh. "Thanks," I said.

"No, you." He bounded into the gym, then turned and walked backward. He pointed to me and mouthed, *Thank* you.

I stood in the gymnasium by myself. As much as I dreaded seeing Moni, I really didn't want to cheer alone. A few minutes later Moni arrived. I was so relieved that—like an idiot—I waved. She didn't wave back.

"Don't get the wrong idea," she said when she dropped her coat beside the bleachers. "I'm only here because of Rick."

"Bethany! Moni! There you are!" Mrs. Dunne called. In response to the enthusiastic greeting, both Moni and I plastered on our best "school spirit" smiles. *Chalk another one up for cheerleading,* I thought. At least now I could be insincere with the best of them.

Mrs. Dunne, wrestling mom extraordinaire, handed me a pillow made of purple and gold satin with matching fringe. She gave the second pillow to Moni.

"They're yours to keep," Mrs. Dunne said. "The gym floor must be hard. Of course, we hope you'll put them to good use next year." She urged us closer with a crook of her finger. "This is strictly confidential. Coach Donaldson and Sheila want to give you a formal invitation, but mark your calendars for the end-of-season banquet."

I forced another smile. Moni did the same. I'm not sure it was enough to convince Mrs. Dunne that attending the wrestling team banquet was a lifelong dream.

"These are nice," I said when Mrs. Dunne left.

Moni responded with: Nothing.

We positioned ourselves in our usual spots, our knees on the new pillows. The fringe on them flirted with the edge of the mat, and our pom-poms rustled each time one of us shifted. Moni didn't look my way while we waited for the first match to start. And once again I wondered why the hell I even bothered to show up.

When the first of my five freshman boys took the mat, I knew. It wasn't school spirit. It wasn't any obligation I felt toward the squad or even toward Sheila. It was those boys in the lobby. *That* was why I was here. They mattered. Not just basketball stars and senior hotties, but the skinny freshman wrestlers, too.

How Moni and I did it, I couldn't say. One of us would start a cheer and the other would join in. My voice sounded tinny and cracked once or twice, but no one seemed to notice. Then it was Andrew's turn on the mat. I yelled so hard that my throat ached. When he finished with a pin, I did a double jump, herkie included.

And I nailed it.

The meet ended with a victory for the Panthers and a personal best for Rick. When he swaggered toward us, Moni sprang up, grabbed her set of pom-poms, and met him halfway.

"Hey, spark plug," he said, before smacking Moni on the rear. She squealed, and they walked toward a group of seniors. Moni never looked back. But Rick did. He glanced at me over the top of my former best friend's head; his expression was confident.

I scooped up my pom-poms, the pillow, and my winter coat and hugged them all tight to my chest. My head buzzed. I felt dizzy. The crowd in the lobby was too loud and too close. I headed toward the back entrance and quiet.

I parked myself at the top of the flight of stairs that led to the band and choir rooms. My pom-poms slithered down the steps, but I ignored them. Instead I closed my eyes and traced the pillow's pattern, memorizing the embroidered knots and swirls with my fingertips.

"Go Panthers," I whispered.

A throat cleared, and I jumped. When I opened my eyes, I found the pack of freshman boys, all five of them.

"You okay?" Tyler asked.

"Sure," I said.

They pushed one another, like that first day in the weight room, until Andrew ended up front and center. "Well, it's just . . . ," he said. "We hear stuff. In the locker room." His words came out in short bursts. "Stuff about . . . stuff. And we were thinking. The five of us could probably take him. Maybe."

I looked at them, a gaggle of sweaty boys, purple singlets, and knobby knees. It was a pretty big maybe.

"Awww," I started, then stopped. Their wide eyes and the little-boy concern on their faces made my throat close up. "You guys are great," I managed. "Really great. And I—"

And I lost it, totally. Tears sprang to my eyes. I tried to hide my face, but teardrops darkened the purple and gold satin in my lap. Andrew's hand came to rest softly on my shoulder.

The sobs that racked my body were stronger than any I had cried at home.

14

From *The Prairie Stone High
Varsity Cheerleading Guide*:

Sometimes being a Prairie Stone High varsity
cheerleader brings you more attention than you
want. It can be thrilling when all eyes are on you—
or terrifying. Not everyone will be happy that you
made the squad, especially if they didn't. Don't
respond to petty jealousy and infighting. Let your
school spirit raise you above all that.

It was the following Monday before first bell when the taunts
came from the gauntlet. I'd been whispered about and
pointed at so much in the past week that at first, I barely
noticed this new round of insults. They weren't aimed at me, and
that was enough. The cafeteria was serving oatmeal again. And I
was buttoning Todd's shirt. Again.

Once he got over the disappointment of losing his celebrity endorsement, Todd had been my biggest support. I didn't know how I would have made it through the weekend without him—or without Geek Night. Who says you can't go home again?

In return, I was helping him lay the groundwork for his campaign. I liked to pretend it kept my mind off of everything else. It didn't. Not really. Still, I was grateful for any distractions—be it the scientific evaluation of hair gels or debating the pros and cons of wearing Wookie shirts.

The voices rose again and halted my fingers mid-buttonhole. Todd looked around me and over my shoulder. "Uh-oh," he said.

"Uh-oh?"

"I thought Mangers and his bunch were bad." He shook his head. "They're nothing compared to you girls."

"Hey!" I slapped his chest and let the mismatched buttoning remain. Then I turned.

Chantal, Traci, and their wannabes had someone cornered near the stairwell. Traci blocked the escape route down the hall, while the others fanned out. Chantal stood at the apex, hands on her hips, blocking my view of the victim. A surge of sympathy shot through me. I didn't care *who* you were or *what* you'd done, no one deserved an all-out gauntlet-girl assault.

"I'd rather be body-slammed into a row of lockers," Todd muttered. "At least that's honest."

I gave him a look.

"Well, it's over quick anyway."

"Whatever." I sighed and picked up where I'd left off with Todd's shirt. Really, someday he would have to learn to dress himself.

Todd rose up on his toes, and his eyes narrowed.

"What?" I asked and moved to turn.

He put a hand on my shoulder to stop me. "It's nothing. No one we know."

Right. We knew *all* of Chantal's victims, didn't we? A lot of them shared a lunch table with us. Come on, it hadn't been that long since the two of us, plus Moni, had been trapped in the gauntlet.

Oh, no.

I jerked from Todd's grasp and spun. I held my breath and danced from foot to foot, trying to get a better line of sight. Finally Traci shifted. A flash of blonde.

Not . . .

That earlier sympathy congealed into a mass of dread. I couldn't hear the words, but I could feel them, every tiny verbal cut. Each one on its own might be harmless, but strung together, the victim could bleed to death before she ever knew what hit her.

Moni?

I took a step forward, but Todd pulled me back. I stumbled and fell against his chest. I stood there in Todd's strange embrace, not sure what to do, what to say, what to think.

"You don't owe her anything, Reynolds," he said. "Maybe if she'd held up her end of the deal, but—"

"Her end of the . . . what?" I asked. I stepped back, but Todd still held my shoulders.

"You know—chicks before dicks," Todd said, "or, in this case, pricks."

I yanked free and stared at him. "How do you even *know* about that?"

"Strategy."

"What?" I asked, craning my neck to get a clearer look down the hall.

"Women are often the swing vote," said Todd. "It's my job to be in touch with my feminine side."

I pushed back my hair and tried to come up with an appropriate response. At that moment, Chantal turned. Her eyes met mine. For an instant I thought I saw a question in them. Then she shrugged. Like it didn't matter that I stood there, only twenty feet away. Like Moni didn't matter. Not to me. Not to anyone.

But that was just it. It *did* matter. I mattered. So did Moni. It went deeper than friendship. *Everyone* mattered. Geek girls and jocks. Skinny freshmen, and God help me, maybe even the gauntlet girls mattered to someone. We all mattered.

A lot.

I looked at Todd.

He glanced down the hall. "You're not seriously going to . . . are you?"

I nodded. Then I was off. From behind me, I heard Todd's whisper.

"Damn, girl."

I was two feet away when I finally saw Moni, her face pink and shiny with tears. I reached for Chantal's shoulder and tugged her away from everyone, so it was just the two of us.

"Stop," I said. Not loud. Not threatening, but the chattering around us died.

"Cut your losses, Reynolds."

Good advice, but I wasn't going to take it. "Stop," I said again.

"Whatever." Chantal tossed her hair, the strands of it whipped me in the face. "So, pest," she said, returning her attention to Moni. "We all know what it means when Rick Mangers dumps a girl."

We do?

"Sometimes it means he wasn't getting any, but usually—"

Oh God, poor Moni. "Stop, or I'll—"

Chantal glared at me. "What?"

Good question. I could mention Chantal's one-night stand with R.J. Schmidt, but I wasn't sure it would wound her much. It probably wouldn't even scratch. So—how did you defeat an enemy? According to Sun Tzu and his *Art of War*, you attacked the weakest spot. Even a head gauntlet girl had to have one of those.

"So," I said, softer. "My dad uploaded a family website last night."

"And?"

"A family website," I repeated.

"What are you talking about, geek?" Chantal glanced around for support, but I spoke so low, no one else knew what I'd said.

"You know, a website, like a place on the Internet that anyone can see," I said. "He put a bunch of pictures on it. Even movies."

"Like I care?"

I shrugged and continued as though Chantal hadn't spoken. "Family vacations." I ticked the items off on my fingers. "Graduations. Weddings." I locked eyes with Chantal, making certain I had her complete attention. "Dance recitals."

The air went cold while Chantal stared at me.

"It's www dot—," I started, loud enough now that Traci swung around and leaned closer.

Chantal held up a hand to halt me.

"Stop," I said. "Permanently."

Chantal took a step back and surveyed her group, then scanned me with contempt. I had to hand it to her; she was still the queen of cool.

"Come on," Chantal said. Hair toss: check. Eye roll: check. "We've got better things to do."

And then she left. Traci frowned at the spot where Chantal had stood, but she followed. They all followed, abandoning the gauntlet—that prime bit of real estate—and leaving me and Moni alone.

A couple of freshman girls exchanged glances, then took a cautious step into the lobby. Todd bowed to me, low and sweeping, with a flourish of his arm. Then he hurried after the freshman girls, probably to start acquiring that swing vote. A few undersized wrestlers punched one another's shoulders. I saw Andrew, and he threw me an ice-melting grin. The crowd outside the cafeteria resumed its chattering. In a delayed reaction, my palms went clammy, and my legs felt like noodles. I all but collapsed against the lockers.

I looked at Moni, thinking I'd make a joke of it. Everything else had been, why not this? But she ducked her head. Without a word, she ran down the hall, leaving me too breathless and too startled to call after her.

On Tuesday I was still feeling the aftershocks of the gauntlet. In class Moni never looked my way. I hadn't seen her at lunch. That afternoon, the figure leaning against my locker made my heart skip a beat, but only for a second. Far too tall, too slim, and too sophisticated for Moni. No, instead Chantal Simmons stood there, all alone. Not a groupie or wannabe in sight. Without the others, Chantal seemed smaller, less of a threat, friendly. Well, almost.

"I need to . . ." I waved a hand at my locker.

Chantal scooted, just enough so I could run through my combination.

"You know, Reynolds, you're in those pictures too."

"I have Photoshop, and I'm not afraid to use it." I pulled my German book from the top shelf and added it to the pile in my arms.

The start of a smile lit Chantal's face. I thought she might actually laugh. Instead my former friend grew serious. "Then I don't suppose you'd send me some," she said.

"Some what?" I asked, sure that I'd heard her wrong. "You want pictures?"

"Just copies. They're all digital, right?"

I nodded, slowly, still not understanding. "You mean, like pictures of you and me?"

"And Madame Wolsinski. Do you have any of those?"

Oh yeah, I did, including one where Madame Wolsinski had brought her cane down on the barre—right between my foot and Chantal's.

"I do," I said at last. "But—"

Chantal shrugged. On her, the motion looked incredibly cool. Chic, even. "My mom," she said, then blinked a couple of times. "She lost them—at least, that's what she said. Maybe she just got rid of them. Whatever. I don't have them anymore."

My own parents were embarrassingly proud of everything I'd done. Even my graceless years at Madame Wolsinski's. Maybe the confusion showed on my face. Maybe Chantal knew how strange it sounded to me. For whatever reason, she spoke again.

"It's no biggie. I mean, let's face it, Bee, the world doesn't need pictures of me looking like that. I was ugly."

I shook my head. First, at the sound of my old nickname coming from Chantal Simmons's lips and then because, well, Chantal was never ugly. A little chubby maybe. A little ordinary, but not—

"I always thought you were pretty. I mean, before." I stopped. "Not like you're, uh, not like—" I was babbling. "That is, well, you're—"

Chantal laughed. "Yeah. You'd be surprised what money can buy."

"Then . . . can I ask?"

"No," she said. "But you can guess."

I pointed to my own chin. Surprise flickered in Chantal's eyes.

"You're smart, Reynolds. Everyone always says the nose." She chased strands of hair from her shoulder. "But that didn't happen until after the accident."

That made sense. I'd noticed a change once the swelling on Chantal's face had gone down. "Your old nose was fine."

"Not according to my mom."

"And the rest?"

"Right after eighth grade—actually, two days after our last dance recital—they broke my jaw and took out two pieces. Here"—Chantal touched one side of her chin—"and here." Her fingers lighted on the other. "And then it was wired shut for six weeks. It's pretty much why I never called you that summer. By August I had to buy a whole new wardrobe because I wasn't exactly sucking down milkshakes."

It sounded like torture, even with the new clothes. "That could turn anyone into a bitch." A second later I realized I'd said that out loud. "I mean—"

But again, she just laughed. I wondered how much of the Chantal I once knew lingered beneath her shiny new surface. It made me wonder too: How far would any one of us go to feel like we mattered?

"So what do you say?" she asked. "Think you could send a couple JPEGs to my PQ account?"

"You have a Party Quest account?" I still hadn't signed up. The idea that Chantal Simmons could outgeek me was bizarre.

"Emerson turned me on to it. I figured you knew."

I tried to picture it, but I just couldn't imagine Chantal Simmons as an avatar, saving the world one level at a time. Then I realized it was probably good practice for turning Todd—and boys like him—into puddles of boy hormones.

Dorks.

She scribbled the address on a scrap of paper. "This gets out, I'm freaking slaying your reputation."

Now *I* laughed. "Some threat. I don't have a reputation."

"You don't?" But that was all Chantal would say. She pushed from her pose against the lockers and glided down the hall, her velvet clogs, with sequins, clomping against the tile.

I studied the scrap of paper with Chantal's address. If she had a PQ account, could she be hiding mad Photoshop skills too? I didn't have to send her any photos. Maybe . . . maybe I'd just think about it.

"Hey, Cee," I called, her old nickname sounding as strange as mine did.

Chantal turned.

"Nice shoes."

15

From *The Prairie Stone High
Varsity Cheerleading Guide*:

One of the secret advantages to being a Prairie Stone
High School varsity cheerleader is in the lifelong
friendships you will form. No one knows better the
effort it takes and the work you do—on and off the
court—than your fellow cheerleaders.

The gauntlet. A week had passed, but on the following
Monday, it was still a pretty important bit of real estate.
Sadly, the few sophomores who loitered there now didn't
seem to know what to do with it. I peeked through the cafeteria
doorway, but that morning Jack Paulson wasn't at one of the tables.
It figured.

I stalled by Moni's locker, hoping to catch her before the
bell. Since the breakup with Rick, she was silent in class and

invisible online. She'd used her last cheerleading skip privilege at Friday night's basketball game. And, of course, she still wasn't answering my calls. After a few minutes, I gave up and walked to the lobby.

In the corner by the trophy cases, the dance team was raising money for new outfits by hosting a rose sale. For three dollars you could buy a rose to be delivered on Wednesday, Valentine's Day. Between the flower sale, Friday's rematch with the Wilson Warriors, and the Sweetheart Dance planned for afterward, no one could talk about anything else.

Which was depressing.

I inched over to the table, snatched two note cards, and retreated to a quiet spot by the stairs—all before I could convince myself this was the worst idea ever.

I thought about Jack and his mysterious fight with Rick. Not once in this whole bet/joke thing did he ever really pull a move. Sure, there was some serious kissing. *Oh*—I tapped my pen against my teeth—*serious kissing*. But Jack never tried anything else. If it was really a race with Rick Mangers to see who could get the furthest the fastest . . . well then, Jack lost. Big-time.

On purpose? If that was true, then why hadn't he tried to defend himself, or at least tried to explain?

Maybe it was hard to explain *anything* when you believed you'd lost your last chance at *everything*. I thought back to that night in the cold. Maybe Jack *had* tried to explain. Maybe it was in the way he pounded those baskets. Or in his desperate kiss.

There's smart in your head, and there's smart in your heart. I'd once wanted to tell Jack that, but maybe I was the one who needed to be told. I'd listened with my head all my life. Maybe it was time to give my heart an equal chance.

I looked down at my note cards. I could do this. Just like an essay test, or my Life at Prairie Stone columns. Only harder.

Could I write something that would bring Jack and me together again? Probably not. But if I could close just an inch of the space between us, then maybe, just maybe, it was worth it. After all—no risk, no reward.

The dance team wasn't up to gauntlet-girl caliber in the mean-girl department. Still, anything sent to *the* Jack Paulson would be noted *(Oh, my God, what a total loser!)*, scrutinized *(Can you believe she really wrote that?)*, and subsequently spread around school.

I didn't need the grief—or multiple sets of acrylic nails prying open any note I might write to Jack. But then, *I* wasn't writing to Jack.

Dear Jack,

I was wondering.

Are all bets off?

Your friend,

Elizabeth Bennet

P.S. I'll be cheering for you on Friday.

I pictured the entire dance team huddled over a yearbook, trying to determine just who this Elizabeth Bennet was. Good luck with that. Then I thought about my copy of *Pride and Prejudice*. Did Jack still carry it in the pocket of his letter jacket? Whether he did or not, I guess it didn't matter. Even if no one else could figure it out, Jack had never been the dumb jock he pretended to be. He'd get it.

The second note was harder. I'd spent half the night brainstorming what to say, but all I kept coming back to was how stupid it was that Moni and I *still* weren't talking. So I wrote:

I was thinking.

The Gauntlet +

Geek Night +

Cheerleading =

Worth throwing away because of one prick?

I didn't sign this one. I didn't have to. Moni could do the math. I hoped whatever answer she came up with, it would be the right one.

On Wednesday roses sprouted all over Prairie Stone High. They bobbed in line in the cafeteria, were greeted with squeals in the classrooms, and seriously disrupted study hall. One rose wasn't such a big deal. After all, girls banded together, made sure everyone in their group got one. It was something that, in the past, Moni and I vowed never to do.

But more than one flower? Then it was a sure thing. You were cool.

By noon I had collected exactly zero roses. I still hadn't seen Moni. Coach Miller pulled all the basketball players out of class for extra practice. If the team beat the Wilson Warriors, they'd go to the regional tournament. But that meant Jack's desk in Independent Reading sat empty.

I was walking down the hall, my mind on three-dollar roses—and what a deal that wasn't—when I almost missed her. Moni stood near our old meet-up spot just down the hall from the cafeteria doors. She held a folder to her chest, a single rose in her hand. She looked like she was hoping I'd walk past and not look back.

"Hey," I said.

Moni turned from me. She tried to slip away, but I grabbed her arm. "This is ridiculous," I said. "The least we can do is talk. Come on, if it makes a difference, I know just how you feel."

"Yeah right," Moni said. "No one's talking about you."

Not now, of course. But the halls *had* been thick with gossip about Jack and how he'd dumped me. "They were," I said.

"And half the guys were saying how dumb Jack was for doing it."

"No way."

"Way," said Moni, and I glimpsed a sadder version of that Moni Lisa smile.

"So what do we do now?" I asked.

Moni closed her eyes and hugged her folder tighter. Talking in the hall wasn't getting us anywhere. The gauntlet was empty, and for now, the path to the girls' bathroom was clear. "Come on," I said. I walked across the hall and into the restroom, hoping Moni would follow.

At first she didn't. But by the time I'd checked under the last stall—just in case—I caught Moni's reflection in the mirror. I studied her face. Nothing about it looked right. Nothing about this whole deal felt right.

"Talk to me?" I said. "Please. If you don't want to be friends, that's fine." Not really, but not knowing was worse. "At least say it."

Moni slumped against the mirror. "You're the one with everything to say. Why don't you start with 'I told you so'?"

I kept quiet, not because I didn't have a right to say those words, but to prove to her that I wouldn't.

"I thought . . ." Moni closed her eyes. "I thought this was it. You had Jack. I had Rick. Everyone else had a sparkly new life, my mom, my dad. Why not me? But it was all . . ."

A joke, I thought. "I know," I said.

"I'm sorry I didn't believe you," Moni said. "Rick said you sent Jack after him—"

"I did what?"

"You didn't know?"

"It's pretty sad. My source for gossip these days is Todd."

That got a half smile, but it didn't last.

"Everything's just so screwed up," Moni went on. "I don't know what's true anymore and what's fake. Except Rick. That was pretty much all fake. And the ironic thing is, *real* is the reason I started liking him in the first place."

"I thought it had to do with that wrestling uniform," I said, but my lame attempt at a joke made Moni's eyes turn watery.

"That's what everybody thinks. But it wasn't because he was so hot. I thought *Brian* was cute. And it wasn't because he was popular or whatever. I really *liked* hanging out with the kids in Math League and the debate dorks . . . and you. It didn't take me very long on the cheerleading squad to figure out I didn't need new friends. I needed . . . I don't know. Something to hold on to, I guess."

I wanted to be supportive, to say the right thing, but I didn't have a clue what she was talking about.

"I needed skin," she said finally. "And bones. And yeah, the muscles didn't hurt either. Do you know that in all the time that I was Brian's online girlfriend, he never touched me, didn't even try to hold my hand, not even once? And then there was Rick. The minute I met him he had his arm around me. It felt solid. *Real.* Like something that couldn't just disappear. But now, poof."

"I'm so sorry," I said. And I was. If anyone deserved the real thing, it was Moni.

"I wish we'd never tried out for cheerleading." She turned the rose by its stem. "Oh yeah. It paid off. Big-time."

"I don't know what you're talking about," I said. "At least once a week, we don't have to worry about what to wear." I shimmy-kicked and shook invisible pom-poms. "And I don't know about you, but my school spirit is really shiny these days."

Moni snorted. It wasn't a laugh, but it was close.

"So?" I tried. I thought we were almost there, almost back to what we had been. But a look at Moni's face told me: *Not yet*.

"What you did for me with Chantal . . . ," she started.

"What about it?" I asked.

"The thing is, if it was the other way around?" Moni shut her eyes for a moment. "I'm not sure I would've done the same thing."

"Oh."

"Yeah. Oh."

"Maybe you would," I said. "I mean, I didn't know until I did it."

Moni laughed. That was good, except it didn't sound so happy.

"So why *did* Jack go after Rick?" I asked, partly out of curiosity, but mostly just to change the subject.

Moni shrugged. "I'm not sure. But I do know I was supposed to be 'grateful' to Rick because he fought over me."

The way she used those air quotation marks around the word "grateful" confused me. "Oh. *Grateful?*" I said when I finally plucked the alternate meaning from my mental vocabulary list.

"Yeah," Moni said, "really grateful."

"And . . ." I looked away. "How grateful were—?" As soon as the words came out, I wished I could stuff them back in.

Moni closed her eyes. "Don't worry."

"You sure?" I said.

"Rick Mangers can really be a prick." Moni opened her eyes. And for the first time, I thought I saw a spark there. "But at least he's a prick who understands the word no." A single tear slipped down her cheek.

I pushed past the folder, past the rose, and gave my best friend a hug. The rest could come later. But right now, she needed something real.

Sheila canceled cheerleading practice that afternoon. Then I remembered it was Valentine's Day. Anyone with glossy red hair and perfect nails probably had better things to do. Besides, Moni and I would've been the only ones to show up anyway. I'd spotted most of the other girls on the squad—collectively they could have opened their own flower shop with all the roses they'd received.

For the first time since November, I didn't have much to do once school got out either. Girls' basketball, the gymnastics team, and the wrestlers all had away meets this week. The boys' basketball team wouldn't play until the rematch with Wilson High on Friday. My homework was caught up. I'd even finished my latest Life at Prairie Stone column.

I did have to fix dinner for Shelby, though. Mom and Dad had taken the day off to eat piroshkis and catch a matinee at the Guthrie Theater. Only in Minnesota could oniony Russian hamburgers be considered a romantic meal.

Shelby and I polished off our reheated tuna noodle hotdish,

and she headed to her room to categorize the valentines she'd received at school that day. I turned on my laptop and opened my IM program. Moni pinged me right away.

QT_Pi: Watcha doin?

Book_Grrl: It's Valentine's Day, so—nothing. How about you?

QT_Pi: Starbucks Boy is organizing a special poetry reading at the coffee shop tonight. He and Mom invited me to come along.

Book_Grrl: That sounds . . . excruciating.

QT_Pi: Tell me about it. Wanna come?

I wasn't exactly thrilled about watching Moni's mom and her boyfriend make goo-goo eyes at each other. The probability of bad love poetry didn't excite me either. But if it meant spending time with Moni (and it didn't start until after my parents were due home), then . . .

Book_Grrl: Sure.

The poems were at least as agonizing as I'd guessed they would be. Who knew so many words rhymed with hearts? Well, if you count K-Marts and Descartes, that is. The goo-goo eyes between Moni's mom and Starbucks Boy—as well as the other couples there—were at least as painful. But if Valentine's Day had to suck, it sucked a little less sitting beside my best friend. And hey, we finally had the chance to drown our sorrows in white chocolate mochas. We even ordered the extra whip.

Thursday, the worst possible thing happened. Coach Miller did *not* pull the boys' basketball team for extra anything, and Jack's desk did *not* go empty in Independent Reading.

For the past two weeks, the only decent thing about the class had been watching the *Pride and Prejudice* miniseries. One hour each day, the lights were low, the show took my attention, and if I never really forgot Jack was sitting next to me, well, at least I could pretend to. On some days, the miniseries was the only decent thing about school, period.

That morning Jack entered the classroom at the last second, right as Mr. Wilker dimmed the lights. I tried to concentrate on the end of the show, the very best part. My mind strayed to that stupid rose and the even stupider note I'd sent Jack. Now he wouldn't even glance my way.

Geek Girl, meet humiliation.

Far too soon, the credits rolled on the last section. Mr. Wilker thumbed the remote control and pointed at Ryan Nelson to get the lights. Reality, welcome back. I wondered if Mr. Wilker would let me off the hook for the Q&A. Sometimes no one would say a thing unless I raised my hand first.

"He was an ass."

We hadn't even started the discussion yet, so the words, and especially *that* word, made everyone whisper. Even more so, since those words came from Jack. He never spoke up in class unless he was called on. Sometimes not even then.

"Well." Mr. Wilker hitched up his pant leg and sat on the edge of his desk. "Tell us what you *really* think of Mr. Darcy."

Jack was staring straight ahead. His hands were clenched on each side of his desk. "I'm just saying, he was a jerk to treat Elizabeth like that. What's up with the whole 'I'm asking you to marry me, even though we both know you're beneath me' thing anyway?"

I swear I only moved a finger, but Wilker was on it. "Ah, Bethany. I pegged you as a Mr. Darcy supporter," he said. "Care to weigh in?"

"It's . . ." *Gah.* "It's hard for us to understand how far apart the two of them were on the social ladder back then. It was a huge liability for Elizabeth to have relatives work for a living, or to not have any dowry, or to be stuck with a mother like Mrs. Bennet. I mean, if you think of it like high school, it's easier."

Mr. Wilker laughed. "Go on."

"It's like the preps and the losers, the jocks and the . . ." I didn't need to say the word; everyone knew the way the sentence should end. "There's always been an aristocracy. There will always be people who are, um, above other people. Like, imagine a goth kid getting together with the president of the Student Council." Or the star basketball player hooking up with a geek extraordinaire. "Not gonna happen."

"If he really liked her," Jack said, "none of that stuff should've mattered."

"In the end, it didn't." I shuffled the pages of my novel, like my fingertips could pull the words I needed from there. "Look at what Darcy did for Lydia."

"Good point, Bethany," said Mr. Wilker. "It might seem strange to us now, but Lydia running off with Mr. Wickham and having, um, relations was, well . . . and then Darcy fixing her—her honor—yes, Ryan?" Mr. Wilker pointed to Ryan Nelson in the back row. "Your take?"

"Do you think Elizabeth was kind of like a gold digger?"

Jack shifted in his desk chair and scowled.

Mr. Wilker cleared his throat. "What makes you ask that?"

"'Cause it's only after she sees Darcy's house that she starts being into him."

My arm nearly left the socket when I raised my hand this time. God, I was *so* being teacher's pet. But once upon a time, Jack Paulson said he wanted to talk about *Pride and Prejudice*. Maybe that had been a joke too. Good thing I knew the punch line.

Mr. Wilker nodded, my cue to go ahead.

"We know right from the start that Mr. Darcy has money. It's no big secret," I said. "Then Mr. Collins comes along and we find out Lady Catherine is rich too. Their two estates are, like, contrasted in the story. Lady Catherine's house is a symbol for everything that's wrong with the ruling class. But Mr. Darcy's," I continued, "represents everything that's right."

I wondered if Jane Austen ever faced down a gauntlet-girl brigade. I knew Elizabeth Bennet had. I stole a glance at Jack. He no longer stared straight ahead. No. Now his full attention was focused on me. For a moment I forgot about roses and humiliation and simply stared back. *Such fine eyes,* as Jane Austen would say. With my voice faltering, I added, "Seeing this other side of Mr. Darcy is why Elizabeth falls in love with him."

"Interesting. Ladies and gentlemen, take note." Mr. Wilker pressed two fingers against each temple. "Thanks to Bethany, I feel an essay question coming on."

Groans erupted. A few seconds later a ball of crumpled paper smacked the back of my head. It fell to the floor and came to rest between my desk and Jack's. He snatched the crushed paper, glanced up at Mr. Wilker, then shot a look down the aisle. With a flick of his wrist, he fired the ball toward the back desks. It struck his target's forehead with a solid smack.

"Too bad you couldn't do that when it counted, Paulson," someone said.

Jack looked cool, not angry or embarrassed. No smile. No frown. No game face. Just a slight tilt to his chin, the only hint of his pride.

On Friday, Prairie Stone High erupted once again with roses. Because one day of mortification simply wasn't enough. Actually, someone on the dance team over-ordered, and they had dozens left over from Wednesday. They were selling them at a discount—

just one dollar today. The line in the lobby was filled with boys who'd forgotten Valentine's Day. Like a two-day-old rose would fix that.

I was trudging toward my locker after school, but the sight of Moni with two roses made me run. I skidded to a halt, and the back of my skirt flipped up. Purple Butt, meet World.

"What? How? Who?" I asked.

"They were on my desk last period." Moni turned the roses in her hands.

"And?" I asked.

"Well, there's one from Brian." Moni handed me a note.

I examined rows of zeros and ones. "What's this supposed to be?"

"It's in binary," Moni said, and wrinkled her nose. "He's asking me to meet him here, after school."

Okay, so we were still dealing with computers, but at least it was paper and ink and not pixels. Not to mention a real rose. It was a start.

"Lucky for him you're a math geek," I said. "The other one?"

"Rick Mangers."

"No."

Moni shook open the note to reveal a single, one-word sentence.

You.

R.

"Well, you know," I said, "jocks are all about the one-word sentences. At least it doesn't say, 'Me'!"

Moni laughed. "Any idea what it means?" Her hand skimmed over the top of her head. "'Cause he kinda lost me."

"Not a clue." I glanced down the hall. "But I think you might find out." For once, Rick Mangers didn't appear out of nowhere. He walked toward us, his swagger only slightly hindered by a backpack full of books.

"Hey," he said, including both of us.

Moni's face went blank.

"Could I ask you something?" Rick said to Moni. I backed up a few steps and turned toward my locker. "I need to—," he started, but Todd yelled my name from down the hall, drowning out Rick's next words.

I watched Rick pull one of the roses from Moni's hand and touch it to her nose. He was good, I had to admit. A real player. But this time he looked . . . sincere? The two of them talked quietly together. I didn't want to eavesdrop. Okay, I only sort of wanted to. Todd didn't give me that option.

"Reynolds," he shouted again.

I held a finger to my lips and hissed, "Shhhh."

But Todd Emerson? Totally shush-proof. He approached, buttons all in place for once.

"I need to bounce something off you." He touched me on the elbow and led me toward the stairwell. "I've been thinking," he said, and leaned in close. "We should make this a two-pronged attack. Next fall I want you to run for homecoming queen."

"For what?"

"Hear me out. I mean, let's face it, you're one of the prettier girls in school."

"Oh, sure." I rolled my eyes. "I bet you say that to all your muses."

"This cheerleading thing has paid off."

"Big-time," I added, with another look toward the ceiling.

"You've had some exposure," he continued. "People know who you are, yet you're still one of the masses."

Chalk another one up to cheerleading.

"Put a name to a face and boom." Todd clapped his hands. "Instant homecoming queen."

Just add water. "Have you considered that maybe I don't *want* to be homecoming queen?"

"Did you want to be a cheerleader?"

Okay. So I didn't have an answer for that.

"Some people are born to greatness," said Todd.

Oh, I knew who he included in that category, and I was looking right at him.

"Others have it thrust upon them." Todd peered at me over the top of his new narrow-framed glasses. "Just think about it, Reynolds."

He was crazy if he thought I'd try for homecoming queen. I was crazy for letting it cross my mind.

Todd's gaze traveled over my shoulder to the hall behind me. "Oh. My. God."

I had to laugh. Maybe cheerleader cooties really were contagious.

"I told him," Todd said, "*no matter what*, do *not* wear the cape."

Cape?

I turned and followed Todd's line of sight. Moni still stood
beside her locker, but Rick had been replaced by a kneeling Brian.
At least I thought it was Brian. It was hard to tell with the massive
purple robe and the hood that obscured his face.

He held something shiny out to Moni that appeared to be
some sort of golden stick. The top of it was adorned with . . . was
that a Christmas tree ornament? Ribbons coiled the length of the
staff, supplemented at intervals with what looked like miniature
purple and gold cheerleading pom-poms.

"Is he . . . is he doing what I think he's doing?" I asked.

"That depends," Todd said. "Are you thinking he's spent the
past two weeks creating an exact replica of a Party Quest wand for
Moni, and now he is presenting it to her? Then—yes."

Brian stood and placed the wand into Moni's outstretched hands.

"Now go in for the kill," Todd said under his breath.

Whatever "the kill" was, it didn't look like Brian was going for
it any time soon. Unless it involved turning whiter than the usual
Minnesota pale and shaking so hard that we could see him tremble
from our spot near the stairs.

"Come on . . . *come on* . . ." Todd seemed to will the words as
much as say them.

Maybe it was some kind of nerd-boy mind meld, but something spurred Brian to stop shaking. He threw back his hood and swooped in for a kiss. It wasn't the smoothest lip-lock on record, but it was real. It appeared that Moni thought so too. In any case, she leaned in and kissed Brian back.

Then it was all fist pumps and woo-hoos as Todd ran to meet Brian in a midair chest bump. The boys clomped down the hall together, stopping every few steps for another round of high fives.

"So," I said when I reached Moni.

"So," she said back, and that Moni Lisa smile spread across her face. She repeated every word of Brian's conversation, the grin never leaving her lips.

"And Rick?" I asked when she was done.

"He asked me to the dance."

"No way."

"Way," Moni said, "and he apologized. Sort of."

"Are we talking about the same Rick Mangers? About this tall?" I raised my hand. "Senior hottie, but kind of a prick?"

"Who knew, huh?"

"And?" I asked.

Moni worked the rose stems into the ribbons that coiled the wand, then sniffed the tiny bouquet. "Not bad for one-dollar roses."

"Come on," I said. "Tell me."

But Moni changed the subject. "My dad called last night and asked what I wanted for Valentine's Day. I told him, 'A Monica-free weekend.'"

"And?"

"And he's coming down for the game, then we're leaving right afterward." Moni shrugged. "I won't even *be* here for the dance, but I didn't tell Rick that. I just told him no."

"It'll build his character," I said. "Once he gets over the shock."

"I just figured maybe I need some time to think. I mean, I've got this great big brain here." She tapped her forehead. "Maybe it's time I used it. Besides, if Monica's cool about this weekend, then maybe she's not totally awful."

"And if she's not cool with it?" I asked.

Moni grinned. "Then this will probably be the beginning of the end," she said, but a moment later her smile faded. "What about you? Did Todd—?"

"What?"

"Ask you to the dance?"

"Right." I pushed off the lockers and headed for my own.

"Come on." Moni jumped in front of me. "I thought for sure. Seems like there's something going on between you two."

"I'm just a muse."

"You're amused?"

"Forget it," I said.

"You sure there's nothing—?"

"Nothing but delusions of grandeur."

"Whatever." Moni drew a breath, and her eyes widened. I turned to see where she was looking. Todd was at the end of the hallway, waving at Chantal. Apparently he was courting the gauntlet girl vote.

"She'll eat him alive," Moni predicted.

"I don't think so," I said. At least, not if he had something she wanted.

Chantal fell into step beside Todd. A hand on his sleeve, that hair shimmy thing. It was hard to tell from so far away, but I thought she gave him the look, the one reserved for seniors of the opposite sex—or quite possibly future presidents of the student body. And he didn't even dissolve into a puddle of boy hormones. What had he promised her? I suspected it had something to do with the homecoming court.

"He'll be just fine," I said.

16

From *The Prairie Stone High Varsity Cheerleading Guide*:

It's been my honor and privilege to guide you through this season as Prairie Stone High School varsity cheerleaders. Whether it was for one season or many years, you'll never forget your time on the squad. No matter where life may take you, always let your (school) spirit shine!

My legs trembled. My voice was hoarse. I had lost five pounds in sweat—five pounds that had magically transferred to the pom-poms. How, exactly, *did* fringe get to be so heavy?

And it wasn't even halftime.

Jack looked as sweaty as I felt. But tonight he owned the court.

"Man," Moni whispered. "It's like he's on some sort of mission. Has he missed a shot yet?"

Well, yeah, he had. Even Jack Paulson couldn't make every basket. But it was good to see him play so well. And it was good to have my mom, my dad, and especially Shelby in the stands, even if I wasn't sure who she was there to watch. Was it me or Jack she grinned at most?

I had just sneaked a look back at the court when I saw it, and I hoped the referee saw it too. Jack sprang for a rebound, arms high in the air, leg muscles taut. An elbow from one of the Wilson Warriors struck him in the midsection. The ball left his fingertips, hit the rim, then ricocheted into the crowd.

Jack fell. His legs buckled beneath him, and he crumpled to the ground. A gasp echoed through the gym, followed by boos, then the shriek of a whistle rising above both. I lurched forward and gripped my pom-poms, feeling helpless. The refs hovered. Coach Miller rushed the court, a concerned frown on his face. He knelt and spoke to Jack, but the words were lost in all the noise.

No one moved. Not Jack. Not Coach. Not the referees. Cries from the crowd died down, and everyone waited. *Please let him be okay,* I chanted over and over to myself. I would have traded a thousand one-dollar roses just to see him move.

Jack rolled to his side. A wave of rhythmic clapping surged through the gym. It grew louder and faster as he made his way to his hands and knees. When he stood, everyone went wild, stomping, clapping. The roar was like a living, breathing thing.

The other cheerleaders jumped up and down. I stepped forward. My toes flirted with the boundary line, and I looked down the line of fringe. For once, no one yelled at me for not cheering.

Coach Miller probed Jack's stomach. Jack winced, waved him off, and walked to his place at the free-throw line. The ball thumped against the floor, a blur of orange against the honey-colored wood. The crowd hushed. Even fans from the opposing team fell quiet.

His first shot circled the rim but rolled off. Nope. Not even Jack Paulson could make them all. He dribbled the ball again, the crowd still silent. The score was tied, with three seconds left before halftime.

The thudding stopped. Jack held the ball, his sights on the basket. Then, suddenly, he looked toward me. I didn't know what else to do, so I gave my pom-poms a shake. That little-boy grin spread across his face. It seemed like his eyes never left mine. But they must have. The ball spun through the air. It floated above the rim. Then it slipped through, nothing but net. The Panthers headed into halftime up by one point, and I felt a blossom of hope in my chest. Just as quickly, I tried to talk myself out of it.

"Whoa." Moni's breath left her with a whoosh. "Call me tonight. I don't care if it's three in the freaking a.m. Call. Me."

"What do you—?"

"You're kidding, right?" Moni shoved me. "You saw it. I saw it. The whole school saw it. Don't believe me, go ask someone. I bet even Todd saw it."

"Do you think—" There was that hope again. I sighed.

"Yeah, I do." Moni gripped me by the shoulders and frowned into my face. "Just promise me one thing. If he asks if you're going to the dance, this time, *say yes*."

The boys streamed toward the locker rooms, the crowd poured from the stands, people headed to the restrooms, and the Student Council went to man the snack bar in the lobby. But my feet refused to budge. I stared at the doorway long after Jack had vanished. People bumped me, but I barely stumbled. Only Sheila, collecting my arm and Moni's, got me moving again.

"Can I talk to you two?" she said.

Like we had any choice. She escorted us to a space beside the bleachers, reached out, and fluffed each of our pom-poms in turn.

"I've been wanting to tell you." Sheila's eyes sparkled with—*were those tears?* "To tell you how proud I am of you. I know it hasn't been easy. And that you had to really dig deep at times. But I was right about you girls from the start. Your school spirit just shines!"

Moni and I watched her walk away. Sheila stopped by Cassidy and held a perfectly lacquered hand in front of the captain's mouth. Cassidy shook her head at first, then, eyes downcast, pulled out her gum and dropped it into Sheila's palm.

Oh yeah, our coach really could strike fear into the meanest mean-girl cheerleader. We tried not to laugh, and managed pretty well until Sheila hit the gym doors. Then we exploded. Cassidy darted a look at us, but she started laughing too. Moni waved to her and shouted, "Bee and I have considered Death by Pom-pom; you want to join us?"

"I heard that," Sheila called from just outside the doors.

We froze in place.

But Sheila just flipped her hair and glanced over her shoulder. "Next year, Moni, no excuses. We're seriously going to work on those splits."

The gym door opened and shut, bringing bursts of music and the occasional rose petal out into the lobby. Tonight laughter and talk made up part of the melody. Maybe it was leftover vibes from Valentine's Day, or maybe the fact that the Panthers won by three. Regionals, here we come.

No one stood in line for the phone, not even me. Mom and Dad pried Shelby loose from the pom-poms. They looked toward the gym doors, then back at me.

"So?" they both said at once.

"I—I think I'll stay," I said. No risk, no reward, right?

After they left, I shared the lobby with a few others. In one corner, some freshman boys debated the merits of attending the dance. When a group of girls headed inside, the boys trailed after them, deciding the two-dollar cover charge might be worth it.

Then, out of nowhere, Rick Mangers appeared. He walked right up to me as if the past couple of weeks had never happened. "You talking to spark plug tonight?"

"I'll be talking to Moni," I said.

Rick laughed. "Yeah, well, tell her I went inside *alone*." He nodded toward the gym.

"But will you be leaving alone? That's the question."

"Guess you'll have to stick around and find out."

"*To* find out," I automatically corrected.

"Metaphor?"

"Grammar."

Rick swore and went silent. Then he looked at me. "So, you really tutor anyone?"

"Anyone who shows up."

He nodded and headed for the gym door, that swagger still in place. The way I figured it, when he was ninety and used a walker, he'd still find a way to swagger. Before he slipped inside, he glanced over his shoulder.

"Hey, Bethany," he called.

I was reminded again that how a guy said your name meant something, and Rick had my attention.

"You still don't know what you think you know, you know?"

What? "You're right," I said. "I don't know. Why don't you tell me?"

But he didn't. He paid the cover charge, but before slipping inside the gym, he turned and winked.

Some things never changed.

The door to the Little Theater rattled. Todd emerged, looking strangely dapper—that was really the only word for it. He and Mr. Hair Gel had finally become properly acquainted. He wore a correctly buttoned (and nonplaid) shirt for a change. He almost had the wow factor.

"Getting ready for the ball, Cinderella?" I asked.

Todd scowled and pushed up his glasses. "Figured if I'm running for student body president, I should experience what the student body does."

"Something about that sounds wrong," I said.

"Tell me about it." Todd gave me a thoughtful look. "What about you? Fielding offers?" He nodded toward the gym.

"None so far."

"It'll happen."

"I don't know." I pushed down a sigh. Jack never took this long to change. I wondered if he regretted that free-throw look. I wondered again if it had even happened.

"You can still come inside." Todd nodded toward the gym again. "Join me, in official pre-election capacity, of course."

"Oh, of course."

He took off for the door. When he reached the entrance, I called after him. "Hey, Emerson!"

He raised an eyebrow.

"Just don't do the robot dance, okay?"

He pointed at his chest and mouthed, *Who, me?* Then he paid, stood straight, bent his arms like they were on hinges, and walked mechanically inside the gym.

He was *so* going to blow the election.

Footsteps from the locker room hall made my heart leap. I sucked in a breath and let it out. But the boy who rounded the corner was Ryan Nelson, not Jack.

"Oh, hey," he said, and nodded over his shoulder, toward the locker room. "I—I mean, Paulson . . ."

He trailed off, like he was torn. I had no idea if Jack meant for me to stay, or sent Ryan to get me to leave. Maybe he didn't even know himself.

"Can you get me a basketball?" I said.

"A what?" Ryan looked at me strangely, like I'd just asked him for lip gloss or something.

"You know." I dribbled an invisible ball. "They're round and orange, and they bounce."

"Uh, sure."

I followed him to the equipment room. Ryan tossed me a ball and didn't seem surprised when I headed away from the lobby and the gym. "I'll be out back," I told him.

Icy air frosted the bare skin on my legs. The cold stole my breath, but I went for it anyway. I dropped the pom-poms at the edge of the makeshift court. A breeze made the fringe whisper against the asphalt. My breath and the *thump, thump, thump* of the basketball were the only other sounds.

I aimed for the basket. I tried to mimic what Jack did, how he moved on the court. The ball left my fingertips. It wobbled around the rim before slipping through the chain links. The ball bounced once, but before I could catch it, it vanished in a blur. And that same blur went in for a layup, shook the backboard, and hit the ground in a solid slap.

Jack.

"Are you okay?" I asked.

He rolled the basketball between his palms, then looked at me. "What?"

I waved a hand in front of my stomach. "From tonight. Are you hurt?"

"Oh, that. Had the wind knocked out of me. I feel like a wuss."

"Don't—it looked scary."

Jack shrugged.

"I was worried," I said, the words leaving my mouth before I could weigh them.

Jack let the ball drop and approached, a hand in his letter jacket's pocket.

"Been meaning to give you this." From that pocket, he tugged my copy of *Pride and Prejudice.* "I finished it." He studied the cover, and his eyebrows drew together. "It's kind of about second chances, don't you think? I mean, once Darcy got over himself."

"Elizabeth made mistakes too."

Jack shook his head. Something told me he loved Elizabeth Bennet as much as I did.

"It's funny," he said. "The difference between books and real life. I figured, heck, if it worked for Darcy—"

"If what worked?"

"Remember when he went after Wickham to make him do right by Lydia?" Jack touched the yellowing remains of his black eye. "Rick was talking shit about Moni that Saturday after practice, and I went after him. I was so pissed. At him. At me." He shrugged again.

"Seemed like the thing to do. Besides, the way I figured it, I was about to lose a hundred bucks." His grip tightened around the book in his hands. "I still can't believe you showed up for that last meet." He paused as if considering something. "Neither could Mangers."

Neither could I. But . . . my mind whirled, and I struggled to pull all the pieces together. "So, that bet?" Maybe I really *didn't* know what I thought I knew, which made Rick Mangers right about something.

Jack turned away. For a moment I thought he might walk away, and that would be it. I swallowed back panic and tears. But then he looked at me.

"Which one?" he asked.

"Which . . . one?"

He held my gaze. "There were two, Bethany. One about whether you and Moni would cheer for every wrestling meet. And one about—" He stopped speaking but still looked into my eyes.

"Right," I said.

"Yeah. But for what it's worth, I think Rick's serious this time. R.J. Schmidt made a crack about Moni the other day. Mangers nearly beat the crap out of him."

Not that R.J. Schmidt didn't deserve a good beating. "So, when you fought Rick . . . ?"

"I wanted to prove that I was . . . serious, that it was never a joke."

"Never?" And no matter what, I couldn't keep the skepticism from my voice.

"Okay, it started that way for Mangers. But I thought, if we were supposed to, you know, I could use it as an excuse—"

"You never needed an excuse," I whispered.

Jack studied the ground, kicked the toe of one shoe with the other. "By the time I figured that out, I'd screwed the whole thing up." He looked at me. "It was too late."

"Who says it's too late?"

"Then here." He pushed the book at me.

I took it and turned it in my hands. The novel felt lumpy, unaccountably so. The pages fell open. In the crease sat a ring. I stripped off my mittens and held it between my finger and thumb. Beneath the yellow lamplight, the opal glowed in its setting. The slender gold band was engraved CLASS OF '89.

"It was my mom's," he said.

My lungs held zero air. I couldn't breathe, couldn't think. I shook my head, hoping to shake away the tears. "I can't—I mean, it's way too special. I—"

"My dad said the right girl would say that." Jack gave me that little-boy grin. "It's mine. He gave it to me a couple of years ago, and I want you to have it. I couldn't think of anything else that would prove—"

"A rose would've worked. Even a two-day-old one."

He laughed. "Maybe. I really liked mine. It got me thinking, you know? About everything." He stepped forward and took the ring from my hand. "Will you wear it?"

At some point I must have nodded or said yes. It was the only explanation for how the ring came to rest on my finger and for the quick, soap-scented kiss from Jack.

"So," he said, his eyes warm and mischievous. He glanced toward the school. "You going inside?"

He scooped up the basketball, his gym bag, and my pom-poms, and we raced through the cold to the back door.

At the gym entrance, I tugged some loose bills from my coat pocket while Jack pulled out his wallet.

"Let me?" I asked, four dollars in hand.

His chin tilted with that hint of pride, but his face softened. "Next time, okay?"

Jack opened his wallet. Inside were five twenty-dollar bills.

I felt my eyes go wide. "What the heck?"

But Jack only grinned. Without another word, he pulled me inside the gym. I dumped my coat and pom-poms in a corner, one not far from where Todd stood, surrounded by debate dorks, a few freshman wrestlers, and oddly enough, a couple of gauntlet girls. Okay, so they were third-tier gauntlet girls. Still, apparently the wow factor had kicked in.

Maybe some things did change.

The DJ cued up a slow song. "This one goes out to all the girls on the Prairie Stone High School varsity cheerleading squad."

The dedication echoed through the space. A squeal went up from the center of the gym. I rolled my eyes. Jack laughed.

Then again, some things never changed.

Jack tugged me toward the dance floor. He hadn't shed his

letter jacket. He pulled me close, pulled me into the jacket itself. My arms went around his neck, my head rested against his chest, the cotton T-shirt soft against my cheek.

Geek Girl, I thought, and snuggled closer to Jack.

Meet World.

About the Authors

CHARITY TAHMASEB was a 2003 Golden Heart finalist, and one of her short stories was nominated for a Pushcart Prize. She lives in Minnesota.

DARCY VANCE's essays on family life have appeared in regional newspapers, and her first novel was a finalist in the Get Your Stiletto in the Door Contest. She lives in Indiana.

Here's a peek
at another book you'll love:

giving
up
the
V

By Serena Robar

Where does the underwear go?

I, Spencer Davis, was naked from the waist down. I'd folded my jeans and put them on the single chair in the corner of the exam room but wasn't sure what to do with my underwear.

Should I hide them under my jeans or fold them neatly on top? If I hide them, then maybe the doctor will think I'm embarrassed about my body, but if I lay them out, then he will assume I have no problem with people staring at my underwear.

There was a knock at the door. I muttered a profanity and crammed the white cotton undies under my jeans. I made a running jump toward the exam table and miscalculated the distance.

Son of a bitch!

My knee slammed into the side and shifted the entire thing a good foot.

Doubling over in pain, I pulled my knee tightly to my chest, exhaling loudly in an effort not to cry out. The nurse knocked again.

"Everything all right in there?"

"Fine," I choked out. I pressed my forehead into my thigh and took several deep breaths to steady myself. "Everything is fine, give me just a minute."

Ow, ow, ow.

I limped toward the counter, grabbed a paper towel, and held it under the faucet of the sink. Turning on the water, I shivered as it saturated the paper and ran through my fingers. Goose bumps prickled up and down my naked legs.

This is so not my morning.

I balanced on one foot and pressed the cool compress to my swelling knee.

How did I end up here? This is totally insane.

Naked from the waist down, holding a flamingo pose as my knee throbbed, was not how I wanted the doctor to find me. I eyed the sterile-looking exam table critically. Of course, lying flat on my back, legs spread open for all to see, wasn't exactly the way I wanted the doctor to see me either.

Had anyone else ever spent their sixteenth birthday in this position before (no pun intended)? I snorted. Most sixteen-year-olds celebrated this milestone birthday with a big bash and amazing presents, like a new car.

My present was my first ob-gyn exam, courtesy of my forward-thinking mother, who thought birth control pills were a girl's rite of passage into adulthood. Mom used to teach Marital and Sexual Lifestyles (aka "Dirty 230") at Washington State University. I think her technical title was professor of women's studies, but since Dad moved us to the other side of the mountains for his job, her only outlet was volunteering at Planned Parenthood and trying to educate the unwashed masses about effective birth control and preventing the spread of STDs. Because my sister was in college (she'd wisely chosen an out-of-state school) and I was still at home, I got the brunt of her educating impulses.

Like my sister before me, soon I would lie on the exam table, feet in stirrups, dying of embarrassment as our family doctor looked up my *yoo hoo*.

That thought almost made my knee injury pale in comparison. I hobbled over to the table and carefully took a seat. There was a paper drape within reach, so I covered my lap and sighed.

Another soft knock.

"I'm ready," I called out. *Ready to die of embarrassment*, I silently added.

The door opened to reveal a twentysomething blond nurse wearing blue scrubs, her hair clipped up haphazardly.

"I was starting to wonder if you were trying to make an escape or something," she joked, eyeing the window. She removed the stethoscope hanging around her neck and took my arm. "Let me just get your vitals and then I'll call the doctor in."

The drape was still over my lap but shifted toward my waist as I slid down. I had an excellent view of the doctor's head and shoulders when he popped on a mask and perused a tray the nurse had prepared next to him.

"Spencer, you're going to feel my hand on your knee now, so just relax. I'm going to slide it down and then you'll feel some pressure when I insert the speculum. Nurse, can you hand me that?"

What was up with the kitty poster on the ceiling? Hang in there? Was that a joke? I wondered if anyone had died of mortification on the exam table before. The instrument was cold and intrusive. I couldn't help wincing.

"Spencer, I know this is uncomfortable, but I need you to relax. Push your lower back down toward the table. That will loosen up the proper muscles."

I forced myself to do as he asked and felt the metal speculum slide in. It was official. Our family doctor had just made it to third base with me.

"I'm going to open it up now. Very gently." The pressure increased, and I heard a squeaky sound, like a wheel that needed to be oiled.

"We're gonna need some WD-40 down here," my doctor joked.

I bit my lip in horror. It was sticking? I *had* to die. Right now. *Omigod, it's sticking, get it out!*

"Nurse, pass me the mirror. Spencer might want to see what we're doing."

"No!" I practically screamed. He raised his head, from between my legs, no less. I made a point of calming my voice down. "N m good. Let's keep the mystery alive, okay?"

He nodded and went back to work. He told me he w wabbing my cervix (ew), and I breathed a sigh of relief when finally removed the speculum, ending my torment. The nurse ped me into a seated position.

"We should have the results of the Pap in no t . If there is anything abnormal, we'll let you know."

I nodded, surprised when tears filled my eyes. d no idea why I felt like crying. Maybe it was the relief that "ordeal"—as it would forever be known—was over. Or mayb was the complete lack of control I felt at this moment.

Dr. Taylor put a fatherly hand on my s ulder. "You're a young woman now, Spencer, and taking care of ur body is part of being a woman."

He turned away so I could wipe eyes in private. The nurse diverted her gaze to the chart in h nands. When I'd once again regained my composure, the doct was writing something down on his notepad.

"I'm sending your prescrip n to the pharmacy, but here's a couple months' supply of the l to get you started."

The nurse produced a wn paper sack filled with a three-month supply of birth cor ol pills.

"Do you have any qu stions?" he asked kindly.

"Yes." I tried for hu or. "Is it possible to die of humiliation?"

Dr. Taylor chuckl l. "Well, I haven't heard of any documented cases." He looked me in the eyes. "Does your boyfriend know you were coming here today?"

"I don't have a boyfriend, Doc. This is sort of a rite of passage in the Davis household. My mother thinks all girls should be on the Pill when they turn sixteen. Sort of like a pre-emptive strike. It doesn't matter that the girl in question isn't even interested in giving up the V yet. It's all part of the status quo."

He nodded in understanding. He knew my mom well enough and was familiar with her liberal thinking. "We're going to leave you alone so you can get dressed. There's some tissues if you need to clean up. When you're all dressed, just crack the door, and I'll get your mother and we'll all have a little chat. Okay?"

I nodded, and they finally left me in peace. I spent several moments immobile on the table, paper draped across my naked legs, goose bumps rippling over my body. So this was what abject horror and humiliation felt like. Nice.

Not.

I slowly slipped off the table, cringing when I felt the jelly squish between my thighs (can you believe they lube up that metal thing?). I hobbled toward the desk for tissue, legs spread wide, trying not to make a bigger mess. The tears started again as I wiped off the offending goo. What was with all the tears? Did everyone spontaneously burst into tears after a pelvic? That was something my sister had failed to mention.

This could very well be the most memorable sixteenth birthday in history. And not the good kind of memorable.

It was *my* body, for God's sake. I should have the final say about what happened to it. I wasn't the least bit interested in having sex, and there wasn't even a guy in my entire school that piqued my interest. I was the reasonable one. I was the one everyone came to for advice. I wasn't the girl who fell on her back whenever a cute boy said hey. I tried again to stamp down the feeling of resentment toward my mother that wouldn't be totally squelched. I loved my mother, and I knew she did what she thought was best for me, but today was, well, this wasn't it.

When I was ready to face the world again, I took one last look in the mirror above the sink and tried to decide if I looked different. My ponytail was a bit mussed, but I had naturally curly hair, so when didn't it look mussed? I quickly redid it. Other than that I looked the same.

But I wasn't. I would never be the same again.